In
Your
Name

The Mechanic Trilogy Book 2

Rob Ashman

For Maureen

Chapter 1

Friday 27 May 1983
Tallahassee, Florida

The warm spring rain drummed hard against the umbrellas as the sun scorched steam off the grass. Only in Florida could that ever be considered normal weather.

Lucas stared blankly ahead completely immune to the fifty or so faces staring back at him. He had no more tears to cry, no more emotion to give. His hands shoved deep into his pockets, letting those around him do the job of keeping the rain off. His crushing sadness permeated everyone that was there.

The priest read from a book and the words floated past Lucas without being heard. The ground was awash with white flowers, all with handwritten cards stuck between the folds of cellophane. In stark contrast the mourners all wore black.

A pale wooden casket stood above the grave. Raindrops danced off the coffin onto the grass.

The priest was coming to the end: '… and so we commit this body to the ground. Earth to earth, ashes to ashes, dust to dust.'

There was a soft whirring sound and the coffin descended out of sight.

'So let us go in peace to live out the word of God,' the priest continued from his script, crossing himself.

Lucas stepped forward, scooped a handful of wet soil and dropped it into the grave. The dirt rattled against the wood. Pain shuddered through his body and he struggled to keep his balance. He stood motionless while the rain cascaded down his face, dripping from his eyelashes. He didn't blink, staring into the middle distance. An arm reached around his shoulders and guided him back under the umbrella.

Others filed past the grave, wearing their masks of grief and allowing soil to spill through their fingers onto the coffin lid. Lucas was escorted back to the black limousine. The crowd milled around chatting as the car silently pulled away.

Lucas twisted in his seat and looked out of the rear window. He could just make out the white marble headstone with black writing.

There was no way to come back from this.

Chapter 2

Nine weeks earlier
Las Vegas, Nevada

Eight months is a long time to go without killing someone of consequence, and the only victims of consequence for Mechanic to slaughter were Lucas and Harper. Her dreams were a random cascade of severed limbs, broken bodies and lifeless eyes, but revenge would have to wait. She had other more important things to occupy her time.

Getting out of Florida and evading the police had been straight forward – sliding off the grid was easy for a woman with her talents, the hard part was agonising over what to do with her sister, Jo. It was a gut-wrenching decision. Her every instinct screamed at her to get away but she couldn't simply leave Jo. Eventually Mechanic headed west to the place where she knew she could find work and people didn't ask too many questions: Las Vegas, Nevada.

The trauma of what had happened to her sister had an unexpected outcome; the voices in her head were silent. Daddy no longer patrolled the labyrinth in her mind compelling her to take the lives of seemingly happy families. But that did not eliminate her need to kill. It was a constant itch which needed scratching.

Eight months is a long time to go without killing someone of consequence but that doesn't mean not killing at all. It had to be satisfied by something else, and that something else was drug dealers.

They were ready-made fodder with built-in motives. Turf wars were common, with rival gangs clashing over territories. The police must have thought it was Christmas every week – bad guys shooting bad guys. What could make you smile more? Of course, they investigated the cases, but only superficially, there was never a serious commitment to bring people to justice. In fact, from their perspective, it was a practice which should be widely encouraged.

Mechanic had an important assignment coming up and needed to be clear-headed. She needed to be professional. She needed a kill fix, and that meant going cruising.

She drove around the rundown parts of Vegas looking for a credible target. It needed to be in a location where drugs were openly sold on the street, which signified a zero police presence. It also tended to suggest a lack of passing traffic, since the only people around were those looking for business.

It didn't take long to locate the perfect candidate and for the past three nights she'd kept a watchful eye on the proceedings.

It was the same set-up every time. On a four-way road junction sat a big fat guy squashed into a white plastic chair, the legs bowing under his weight. With his back to the corner he had three-sixty-degree vision. He was on lookout.

A second guy with a tall, athletic frame leaned against the bare brick wall opposite sucking on thin cigars, blowing plumes of blue grey smoke into the air. He held the gear.

The third guy was thickset, with a shaved head and homemade tattoos running across his chest and down his arms. He jogged and danced on the spot to the sounds in his head. He was the psycho of the team, the one who killed for fun.

One was white, one was black and one was Hispanic. This drug cartel obviously valued diversity.

Mechanic parked her car out of sight about two hundred yards away and walked up the street towards them. She wore a black baggy sweatshirt with the hood pulled forward, dark jogging pants, work boots and black gloves with rubber-grip palms.

Her breathing was slow and deep.

Her head clear as crystal.

Adrenaline coursed through her body but she maintained a relaxed appearance. She looked like someone taking a casual stroll in the wrong part of town.

She approached the men and could hear the unhinged bald one beat boxing and snapping his fingers as he danced in the road. The fat one made a sound like 'Yo!' and dancing boy turned to face her.

'Hey, Holmes, you looking for some shit? Cos you've come to the right place.' When he pronounced the word 'right' his voice rose in pitch to top C. He swaggered around waving his arms. Mechanic said nothing and continued walking.

'Hey, Holmes, don't ignore me when I'm smiling and being nice.' Dancing boy stepped in front of her about six feet away blocking her path. He was about the same height but half as wide again. 'You want gear? We got great gear. Good shit, Holmes. Good shit.'

She kept her head down and tried to step around him. He let her pass, only to run in front, again blocking her path. She was now level with the other two who regarded her with disinterest.

'I said, you want gear, we got gear, if you don't want gear well ...' Dancing boy jigged about. 'What the hell you doing on our street?' He held his thickly inked arms outstretched to prevent her going any further. She went to move around him but he shifted position, the stink of garlic and tequila wafted around her as he stepped in close. He reeked of stale sweat and dirty clothes.

'Where you going in such a hurry, man?' He flicked her hood back and she stared him in the face.

'Wow, es una chica!' The others looked over. 'Look guys, it's a girl.' He let the word 'girl' rise to top C, whooping as he spun on his heels. 'Ella es muy bonita,' he yelled to the others, wolf-whistling and rubbing his chest.

Mechanic stepped forward but he cut her off. The tall, athletic one pushed himself off the wall. He was now interested.

This was getting close.

'Let me pass, please,' Mechanic said trying to move to the side. Dancing boy pushed his body against hers, his face greasy and deeply pockmarked where acne and poor hygiene had marked him for life. Scored across the indents in his skin she could see the scars of past encounters. His stinking breath was hot on her cheek. Mechanic looked at the floor as he whispered in her ear.

'So what's a piece of pretty white pussy doing walking down my street, eh?'

'Just let me pass.'

'Not sure I will, cos I got something here that needs attention. What do you say?' He grabbed his crotch. 'And my friends, they love the taste of white meat. I figure you could help them too.' He curled back his lips to reveal an uneven row of broken yellow teeth.

Mechanic glanced to the side and could see the tall guy moving in.

'You think she's good to go?' Tall guy said laughing. 'She's gonna take all of us, right?'

'I guess so.' With that, dancing boy circled around Mechanic and gripped her in a bear hug from behind. He was strong and clamped her arms to her sides.

Mechanic didn't struggle, she slackened her grip on the eighteen-inch knurled metal bar concealed in her sleeve and slowly slid it down. When she felt the burred serrations at the end she tightened her grip.

Tall guy shifted his gaze and saw the weapon.

'Hey what the f—'

Mechanic jerked forward from the waist causing dancing boy to lean over the top of her. Then she snapped her head backwards, smashing him square in the face. Blood sprayed in the air as his nose burst open. She repeated the move and the back of her head caught him on the side of the jaw as he tried to pull away. He yelled in pain and clutched at his shattered features with both hands. She raised her right arm and slammed the metal bar down hard against his right knee. There was a loud crack as his leg bucked and he collapsed in a heap.

Tall guy levelled his gun and moved in close. Mechanic darted to the side and smashed the bar into his forearm sending the weapon clattering to the floor. She spun and kicked him in the chest. A rasping gasp of air escaped as he staggered backwards under the force of the blow.

Tall guy screamed in pain as his splintered arm sent delayed pain signals to his brain. She stepped forward and swung the metal bar again, striking his left collarbone. He fell to the ground as his legs gave way.

Mechanic turned to face dancing boy who was struggling to right himself with only one working leg. The bar swished through the air and cut a deep corrugated groove in the top of his head.

He catapulted backwards. Dead before he hit the ground. Staring at the sky with his mouth gaping open.

Mechanic kicked the gun to one side and approached tall guy who was kneeling on the floor. His eyes were the size of pool balls as he tried to get his useless arms to do something to protect himself. They flapped at his sides, dripping flecks of blood onto the sidewalk.

She surveyed the damage. 'You're not quite done are you? One more I think.' The jagged end of the bar ripped through his throat as she swung it horizontally. He keeled over sideways with the same look as his partner. A halo of dark blood grew around his head.

Mechanic fixed fat man with a stare that made a trickle of piss stain the crotch of his pants. He was stuck in his chair.

She picked up the gun and walked towards him with the grip outstretched.

'Take it.'

He tried to free himself from the plastic sticking to his skin.

'You obviously don't have one, so take it.' She offered him the butt of the revolver. 'Take it.'

He reached out with a shaking, fat hand and took the weapon. His flabby fingers curled around the contoured grip. She watched as fat man's cogs turned, trying to figure out what was happening.

'You are in bad need of exercise,' she said looking at his ass poking through the slats in the chair.

Fat man pointed the muzzle at Mechanic.

'So I'm going to do you a favour.' She snaked out her right hand, seized the barrel and yanked the gun from his grasp. He screamed as his finger snapped against the trigger guard.

'I always like to give people a chance, and you just blew yours.' Fat man stared at his finger sticking out at right angles to the back of his hand.

'It's dislocated and broken. That will hurt like a bastard,' Mechanic said casually. 'No time for that now, it's time for your run.' She stamped the sole of her boot into the side of his head sending him sprawling to the ground. He landed on the sidewalk with a sweaty splat, crying out as he landed on his busted hand.

'Go on, run,' she chanted, 'run, fat boy, run.' Mechanic waved her hands in front of her as if she was shooing away a cat about to crap on her lawn.

He scrambled to his feet and heaved himself into an unsteady walk. Mechanic let him go, watching him waddle and flap his way up the road.

She bent down and unclipped the knives attached to her ankle. She stood up, took a calming breath and hurled the first blade. It buzzed through the air and embedded itself deep into the middle of fat man's back.

He stopped and let out a high-pitched shriek. His short arms flailed around trying to locate the knife but without success. He could hear the second one coming but it was too late. The silver blade buried itself below his left shoulder. He let out another scream and fell forward, cracking his face on the sidewalk.

Mechanic walked to her victim and could hear his breath rattling as his windpipe filled with blood. He floundered around on his enormous belly like a landed fish, trying to retrieve the blades from his back. Mechanic knelt beside him.

'You really are unfit,' she tutted, pulling the knives from his body. His bulky frame juddered as the blades exited his flesh.

He let out a scream and coughed up blood. Crimson blotches oozed across the back of his shirt.

'Please don't,' fat man pleaded as he thrashed his arms around trying to roll over.

'Don't what?' Mechanic clasped her hand to the back of his head and ground his face into the sidewalk, enjoying the sound of his teeth grating on the concrete. She let him up for air.

'Don't kill me. They make me do drug runs, I don't have a choice.'

'That sounds bad. You should be more careful with the company you keep.'

'Let me go, I need a hospital. I can't breathe. Please let me go. I won't tell. I promise.'

'Are you sure you won't tell if I let you go?' She jerked his head back then smacked it into the floor pushing hard on the back of his head.

'I won't. I promise. Just please …'

Mechanic rolled him onto his back. Leaning over him she stared into his grazed puffy face. 'Are you sure?'

'I promise I won't say a word.'

'Let's fix you up then.'

Mechanic heaved him up with his back against the wall. His head lolled forward and blood spilled from his mouth down his front. 'Wait here, I'll go get help,' she said.

Fat man nodded and wiped his chin.

Mechanic returned to the two bodies lying in the road and picked up the knurled metal bar. Concrete-reinforcing steel made a great weapon. She pushed it up her sleeve and walked back to fat man.

'They coming?' he choked his words out.

'Yes, they'll be here shortly.'

'I can't breathe.'

'They said for me to check your airways to see if they're clear.'

Fat man nodded.

Mechanic knelt beside him and tilted his head back, peering inside his mouth.

'If I let you live, are you sure you won't tell anyone?'

'Ggyesss.'

'Are you sure? Because you don't sound so sure.'

'Ggyess I won't—'

Mechanic jammed his head against the wall face up and forced his jaw down.

'I can't see anything obstructing your airways. You should be able to breathe fine. Can you breathe fine there, fat boy?'

'Grrnoo,' he said with his mouth wide open.

'Then you must be lying and if you'll lie about something as easy as breathing then you'll definitely lie about not telling.'

'Grrnoo I wunt.' His eyes bulged.

'Are … you … sure?' she said banging his head against the brickwork as she pronounced each word.

He winced at each impact. 'Ggyess …'

'Wait a minute, you're right, there is something there, I can see it stuck in your throat.'

Mechanic stood up and shoved her knee into his chest. 'I'll get it out.'

She kept his head tight against the wall and forced her hand into his mouth. She loosened her grip on the bar. It protruded from her sleeve.

'Look at me, fat boy. Keep still now,' she said as his hands tried to relieve the pressure on his chest.

Mechanic drove the bar into his gaping mouth.

The ragged end tore its way through his oesophagus. Fat man's arms lashed out trying to grasp Mechanic's hands. He let out a gagging, choking sound as blood erupted into his mouth.

She rammed it deeper down his throat.

His teeth splintered as he bit into the metal.

Fat man's body convulsed. His hands clawing at her sweatshirt. Then nothing. He was still.

His eyeballs bulged from their sockets, stained red from the rupturing blood vessels.

Mechanic stopped pushing.

She stared into fat man's contorted face, his head tilted back with eight inches of metal protruding from his mouth. Wiping the knives clean, Mechanic snapped them into the leather straps around her ankle and walked back to the other two bodies.

Back at the car she stripped off her clothes, towelled herself down and changed into jeans and a T-shirt. The gloves, sweatshirt, jogging pants and towel were bundled into a white plastic laundry bag marked Hacienda.

Mechanic sat in the car and surveyed her handiwork from a distance. She could just make out fat man sitting against the wall, his head pinned back by what looked like a giant cocktail stick.

She closed her eyes and breathed deeply.

Big day tomorrow.

That felt better.

Chapter 3

Tallahassee, Florida

L ucas's every waking moment was consumed with finding Mechanic and killing the psychotic bitch, though in public he tended to use the phrase 'bring her to justice'. This was a big day for him and, to put it bluntly, he was shitting his pants.

It had been two weeks since his return to work and two weeks since that damn package from Mechanic landed on his desk. It was postmarked the very day he started back at the precinct, 21 March 1983.

He was pleased to be back but knew he wasn't the same man. He wasn't the same police lieutenant who had cracked Mechanic's true identity and had so nearly taken her down. The murdering bitch had broken his body and his spirit – quite literally. She'd beaten him to within a hair's breadth of death and, if it hadn't been for Harper's intervention, Lucas would be dead. He'd spent six months in and out of hospital getting his body put back together and a further two in therapy putting his head back together. Neither of which had been entirely successful.

Despite the best intentions of the force to rehabilitate him back to work, he knew he was damaged goods. He walked with a stick to support his shattered leg, his left lung operated at thirty percent capacity and his right arm shook with tremors caused by the nerve damage he sustained while being hung from the steam pipe.

While his wounds served as painful reminders, they paled into insignificance compared to the demons that played inside his head.

Lucas had become a single-issue cop. He disregarded his wider duties to focus on the single pursuit of catching Mechanic.

Nothing else mattered. Nothing even came close, not even his wife.

The demons were fuelled by guilt and he channelled his guilt into a boiling rage. Rage that there was now a ragged hole deep inside where his friend and partner used to be. Chris Bassano was still very much alive, but the man whom Lucas had worked so closely with was most definitely dead.

Mechanic had attacked Bassano when he cornered her in his car. She tore him to pieces. She smashed his head to a pulp against the dashboard, then almost severed his arm.

Bassano's pretty boy looks were gone, replaced with a misshapen forehead and a spider's web of deep lacerations criss-crossing his face. His arm could not be saved and the amputation ensured he would never again be a cop.

It had changed Bassano irrevocably.

He had become withdrawn, a shadow of his former self. He could no longer cope with living on his own and his parents moved him out of his apartment in Tallahassee and into the family home in New Jersey. He now lived a reclusive lifestyle, refusing to return Lucas's calls or respond to his letters. Lucas blamed himself for what had happened and grieved the loss of the friend he once knew.

Killing the bitch was the only thing that mattered.

He took a deep breath and collected himself. This was a big day.

Lucas tapped on the dark oak door with the inscription 'Commander Chuck Hastings' emblazoned across the top. He hated his boss's office, nothing good ever happened there. He hated his boss even more, though to his annoyance, during Lucas's recuperation he had been a model of support and compassion. Lucas cursed the man's inconsistency.

'Come,' said the detached voice. Lucas entered the room, clasping a red box under his arm.

Chuck Hastings was a large oval man, sitting at a large oval conference table. He was pouring steaming coffee into an oversized cup for a man with short, cropped hair and thick-rimmed glasses whom Lucas didn't recognise.

'Ah, Lucas, glad you could join us,' he said in a frighteningly cheery manner. Lucas noted his boss's shirt buttons were under more stress than usual – the product of too many corporate dinners. 'Let me introduce Jeff Chambers from the FBI.' Lucas shook the man's hand. His name sounded strangely familiar.

'Sir, I …' Lucas stumbled over his words. This was the first high level meeting he'd had since returning to work and he was a little unsteady. The presence of the new guy unnerved him.

'Have some coffee.' Hastings poured another without waiting for a reply. 'Shall we get down to business?' He gestured towards a vacant chair and Lucas did as he was told. He placed the box on the table.

'Sir, I just wanted to—' Lucas blurted out, but his boss expertly cut him off.

'You have a request for us to consider, Lucas, one which is a little off protocol.' Lucas nodded and made a sound which could equally be interpreted as yes or no.

Hastings continued, 'That's why I've invited Jeff. He heads up the Behavioural Science Unit at Quantico and has a great deal of experience in this field.' Lucas nodded in Chambers' direction and the cogs began to whir. 'Would you like to take us through your proposal?' Hastings sat back giving Lucas the floor.

'Sir, two weeks ago I received this.' He opened the box and removed a collection of sealed evidence bags. He held up the largest one which contained a document-sized envelope. 'It's addressed to me and was posted from Baton Rouge, Louisiana. When I opened it these were inside.' Lucas placed the envelope on the desk and held up a number of smaller evidence bags, each one containing a flat white square of paper. 'There are ten in total. The envelope also contained this.' Lucas held up another plastic bag with white granules in it. 'It's sugar, which came from these opened packets. All of this might seem unimportant, and a little screwy, but it relates directly to the Mechanic case.' Lucas paused.

'Go on,' said Hastings.

'You will no doubt have read the case files about Jessica Sells, aka Mechanic, and the slaughter of twenty-four people over two killing sprees – the first in 1979 and the second just eight months ago. She was helped by her sister, Dr Jo Sells, who worked for the FBI. Jo was drafted in to support my investigation but worked against us. Mechanic was never caught and Dr Jo Sells was never apprehended either. There is strong evidence to suggest one of the women is dead, shot in the head by Dick Harper. They are identical twins and the big unanswered question is: which one did Harper shoot? What we do know is Jo Sells had a sugar addiction which embarrassed her. To conceal how many she used, she twisted the packets together like this …' Lucas picked up three sugar packets from the coffee tray, emptied the contents into a spare cup and twisted them together to form a double helix. 'She called them sugar twists and made them automatically every time she had coffee. And she drank a lot of coffee.' Lucas rolled the paper spiral along the table top towards his boss.

Lucas took a deep breath, collecting himself for what he was about to say. 'This letter contained flat sugar packets. When Mechanic tortured me we talked about sugar twists and Jo's addiction. I believe this,' he said holding up the envelope, 'is from Mechanic. She's telling me she's still alive.'

The men on the other side of the table looked at each other and shook their heads.

Lucas's words were spilling out. 'It's postmarked the twenty-first of March, the day I came back to work. She sent me this as a sign. This says she is still at large. It's a reminder that she won in the end. She's taunting me. She's taunting us.'

Both men were silent, looking at the evidence pouches spread out before them. Jeff Chambers broke the silence. 'So you're asking for what exactly, Lucas?' It was a pointless question as he already knew the answer.

'I want to take a team of people to Baton Rouge where this letter came from. I want to track Mechanic down before she kills again.' Lucas could feel the trickle of cold sweat running down the back of his neck.

'This doesn't prove Mechanic is alive, Lucas,' said Chambers. 'It is unusual, I admit, but it doesn't constitute a good reason to mobilise an expensive team to go tramping around Louisiana.'

Lucas stared at him in disbelief. This was fast becoming his nightmare outcome.

'But I disagree—'

'Lucas,' Hastings interrupted, 'we threw everything at that manhunt and found nothing. It was a nationwide alert and we drew a blank. We need something concrete to go on if we are going to start running about the country again. This …' He lifted the bag of sugar from the table, 'doesn't constitute hard evidence, now does it?'

'I know this murdering bitch, sir, and this is just the type of thing she would do. Harper led the first case and Mechanic sent him notes, taunting him that he would never catch her. It destroyed him and his investigation. She tried to do the same to me. She has form for doing this type of thing. I disagree, sir – the sugar packets are a significant development.' He held up the evidence bags, his hands shaking. 'She's sending me a message, sir, I know it. A message that says: 'I'm still alive'. This is her MO, I'm convinced of it. She's fucking taunting us.' Lucas was coming apart at the seams.

'Lucas, I understand your frustration,' said Hastings. 'You've shown extraordinary courage getting back to work and we admire you for doing so, but this isn't concrete enough for us. I'm sorry.'

Lucas exhaled loudly. Droplets of saliva landed on the table.

'But, sir, I know this woman. I know what makes her tick and this is precisely the twisted thing she would do. You have to go with me on this one, sir. She's out there. I just know it—'

'Lucas.' Chambers held up his hand, butting in. 'I've listened to what you have to say and I have to ask myself a simple question: why would Mechanic do this?' Lucas furrowed his brow. 'Put yourself in her position. As far as she is concerned, we don't know if she's dead or alive. We also don't know where she is. So from her perspective she's got away with it – again. Why would she announce the fact that she's alive and give us a possible location? That doesn't make sense, Lucas.'

Chambers softened his tone as if it was time to make friends. He leaned forward: 'You've been under enormous personal stress and I believe it's clouding your thinking. I'm afraid your judgement is flawed on this, Lucas.' Chambers sat back with his arms folded; for him the discussion had come to an end.

Then the light bulb went off in Lucas's head.

'Ah yes, Jeff Chambers. Now I remember,' Lucas said pointing an unsteady finger at him. 'You were the one who sent Dr Jo Sells to be part of my team. You were the one who sent the sister of the serial killer we were trying to apprehend right into the heart of my investigation.'

Jeff Chambers shifted uncomfortably in his seat.

Lucas exploded. 'And you have the nerve to sit there and tell me my judgement is flawed! Before I go further I need to be sure – you're the same guy aren't you?' Chambers nodded and looked at the floor.

'Well, excuse me if I don't find you very credible, Mr Chambers. It's because of you people are dead. It's because of you Chris Bassano has lost an arm and lives the life of a hermit. It's because of you I spent eight months recovering from being beaten half to death – a beating I received at the hands of a psychotic bitch whose fucking sister you sent to help me.' Lucas was on his feet and slammed his hand hard onto the table. 'So, Mr Chambers, why don't you take your flawed judgement and fuck off back to Quantico where you can recruit more relatives of serial killers.'

'Now that's quite enough!' Hastings was also on his feet. 'Lucas, you've gone too far.'

'Too far … too far? How far would you go to catch this vicious bastard, sir? Not as fucking far as Louisiana it would appear.'

Lucas gathered up the evidence pouches, put them in the box and stormed out. He left the office door wide open, not expecting to return.

Chapter 4

Mechanic waited in the main reception of the Hacienda hotel. It was early evening and this was her second visit of the day. Her first had been mid-morning, dressed in a broad floppy hat, tan shorts, flip-flops and a vest top. After a period of casual lift-riding she found what she was looking for on the twenty-first floor – a guest laundry trolley. She deposited the white plastic bag from the previous day among the others and left. The contents would be put through the automated washing process, boiled clean of blood and returned to some bewildered guest in room 2125, who in turn would hand it back to the hotel. It would then sit in lost property until it was either stolen or disposed of along with the thousands of other garments. The best way to hide a needle is to first locate a haystack.

In distinct contrast, she was now wearing a well-tailored black suit and white button-down collar shirt. The therapy of yesterday had done the trick and she exuded confidence and poise.

Her face and hands bore witness to a glowing tan, while the slight bulge on her right hip gave away the .45 in its holster. Her hair was short at the sides and long on top allowing for a sweeping fringe. It was dyed silver and coloured contacts turned her eyes deep blue. Her only jewellery was two silver stud earrings and a military wristwatch. She stood around five feet ten in her flat work shoes and wore a hint of makeup. This was how she liked to look when meeting a client for the first time, business like and elegant.

Mechanic now worked in personal security, a lucrative if not entirely savoury profession, where her unique skills were well sought after. When a high roller arrived in Vegas they liked to know they would be safe. The excesses of the city drew the seedier side of life, like flies around shit, and the clients wanted to be sure they wouldn't spoil their designer shoes by stepping in something bad. That's where Mechanic came in. Bodyguards were typically male and she was in demand.

Most of her clients were women – successful corporate types who flew in for the weekend when their husbands thought they were somewhere else. The women enjoyed their excesses just as much as the men and felt a female minder would be more sensitive with the confidential items on the itinerary. Christ knows why, because every woman Mechanic had ever known couldn't wait to dish the dirt.

Male clients were brazen. Many a time Mechanic would stand guard in a hotel corridor while a parade of semi-clad women were ushered in or out of the room. At least her female clients tended to have dinner first with their procured male company. The men seemed to like theirs with a large helping of alcohol and white powder.

While this assignment was a big deal for her, she was not looking forward to today. A high-stakes guy was blowing into town for three days and his usual minder couldn't take the gig. So, he gave it to Mechanic.

Mr Harry Silverton, or Fuckwit as he was known to those who minded him, was a walking, talking nightmare. He came from Texas and brought with him the smell of oil and money. He had a comic tendency of strutting around in a bright white Stetson and cowboy boots, as if he'd just fallen from a rodeo bull. The problem with Harry was the more he drank the more obnoxious he became. And the more obnoxious he became the louder he got. This was his first time at the Hacienda as the other hotels had been unexpectedly full when his PA called to make a reservation.

Under normal circumstances Mechanic avoided this type of client like the plague, but Harry paid well over the odds and that was hard to turn down. She accepted the job knowing Harry Silverton fully expected to get into trouble and expected his minder to get him out of it. You got paid well but it carried higher risks than normal.

Mechanic checked her watch: 7.25pm. It was usual practice for the hotel to make arrangements for the airport pickup and for her to meet the client on arrival. Silverton was already late, perhaps he hadn't even made it past airport security. The cool fragranced air of the foyer was a welcome alternative to the twenty-eight degree heat outside. Vegas is never the place to be wearing a dark, well-fitted suit.

A black Dodge limo pulled up and the concierge guys ran around like children, opening doors and taking cases from the trunk. Mechanic saw a bright white Stetson emerge from the front of the car and another emerge from the back. One hat stood a good head and shoulders taller than the other. She recognised Silverton.

The two men walked to reception with the smaller man in front. Then it dawned on Mechanic: *Shit he's brought his own security.* That was never good. It always resulted in a turf war about who was in charge. She hated these situations.

Another concierge opened the ornate glass door and they swaggered into the hotel followed by a gaggle of bellhops carrying assorted luggage. The taller guy removed his sunglasses and scanned the interior. The duty manager swooped into action and accosted his high-spending guest with an over-enthusiastic handshake.

Mechanic waited until the initial greeting and small talk had subsided then stepped forward, extended her hand and introduced herself.

'Mr Silverton, I'm Jessica Hudson, welcome to Las Vegas.'

'I'm pleased to make your acquaintance, Ms Hudson. This is Mr Walker,' he said, shaking her hand and pointing to the taller guy in the Stetson. 'He will be accompanying me on my trip.'

Walker glowered at Mechanic.

Silverton and Walker were a sight to behold. The former was a short, stocky man sporting a thin moustache; he was in his late forties, his sweaty face the complexion of putty. The latter was tall, broad and tanned, with a full moustache which reached his chin, Mexican style. He looked like an NFL linebacker dressed in an expensive suit which fitted where it touched. Tufts of dark curly hair protruded from beneath their hats. The two looked like a couple of badly matching bookends.

Walker was bristling with passive aggression. She surveyed him coolly, it was a look she'd seen many times before. Guys like Walker were common in the forces – absolute world-beaters in the gym but scared little schoolboys pissing in their pants when faced with conflict in the field.

Mechanic pushed her way into the exuberant conversation between the hotel manager and Silverton. She smiled broadly.

'Sir, do you have time to take me through your plans for your stay? I can suggest a few itinerary items you might like to consider.'

Silverton waved her away with a podgy hand. 'Walker knows what to do, have a chat with him.' He was too busy having a swell time with his new best friend, the hotel duty manager.

She looked over at Walker. He motioned for her to join him with a wave of his hand and took a street plan from his inside pocket.

Walker met her halfway and placed his left hand in the small of her back. He shook open the map and walked her to a quiet corner of the reception. Walker pulled Mechanic in close and placed his boot on her foot.

'Now listen, missy, and listen real good,' he said in a slow southern drawl.

'Silverton doesn't need extra security. So why don't you make your excuses, smile sweetly and go back to waiting tables or whatever you do to pay the bills. I told Silverton we don't need no girl scout.' He leaned forward stepping hard on her toes. Mechanic didn't flinch.

'And how did that go?' she said looking up into his face.

'What?'

'When you told Silverton he didn't need extra security, how did that go? Because from where I'm standing it looks like he ignored your good advice, which tells me he doesn't rate you, Mr Walker.' She leaned in and sniffed at his lapel. 'And neither do I, you don't smell right to me.'

'What the f—'

'You're wearing a pair of two-hundred-dollar, all-leather shoes – mine have rubber soles. On this marble floor I'd be ten yards ahead of you while you'd still be running on the spot like a cartoon character. Plus mine have steel toecaps, which come in handy when the school bully comes around to stand on your toes.'

Walker looked down and frowned. Mechanic continued, 'And those sunglasses in your top pocket are a fully-fashioned item of beauty, Mr Walker. Things of beauty indeed.' She mimicked his southern drone. 'The problem is the reflective lenses distort the image, making distances difficult to judge.' Walker flashed a glance down towards his hundred-dollar shades. 'That means I doubt you could hit a rolling trash can at thirty yards with those on.'

Mechanic leaned in again and motioned for him to stoop down. She whispered into his ear. 'Take a look under the map.' Walker looked baffled.

She repeated the instruction, 'Take a look under the map.'

Walker moved it away from his body to see Mechanic holding the razor edge of a throwing knife against the front of his pants, the point digging into the fabric.

He went to move away but Mechanic gripped his elbow. 'Now I'm thinking, should I take both, or leave you with one. What do you think?' He swallowed hard. 'You see, Walker.' Mechanic sniffed at his lapel. 'You don't smell right.'

She dug the blade in further. 'For the next three days Mr Silverton has a guardian angel, and that's me. So, while he is gambling, drinking and screwing himself to a standstill I intend to see he does it in complete safety. Are we clear?' She jabbed the knife into Walker's groin, he flinched.

'Now, I'm going to do my job, while you …' she flicked the knife downwards, '… find yourself a new pair of pants.'

Walker recoiled and thrust her away. He looked down at the two-inch gash in the material, right where he kept the family jewels.

Mechanic walked back to Silverton smiling broadly.

'Hey,' he said in a voice slightly too loud, waving his arm in Walker's direction.

'Great to see you guys are getting along.'

'Yup,' Mechanic replied. 'We're getting along just fine, Mr Silverton, just fine.'

Chapter 5

'You were fired?' Harper asked, not quite understanding what his friend was telling him but finding it funny all the same.

'Nope,' replied Lucas.

'You resigned?' Harper had another go.

'Nope.'

'Then what?'

'I'm suspended.'

Harper stifled a laugh. Lucas had the air of a naughty schoolboy telling his mom he had detention.

'Hell man, that's nothing,' said Harper dismissing Lucas with a wave of his teaspoon. 'In my day we used suspensions as a way to give people extra holiday.'

Lucas and Harper were sitting in their usual café. Lucas hated the place. It had an atmosphere which wrapped you in a hundred wet carpets as soon as you entered and left you stinking of stale smoke and bad personal hygiene. Even a short visit ensured your suit went straight to the dry cleaners or in the trash. At least Lucas wouldn't need the services of a dry cleaner, since he wasn't going back to work for a while.

Lucas continued to air his grievances.

'They took my badge and my gun.'

'I have a gun.'

'Yes you have, and I still have the groove in my head where you shot me.' Lucas ran his index finger along the furrow above his right ear.

'So apart from getting yourself suspended, how did it go?' Harper let out a belly laugh and drank the dark sludge from his chipped mug.

'Not good.'

'No shit.'

'They were having none of it. They didn't consider that the envelope and its contents constituted enough hard evidence to restart the enquiry. They point-blank refused to send a team to Louisiana to check it out.'

'Not good then. But that hardly merits a suspension.'

'I think I may have lost my rag and cursed at them.'

'Oh dear, Lieutenant, that will never do.' Harper was poking fun at his friend's predicament. 'So what next?'

'Not sure, what do you think?' Lucas raised his hand to the guy behind the counter to order a coffee. The guy stared straight at him, and then carried on as though he hadn't seen him.

'Are you sure you want to do this?'

'If you mean, am I sure I want to find and kill that murdering bitch? Then the answer is yes. Don't you?'

'I've wanted to take Mechanic down since before you were involved. She cost me everything and there's nothing I want to see more than her face at the end my gun.' Harper swigged from the mug, his hand steady. He was still off the booze.

'You asked me what I think,' Harper continued. 'I think we should go to Baton Rouge and shake a few trees to see what falls out.'

Lucas stared at him and eventually said, 'Do you think they're right? Would we be on a wild goose chase? Do we want this so much it's clouding our judgement?'

'What does it feel like?'

'It feels like we have a lead and should follow it up,' said Lucas.

Harper returned his stare. 'If you figure we should go on the basis of that envelope, you're going to flip out over this.' He reached inside his jacket and pulled out a folded piece of paper. He flattened it on the table under the dim light. 'Two weeks after she evaded capture, Mechanic cleared Olivia Dunn's bank account. You'll recall this was her false identity at the time of the second set of killings. She withdrew the money in a single cash transaction and left the account open with a zero balance.'

'When did you find this out?' Lucas was shaking his head in disbelief.

'Three days ago, and I've had it verified by a guy I know in the bureau.' The term 'a guy' was Harper-speak for the man he occasionally blackmailed for information.

'How come I don't know about this, damn it,' said Lucas.

'Because you, my friend, are persona non grata. They keep this stuff from you to stop you going crazy. Let's be fair, even if you presented them with a fresh set of prints and signed invitation to Mechanic's house you wouldn't be allowed back onto the case. They've known about this for months and you're not in the loop any more. Besides, do you think they want to open all that shit back up? The way they screwed up the first case was bad enough, then they send Dr Jo Sells, Mechanic's twin sister, into the heart of the new investigation – and allow both of them to slip through the net. They don't want that crap raked up, the press would eat them alive. They want to bury the file and get on with making a hash of something new.'

'Shit,' said Lucas lolling back in his chair.

Harper glanced up and felt his pain. He knew what he was going through because the force had done the same to him when the first Mechanic case concluded. It drove him to drink and despair. He was determined that Lucas didn't follow the same path.

'Look at the document.' He offered it up and Lucas took it. 'Read it.'

Lucas scanned the figures and dates and placed it back on the table. 'So?'

'Look at it again, read the letterhead.'

Both men stared at each other and smiled.

'So we are going to Baton Rouge after all,' said Lucas. 'Because that's where she drew the money out.'

Chapter 6

Rebecca Moran pulled her car into one of the designated parking lots marked Private. She looked at the two-storey town house in front of her and smiled. The key to the ground-floor flat was no longer with the real-estate people, it was in her bag.

She checked the rear-view mirror and saw the removals van pass by, closely followed by the Ford sedan containing her mother and father. She cast her eyes to the heavens.

Moran had to concede she'd been a little naïve to think she would have the day to herself, a day spent moving her stuff into the new place and arranging things the way she wanted. Now she would have her possessions put where her mom thought they should be and spend the rest of the week trying to find them.

She could have refused their help but it wasn't worth the trouble. Her mother would pull her 'I'm so disappointed with you' face and sulk for weeks. Anyway, she started her new job in the next few days and could do with the help, even if it did result in some corrective activity afterwards.

Rebecca Moran was a woman in a hurry.

She had graduated with a first-class law degree and had passed her masters in criminology with flying colours. Her parents were spectacularly proud of their only child and dreamed of her soaring up the corporate ladder as a partner in a top law firm.

So when she turned up at the family home one day with a letter confirming her job in the police force there was more than a little upset. Rebecca had always wanted to join the police and had made that career choice perfectly plain but her parents didn't listen. Whenever she said the word policewoman they heard attorney.

Moran tipped the scales at no more than a hundred and thirty pounds and ate like a horse. Her dark brown hair was cut into a stylish bob and her favourite colour was black: black shirts, black suits, black shoes, black everything, even her underwear drawer was totally devoid of any feminine colours.

She had a young face with wide eyes and a bright smile. She seldom wore makeup, preferring instead to adopt the 'I don't have time for that shit' approach to female grooming. It obviously did her no harm and the constant stream of male attention confirmed that Rebecca Moran was indeed a good-looking woman.

Her diminutive stature would often mislead eager male colleagues. She might look like a college kid, but Moran was as tough as they came and fiercely ambitious. She had a competitive streak a mile wide which won her few friends but she couldn't care less. Life was about winning and coming top. She powered her way through her training at the police academy and graduated top of the class. When she was awarded the prestigious Best New Recruit medal her parents were of course very proud, but deep inside they wanted all this police nonsense to come to an end. They simply wanted their little girl to take up that position in the law for which she was destined.

She slid the key into the lock and smiled as the door swung open onto the modest hallway. A two-bedroom modern apartment with a spacious living room and through diner, and the best part of all, it was all hers.

Moran threw herself onto her new leather couch unaware that the focus of her first day at work was being zipped into body bags and taken to the mortuary to await forensic examination. One of the bodies didn't neatly fit into the heavy duty-bag due to the knurled metal spike protruding from his face.

Chapter 7

Keeping up with Harry Silverton was proving to be a real challenge. For a man who looked like he wouldn't last the day without having a coronary, he was a ball of mischief and energy. Most high rollers had a certain composure and an aura that said, 'I don't have to try, life comes to me'. Harry on the other hand seemed to want everything all at once and was perfectly happy to go get it himself.

When he arrived at the Hacienda he didn't go to his suite to freshen up, choosing instead to head straight for the gambling hall. The room was huge, filled with slot machines of every description which filled the place with a resonating cacophony of chiming bells and clattering coins. Running down the centre were the gaming tables and around the outside were the high-stakes rooms filled with green baize tables and attentive croupiers. The low level lighting ensuring the hall remained in a constant state of dusk.

Most people with the spending power of Harry Silverton would sit in a high-stakes room and let the hotel take care of the rest. But Harry Silverton wasn't most people. The normal gaming tables were teaming with people from all walks of life, a ready-made audience for him to play with. Mechanic walked five steps behind as Harry buzzed from table to table trying to make up his mind. He shouldered his way through a crowd of punters surrounding a roulette wheel and demanded a chair. Before anyone could protest he was shaking hands and introducing himself as Harry James Silverton III.

Eventually, a woman who was sitting with her husband watching the game got up and offered him her seat. Harry carved himself enough space with his elbows to sit down. He slid the dealer a billfold of notes big enough to choke a donkey.

'Beer and a JD chaser,' he called, raising his hand in the air.

An attractive blonde waitress appeared in seconds, obviously allocated to provide Harry with his every whim. Mechanic watched her work her particular brand of magic. In her purple mini dress with a split to the top of her thigh, and barely enough material to contain her ample chest, she was in for a bumpy ride.

After a second recount the dealer pushed a wall of chips in front of Harry. 'Ten thousand dollars, sir.' The crowd of onlookers gasped in unison. That's what Harry wanted to hear.

'Hey, thanks for the seat, honey,' he said, flipping the woman next to him a fifty-dollar chip.

His drinks arrived and the pretty blonde with the gaping top manoeuvred herself next to him.

'Mr Silverton,' she said in a Marilyn Monroe voice, 'your drinks.' She leaned hard against Harry as though being jostled by the crowd. This enabled her to squash her right breast against his arm. He lifted the JD from the tray and downed it in one, took the beer and left a chip of indeterminate value in its place.

'Same again, sweetheart,' he said staring down her top. She negotiated her way from the table and considered this was going to be a busy and lucrative shift.

'Here we go!' Harry shouted and threw a handful of chips onto the green baize. Those around him whooped their appreciation. Harry didn't get this reaction playing the high-stakes tables. This was what he craved.

It was at this point that Walker appeared. Mechanic eyed him from across the room noting that his jacket was buttoned all the way to hide the cut in his pants. She beckoned him over.

'Do you do all your own mending?' she asked. Walker scowled at her and walked away. Mechanic smiled. It was only for three days, she may as well have some fun.

The next four hours passed uneventfully. Mechanic watched the proceedings from a distance and marvelled at Silverton's stamina and energy, not to mention his tolerance for alcohol. The pretty blonde Marilyn Monroe waitress was on a constant shuttle back and forth to the bar for drinks and snacks. As Harry made friends with others around the table so the drinks order grew and became more frequent. Despite the tsunami of beers and JD chasers, Marilyn never missed an opportunity to squash herself against Harry, giving him a plunging prevue of what he could be enjoying later. She was a real pro.

Mechanic sipped her tonic and looked at her watch: quarter after midnight. Harry was still performing with all the energy and enthusiasm of a kid on a high-school bus trip. He'd seen off at least six tables of people yet still managed to maintain a significant crowd of onlookers. The lovely Marilyn kept pace with the constant calls for more drinks and would probably be able to retire on the tips. Mechanic couldn't work out if Silverton was financially up or down on the evening, all she knew was that he was spending hard, having a blast and was safe.

Suddenly a shrill electronic whooping could be heard over the noise of the slot machines. The house lights came up and blue xenon lights flashed on the pillars and walls. A fire alarm.

Mechanic moved in and threaded her way next to Harry.

'Mr Silverton, there is a fire alarm, we will need to evacuate the building.' Harry shrugged his shoulders and seemed relaxed about the whole thing, probably because he had a bottle of JD and a crate of Bud inside him. He looked around at the staff who were ushering people out of the hotel.

'Cash me up, we're off to the Stardust.'

'Damn it,' Mechanic kept her mouth shut, *'I thought I was off to bed.'*

Chapter 8

Mechanic hated it when clients brought their own security – it always developed into an argument over driving. She knew the short cuts and ways of avoiding the congestion of the Strip; there was a network of side roads behind the hotels linking one car park to another. Without this knowledge, tourists waited forever at traffic lights and intersections, increasing the risk of an altercation with a drunk passer-by. In Harry's case this was a scenario which was highly likely.

The other reason she hated relinquishing the driving was loss of control. As a bodyguard she had to be in charge of the environment, that was her job. Surrendering the driving duties meant the other person now took the lead and she was forced to follow. This felt extremely uncomfortable.

Sure enough Walker pulled the black limo up outside the lobby and didn't move from the driving seat when Mechanic and Silverton emerged from the hotel. He buzzed down the window.

'You're both in the back. Mr Silverton rides behind me,' he barked his orders as the window slid back up. Silverton was inviting people from the taxi line to come and join him at the Stardust, so Mechanic took his elbow and led him to the car. She opened the door and he fell in.

'You okay with directions?' Mechanic asked as she buckled up.

'Yup,' was all the reply she got. Walker eased the car away from the hotel and down the slip road.

The Hacienda lay at the south end of the Strip and the Stardust at the north. A distance of a couple of miles separated the two, a journey which on the wrong day at the wrong time could take around two hours. Which in Las Vegas, was most of the time. Making use of the back roads was a must.

Walker swung the car across the intersection towards Koval Lane which ran to the east of the main drag.

'No,' said Mechanic leaning forward, 'you're better going I-15, then take Russell and Dean Martin Road.' Walker ignored her and lurched the car across the junction. Mechanic sat back and cursed under her breath.

Silverton was on his car phone laughing and joking with a woman who couldn't get a word in edgeways. He was inviting her to come and play at the Stardust, when the poor woman wasn't even in Las Vegas.

The traffic on Koval was sluggish and tedious. It was a mass of roadworks and the route was littered with stop signs and construction vehicles. Walker was agitated by their slow progress and kept swinging the car around with exaggerated movements to avoid the double-parked cars and obstructions. Mechanic could see him flicking glances at her in the rear-view mirror, then at the clock on the dashboard, then back to her. He was out to prove a point – Koval Lane was quicker than taking the I-15. He was losing the argument fast.

'Hey, Walker, what the hell?' said Silverton, banging down the phone.

'Sorry, Mr Silverton, the traffic is heavier than expected.'

'We're wasting valuable gambling time here. Should have let the lady drive.' He gave Mechanic a theatrical wink. While she didn't appreciate the 'lady' comment, she did like the reaction it prompted in Walker. His face was set in a permanent scowl, he was not happy. Mechanic looked at him in the mirror and smiled. He looked away.

'Come on,' shouted Silverton. 'Get a move on, man.' Silverton nudged Mechanic's arm – he obviously enjoyed baiting Walker. The traffic once again ground to a halt ahead of them. Walker braked hard and swung the car to the right down a side road.

Mechanic leaned forward: 'Hey, Walker, what are you doing? Stick to Koval, these roads are no faster.'

'Thanks,' replied Walker, 'I'll bear that in mind.' He gunned the engine and turned sharp left onto a road running parallel to Koval. Mechanic sat back and shook her head.

'Come on, Walker, put your foot down. The damn place will be shut by the time we get there.' Silverton was much less playful this time.

Mechanic always figured her intuition gave her a split-second warning before things were about to turn bad. This was her split second, something was wrong.

She heard the growl of a big diesel engine as the silver grill of a massive truck ploughed into the side of the car. The impact sent them spinning in the road like a top. Mechanic's side of the car caved in slamming her head into the side window. Silverton cried out as his shoulder cracked against the door. Walker gripped the steering wheel and held on, riding out the collision as if he was at a fairground. Tyres screeched and the car skidded to a stop.

Mechanic was woozy from the blow to her head and she could see two of everything. Walker jumped from the car and yanked opened Silverton's door. He seized him by the back of his jacket and heaved him out of his seat. Silverton squealed in pain.

'What the f—?' he cried unable to find his feet as Walker dragged him along the road.

'Come on, sir, we need to move!' Walker shouted.

Mechanic pulled on the door handle but the crumpled metal wouldn't budge. She slid across the seat and staggered out into the night air. She called after Walker but the words dried in her throat.

The truck circled around and backed up hard against the sidewalk about fifteen yards away facing Mechanic. Walker had Silverton by the scruff of the neck and was frogmarching him away from the car.

Mechanic found her voice. 'Walker!' she shouted. 'Hold up!' But either he didn't hear or didn't want to.

A shot ricocheted off the roof. It was coming from the truck.

A masked man stood on the footplate with the door open firing a handgun through the open window. Mechanic dived back into the car lying flat across the back seat as bullets blew holes in the bodywork. She drew her gun and waited.

'What the fuck is going on?' she said through clenched teeth.

There was a pause in the firing.

She shuffled along the seat and leaned out of the limo, giving her a clear line of sight to the shooter. Her first shot shattered the truck window and hit the gunman in the upper chest. Before he fell, the second hit him square in the face lifting him off the footplate and into the air. He fired two more rounds at the sky and landed on the sidewalk.

Mechanic rolled from the car to see Walker still dragging Silverton along the road. She called after them as another volley of shots hit the limo. She ducked behind the front wheel.

Where the hell did that come from? She snatched a glimpse around the fender to see a second vehicle parked around ten yards away. A masked man was sprawled across the hood with his arms stretched out in front of him. Mechanic recognised the shape of a machine pistol pointed her way. He fired again, the unmistakeable purr of a short burst. The windows blew out, showering her with glass.

This was bad, she was out in the open with only the car for cover. More shells splintered against the bodywork as Mechanic pressed herself tight against the front wheel.

She eased herself back and peered under the car, allowing her eyes to adjust to the lack of light. She could see just enough.

She dug her right elbow into the road and braced her left shoulder against the underside of the car, waiting for the gunman to shift position.

Mechanic blasted off seven rounds, emptying her clip.

The man's right ankle exploded as the sixth bullet shattered its way through the bones and sinews. The following round tore away his calf muscle, the force knocking him off his feet. He fell to the ground clutching his leg.

Mechanic reloaded.

She could hear the gunman cursing as he writhed on the floor. This time she had far more target to work with. She braced herself against the underside of the car and squeezed off two more rounds.

The first hit him in the shoulder and the second in the head. Yes, Mechanic could see just fine that time.

She lay under the car listening. No further sounds.

Mechanic made a break for it, running across the tarmac to the second vehicle. The gunman was wedged between the car and the sidewalk, a stream of blood pooling in the gutter. She put two fingers on his neck to check his pulse then called to Walker who by now had stopped marching Silverton up the road.

'Clear!' she shouted. 'Both men down!' She ran across the street to the truck guy. The missing half of his face made it unnecessary to check his vital signs. Mechanic made a quick assessment of the scene.

Walker was dragging his boss back to the car.

Two dead men were lying in the road.

Sirens were sounding.

Blue and red lights flashed in the distance.

For a serial killer on the run, this was not good.

Chapter 9

Las Vegas police do not like private security operating on their patch at the best of times and like it even less when they leave dead bodies in the street.

The police interview was as intense and threatening as they could make it, but for Mechanic it was nothing more than a casual chat. She was used to interrogations that were administered by professionals, people who thought nothing of throwing in a little physical violence and waterboarding to help things along, tactics which were not allowed in the LVPD playbook.

Her cover held up under close examination, which she knew it would – after all it was designed to withstand the harshest of scrutiny. Mechanic was in possession of the right permits allowing her to carry a concealed firearm, she had the correct licence to practice, and the story of what happened was straightforward.

Walker and Silverton had been released around 4am following some light-touch questioning. Mechanic on the other hand was detained until mid-morning, forced to go over the same damn stuff time and time again. LVPD were making a point.

To the police it was an open-and-shut case: big money guy blows into town making a lot of noise and gets himself noticed by the local hoods. The traffic on the Strip forces them to take the back streets and the bad guys get lucky with the truck. It was a classic case of aggravated highway robbery. But the goons hadn't figured Mechanic into the equation. She was doing her job, protecting herself and her client.

Everyone's story was the same. Everything checked out fine.

Although for Mechanic everything was far from fine.

It didn't seem to occur to the police that both vehicles were stolen the day before, that is the day before Harry Silverton arrived in Vegas. It never occurred to them that the men who attacked them had to be lucky sons of bitches to be waiting at that precise street, at that precise time. And why did the shooters only have eyes for Mechanic and completely ignore Silverton who, after all, was the man with the money?

This situation was far from fine.

It was 11.30am when Mechanic got back to the hotel. She ran a deep bath and soaked away her aches and pains, surrounded by the best soft white towels and toiletries the Hacienda had to offer. Her neck hurt and she had a sizeable bruise on the right side of her head. Fortunately, it was beneath her hairline so didn't show, but she was constantly aware of it because it throbbed like a bastard. Her other injuries were scratches and minor bruising. Nothing a hot bath wouldn't sort out.

Silverton was in his suite with Walker complaining about lost gambling time and already on the JDs. Mechanic was deep in thought: *It's simple. The priority here is maintain my cover, get paid and get out. That's it. Keep it simple.*

But it was anything but simple and Mechanic knew it.

The events of the day churned through her head. They were riddled with inconsistencies. Rule one: if you are going to ram a car you do it on the driver's side. That way you immobilise the driver, who would usually be a security guy. The truck hit the passenger side, suggesting it was meant to immobilise Mechanic. Rule two: always target the money. The gunmen were not interested in Walker or Silverton, they were solely shooting at her. Rule three: if you have a gun, use it. Walker never once drew his weapon. He bundled Silverton away from the scene and stayed there.

This was never about a carjacking or a robbery. Before they had left the Hacienda she'd helped Harry cash in his chips and deposit the money with the hotel; he had about five hundred dollars at most in his back pocket. That's not worth a truck ramming with two shooters.

This had to be driven by a higher price tag, and the only thing that fitted the bill for Mechanic was kidnapping, which led her to one conclusion: Walker had to be in on it.

He was the one who took the route down Koval and then detoured into the back roads. He was the one who escorted Harry away from the limo while the two shooters took care of her. It all fitted.

It also explained why Walker was so hostile towards her when they met. She was not part of the plan and he needed her out of the picture. But she refused to go and his only option was to eliminate her.

With Mechanic out of the way the rest of the kidnapping would have been easy. Walker would receive a knock on the head in the struggle, Harry would get taken hostage and the fun would start. Walker would liaise with the kidnappers, managing the negotiations, and Harry would be returned a million dollars poorer and missing part of his ear. It was a tried and tested gameplay.

Okay, Mechanic thought, submerging her neck and shoulders in the hot, soapy water. *The fact that Walker wants to kidnap his boss and extort money is none of my business. It's only two more days. Maintain cover, get paid and get out – that has to be the plan.*

But that couldn't be the plan and she knew it.

'Shit, what a mess,' her voice echoed around the tiled bathroom.

The logic was crystal clear to her.

By now Walker would have realised that Mechanic was no happy amateur. He'd also have worked out that she hadn't been taken in by the failed carjacking routine and that she could spot the inconsistencies a mile off. This would make Mechanic a loose end, and in her experience loose ends had a nasty tendency of being dealt with.

Her options were limited.

She could run, but that would be a temporary fix. She could use another identity and start over somewhere else, but she had responsibilities now and they had to come first.

There was only one realistic option. It was staring her in the face.

Mechanic had to deal with the loose ends first.

Chapter 10

It's four hundred and forty miles from Tallahassee to Baton Rouge, which on a good run takes around six and a half hours. For Lucas that was six and a half hours in which he could freely obsess about his favourite topic: catching and killing Mechanic. Harper on the other hand had miscalculated and allowed Lucas to persuade him to make the trip.

'Two sets of eyes are better than one,' he had said. 'You got to come.'

The problem was Harper hadn't factored in the journey time. There are only so many times you can listen to Rose Royce Greatest Hits along with Lucas's single topic of conversation and not feel the need to jump from the speeding car. They weren't even halfway and the constant repetitive barrage had Harper reaching for the door handle.

In the end he snapped. 'Look man, I get that you're excited by all this, but you need to get real. You talk like we're going to walk down Main Street and find the murdering bitch sitting there drinking a cold one in the first bar we come to.'

'No, you get real,' Lucas said sharply. 'We know two things, right? She withdrew the money from the American Gateway Bank on 11307 Coursey Boulevard in Baton Rouge. We also know she sent me that letter from Baton Rouge. You're with me, right?'

'Yup.' Harper let out a slow sigh. It was not as though he hadn't heard those two pieces of information at least one hundred times in the last two hours.

'So that has to mean she's there. Or, if not, that's where we need to start, right? So when we get there we need to—'

'Just stop!' said Harper. 'Listen to yourself. I agree with the facts but not with your train of thought. Yes, she cleared out the bank account at American Gateway, and yes she mailed you the sugar packets to let you know she's still alive. And yes both things happened in Baton Rouge. But she is one clever bitch, and she must know you would come looking for her. She's not going to be there, man, think it through.'

Lucas was undaunted by Harper pouring cold water on his logic.

'First we go to the bank and—'

'And do what exactly?' Harper snapped. 'Ask to see the CCTV footage from the day she withdrew the money?'

'That's a start, don't you think?'

'And how will that conversation go? – "Hi, my name is Ed Lucas and this is my friend Dick Harper. Can we see your CCTV tapes for this date and time?" … "Can I ask, sir, is this a police matter?" … "Well, yes it is. I'm a Lieutenant with the Florida Police Department, but I'm suspended and Harper here is an ex-Lieutenant who was drummed out of the force for threatening to punch his boss in the face" – Do you really believe that's going to cut it?'

Lucas clicked his tongue against the roof of his mouth.

Harper hammered home his objections. 'There are several hundred bars, restaurants and cafés in Baton Rouge and any one of them could stock those types of sugar packet. It's a wild goose chase, Lucas. We need to rethink.'

'We'll talk to the bank first and take a chance with the rest. We could strike lucky.'

'But that's my point. You're not listening. What if the bank says, "Okay, sir, here's the CCTV footage, knock yourself out." We know it was her. All it will show is Mechanic standing at the counter receiving a large amount of cash, putting it in a bag and getting the hell out of there. So what? It tells us nothing we don't already know. And what if we find the very same brand of sugar packet in some backstreet joint? We already know she was there. What's the point? Keep your expectations real, that's all I'm saying.'

'Yes, but someone might know something.' Lucas was still fizzing. 'We might speak to somebody who knows her. Knows where she is …' Lucas reached down and opened the glove box. Fishing around he brought out an old photo and a plastic bag and dumped them in Harper's lap. The picture was of Jessica Sells in military dress uniform at her passing out parade. The bag was a red-topped plastic sealed evidence bag containing a single white sugar packet.

'Jesus Christ, Lucas,' Harper said holding up the evidence bag.

'They weren't interested. I thought it would be useful.'

'Tampering with evidence is a crime. It's a spell in jail, that's what it is. Aren't you in enough trouble already?' Harper threw them back into the open compartment and slammed it shut. 'You have to ease back on this, man, and get some perspective or it will destroy you.'

Much to Harper's relief, Lucas sulked and said nothing for the remainder of the journey.

* * *

Just as Harper predicted, the bank was just a bank. The ever-so-helpful junior manager said there was nothing they could do and was positively gushing when he explained to Lucas that he didn't recall the transaction.

No shit, Harper thought, *it was eight months ago*.

After a mind-numbing series of convoluted discussions, with Lucas asking the same damn questions a gazillion different ways, they left empty-handed. The cafés, bars and restaurants were next.

The early start was beginning to tell on both of them as they moved from place to place, looking at sugar packets and flashing around the picture of Mechanic.

'Have you seen this woman?' Lucas asked over and over.

'No, sorry,' was the response every time.

For Harper it was soul-destroying, but Lucas was driven by a childlike expectancy that they would somehow hit the jackpot.

'Let's split up,' said Harper after the seventeenth café. 'Let's go to the hotel, check in and get that picture photocopied. Then I'll take the bars and you can stick with coffee shops.'

'Good idea.'

Harper was relieved he no longer had to endure Lucas's inane questioning. At every venue the patter was always the same.

'Have you ever stocked these at any time?' Lucas would say, holding up the evidence pouch containing the plain white packet.

'No sir, nothing like that,' was the standard response. 'Ours have writing on them.'

'Have you seen this woman?' Lucas would hold up the photo.

'No sir, I've not seen her.'

Harper was enjoying the peace and quiet. Staking out the bars gave him a welcome rest from Lucas's intensity. It also provided him an opportunity to take a small whisky every so often which, because of his prolonged abstinence, now burned the back of his throat and made his head swim. Harper was at risk of sliding off the waggon.

The night was long and predictable. After the cafés closed, Lucas joined Harper on the bar crawl, but each took a different route to cover as much ground as possible. It was one fifteen in the morning when they finally met up to take stock of their progress.

'Big fat nothing.' Harper was not best pleased with his day.

'Same here.' Lucas held his head in his hands.

They were perched on chrome-and-leather bar stools and Harper cleared the glasses to one side. He ordered two drinks and spread a street plan out before them.

'We've been here, here and here.' He drew circles on the paper with his stubby fingers.

'These are all covered. They are the most popular areas and we've got nothing.' He looked at Lucas who was still staring down at the countertop. The barman clunked the drinks down, along with the check.

'I'm tired, let's go back to the hotel and get some shut-eye,' said Lucas. 'We can make a fresh start in the morning.'

Harper shook his head.

'Are you sure, man? I don't reckon she's here.'

'She has to be.' Lucas had more than an edge of desperation in his voice. He took a long slug of beer.

Harper placed his hand on Lucas's shoulder. 'Look man, you carry on. I'll get a rental car and drive back. You stay as long as it takes to get this out of your system. I can rattle some cages at home and see what falls out. There may be other evidence we don't know about.'

Lucas looked at Harper and nodded his head.

'You need to do this, and I need to do something else.' Harper drained his glass in one, slid from the bar stool and left.

Lucas gazed at the froth disintegrating from the top of his beer. It looked exactly how he felt.

Chapter 11

The phone in the bathroom warbled into life. Mechanic woke with a start sending lukewarm water splashing onto the tiled floor. She pulled a towel from the rail and stepped from the tub, sending more water dripping onto the floor. She lifted the receiver from its cradle on the wall.

'Hello.'

'Hudson, this is Walker. Mr Silverton would like to see you in his suite now.' The line went dead before she had chance to reply. It was a quarter after twelve and she was hungry.

Mechanic dressed herself in casual gear and munched on a breakfast bar from her bag. Her work suit was out of commission, it was dirty and torn from rolling on the ground. She holstered her gun. The leather bomber jacket hid it more effectively than her tailored jacket.

The lift doors dinged open and she stepped out into the wide corridor making her way to Silverton's room. She rapped on the door and Walker opened it wide for her to enter. He said nothing. Once inside Walker disappeared into an adjoining room.

Silverton was on the phone laughing and joking with some unfortunate person, taking large gulps of JD from a crystal glass the size of a fruit bowl. The ice chinked as he banged it down on the table and he let out an enormous belly laugh.

'Then she blew them both away!' he boomed. 'Hey, look, got to go. Got some business to attend to.' He hung up.

'Hey, Jessica Hudson I believe!' He crossed the room in two strides and shook her hand vigorously. 'Shit that was something.' He was grinning so widely his head looked as though it might split in two. 'You took those guys out like shooting turkeys in a run. That was quite something, quite something.' He let go of her hand and offered her a seat.

'Sir, please excuse me, I'm not properly dressed.'

'Nonsense, you're fine. I have to congratulate you, that was awesome!' Harry sat on a large sofa which engulfed him. The room was decked out in over-the-top furnishings to complement the over-the-top décor. They sat in a study with a huge glass-topped desk and comfortable chairs. Through the adjoining twin doors she could see an even larger sitting room with a massive TV which was set into the wall. Through more double doors was the bedroom. She calculated the suite had more square footage than her two-up-two-down condo in town. 'Where the hell did you learn to shoot like that?'

'I've done some range work in the past,' Mechanic replied trying to shrug it off.

'When that guy opened fire and the bullets were bouncing off the limo, I thought …' Harry rambled on excitedly, recounting every detail as if it was news to Mechanic. He was highly animated and waved his arms around like a windmill. Occasionally he levelled a pretend gun and fired. 'Bang! You blew his face off from inside the car, and then …'

But Mechanic wasn't listening. She watched Walker pacing around in the other room. He had the phone pressed to his ear and was marching about, at least as far as the cord would allow. His voice was quiet and low. He flashed glances her way but avoided direct eye contact.

'So, what do you think?' Silverton sat on the edge of his seat.

'Of what, sir?'

'My offer, what do you say?' Harry was leaning so far forward Mechanic thought he'd topple over.

'Sorry, Mr Silverton, could you repeat it?' She held her hands up in apology.

'Come work for me,' Harry said with his usual childlike enthusiasm. 'Join me. I could do with someone running my security and I want it to be you.'

She tore herself away from Walker.

'Well that's a generous offer, Mr Silverton, but I'm not sure relocating fits with my plans at the moment.'

'I don't need you in Philly, I need you here. I have business interests in Vegas and regularly fly people in and out. I'd like you to look after them and make sure they have a good time. You would call the shots and organise what you need. When I come to Vegas you would be looking after me. Walker's okay but he's not you. What do you say? I pay well.' He finished the sentence rubbing his thumb and first finger together in the universal sign for money.

'This is a big surprise, Mr Silverton. I don't know what to say. I'm flattered.'

'Then say yes.' He got to his feet.

'I need to know on what basis I would be employed and how that would fit with my private work.' Mechanic's head was working overtime.

'Oh, details, details, details,' Harry said waving his hands around, swatting away imaginary flies. 'Let's assume we're going to get all those itty-bitty details right. What do you say in principle? Huh?'

'Can you give me a minute?'

'Sure, I'm busting for a leak anyway.' He went to the desk and picked up a slip of paper. 'Nearly forgot,' he said handing it to her. 'Let's call this a saved-my-ass bonus. You earned it, girl.' He scuttled off in the direction of the bathroom.

She held the paper in her hand and stared at the scribbled handwriting. It was a cheque for fifteen thousand dollars made out to Jessica Hudson. Mechanic reread it. It definitely said fifteen thousand, it definitely had her name on it and it definitely had today's date on it. She looked at the cheque and then at Walker. He'd finished his call and was reading a newspaper with a coffee in front of him.

He looked up.

Their eyes locked and in that split second Mechanic knew all she needed to know.

She folded the cheque and stuffed it into her jeans pocket. She pushed herself out of the chair and walked over to Walker who was still holding her gaze. As she approached he put down his paper.

Mechanic stood in front of him invading his personal space. 'I'm about to accept an offer to run Silverton's security here in Vegas, which means when you're in town you work for me.'

'I'm gonna talk to Silverton, this isn't going to happen.' Walker went to stand but she held her ground blocking his path.

'Say what you want, Walker, because I don't think he listens to you. I'm going to accept the job and when you're here you'll work for me.' Mechanic placed her hands on the arms of the chair and leaned her face in close.

Walker spluttered another incoherent protest.

Mechanic cut him off.

'You and I need to be clear. I don't do sloppy. And last night was very sloppy. I figure your game was kidnapping with a sizeable ransom.' She stared into his eyes and they flickered. 'Thought so. But it was a shambles, even if you discount the fact that I was there to put a spanner in the works. Your guys were sloppy and so were you.' She paused allowing Walker to digest what was being said.

'I know how to do this stuff and I won't stand for shoddy work. Are we clear?' She stepped away and stood up straight. 'So when this goes down again, it will be on my terms. And please don't labour under any misapprehension, this is not a discussion. You have no option. Are we clear?'

Walker stared at her, open-mouthed.

'It doesn't look like I have a choice,' he said. She smiled and walked back to the other room where Harry had now emerged from the bathroom.

'Mr Silverton,' she offered him her hand, 'in principle, I say yes.'

Mechanic had been taught that all war is based upon deception. When she locked eyes with Walker, what passed between them told her it was time to go to war.

Now was the time to deceive.

Chapter 12

Rebecca Moran's first day at work was nothing like she'd imagined. The normal routine for starting a new job was always a parade of inductions and paperwork, drinking coffee and trying to remember people's names. She'd done none of that.

She'd filled in one form to confirm her new address, signed her name five times, corrected her bank details and said 'Hi' to a handful of people whom she wasn't introduced to. At least she had a badge, a gun and a desk. Presumably the phone would be coming later.

Moran recognised her new boss across the office, he'd interviewed her when she came for the assessment day. Captain Brennan was pushing fifty with craggy features and wore suits that were too big for him, probably the product of renewed gym membership and a reluctance to buy new clothes.

He marched up to her.

'Morning, Rebecca, welcome to LVPD.'

'Thank you, sir.' She shook his hand.

'Do you have everything you need? Is the day going well for you?'

'Well, sir, I was wondering if I could meet some of the—'

'Good, glad that's going well.' He handed Moran a plastic folder. 'Go to the mortuary, they are about to do an autopsy on three drug dealers. See what you think.'

'Thank you, sir. Is there any chance I could meet a few of the t—'

'Better get your skates on, they're going under the knife anytime now. Grace said something about it being unusual. See you later for a coffee.' He strode away in a whirlwind of urgency.

* * *

Forty minutes and three requests for directions later, Moran stood in the reception area of the city mortuary clutching the plastic file. She'd signed herself in and was waiting for Dr Jonathan Grace.

A door opened and a tall middle-aged man with a shaved head and large round glasses breezed in.

'You here to see the three guys? LVPD?'

'Yes. I'm Detective Moran. I have some papers.' She flashed her new badge and waved the file in front of him.

'I'm Jonathan Grace, the medical examiner. I thought it would be good for one of you lot to take a look at this before we do our thing.'

'Okay, well what am I looking at?'

Grace handed her a white coat, overshoes and a hairnet.

'Put these on and I'll show you.'

They walked down a narrow corridor bathed in the sanitised glow from the fluorescent lighting. Grace skimmed a card through a slot in the lock and the door marked Forensic Autopsy Lab clicked open.

Moran entered and was hit by the smell of ammonia, disinfectant and rotting chicken. The room was large and bright with tiled walls and floor. There was a low humming noise from the refrigeration units keeping the guests cool.

'These vics came in a few days ago. All found at the same location, all involved in the selling of narcotics and all with a rap sheet as long as my arm.'

Grace ushered Moran over to three stainless steel tables, each with drain holes at the one end. Hanging from the ceiling were chrome plated weighing scales and water nozzles. On the tables were three dead bodies covered with blue sheets.

Grace stepped forward and drew back two of the covers, one in each hand.

'In the file are the personal details of each vic. It looks like a drug-related hit – you know the form, where one crew decides to muscle in on another.'

Moran's eyes were fixed on the unveiling of the two bodies. This was not what a first day should be like, but she was already feeling the tingling rush of adrenaline.

'The reason for the call is this one.' Grace threw back a third sheet to reveal a large white male, his head pinned back, with a knurled iron bar sticking out of his mouth.

'What the hell is that!'

'At this stage we're not certain, but from what I can tell it looks like the type of metal rod used to reinforce concrete. I think it's called rebar in the trade.'

'Have you seen it before?'

'Yes, there's plenty of it around Vegas with the amount of construction going on, but never seen it used in this way before.'

Moran moved closer. 'What happened to the other guys?'

'That's the interesting thing. This guy died of asphyxiation and blood loss when his throat was ripped out and the other had his skull split in two. They both suffered major blunt-force trauma ante-mortem. And my guess is they were both struck with the same implement. Steel reinforcing bar, here take a look.'

They moved over to the first body, a stocky guy with tattoos.

'See the pattern of bruising. It's the same on both men. I figure when we extract that spike from the big man's mouth we'll find it's got the same pattern as the ridges around the wounds.'

'So whoever did this used the same weapon to kill all three.'

'Looks that way, which, if this is a drug-related turf war, is unusual. Drive-by shootings are the normal way to settle disputes around here, not this.'

'Was any other weapon found at the scene?'

'A handgun. It hadn't been fired. It was found next to this guy.' Grace pointed to the second body, a tall man with a yawning hole where his throat should be. 'We'll know more when we run prints.'

'To have killed all three in this way would require somebody getting up close and personal. This is more like a street brawl than an execution.'

'I agree. The other thing is this.' Grace went to the fat guy and tilted his body sideways. 'Puncture wounds to his upper back. Two of them. Made with a short blade with cutting edges on both sides.'

Moran took a closer look.

'They don't look deep enough to kill him.'

'That's what I figure but until I do more work I can't say. But I think whoever did this ...' he pointed to the metal bar, '... did so when he was alive.'

Moran was buzzing. As first days go, this beat the shit out of meeting the team.

Chapter 13

The journey back to Tallahassee was grim. Lucas's expectations had been dashed to pieces to be replaced with despondency and rage. Days spent chasing down every café and bar to the point of embarrassment had taken its toll.

Several times he lost track of where he had been and visited establishments for a second and third time. He was always greeted politely by staff, who exchanged knowing glances across the coffee tables.

'Weren't you here the other day, sir?' one young man asked him. Lucas stared at him without a shred of recognition. The young man shook his head and smiled. 'I still don't know the woman in the photo, sir, and we still don't stock plain white sugar packets.' Lucas turned and left without uttering another word.

It was an exhausting and humiliating experience.

Harper was right to leave him to it. Despite the complete failure of his wild goose chase, Lucas had to get it out of his system. He had to explore every possibility and if that meant turning up at cafés and asking the same people the same questions he'd asked two days earlier, then so be it. His legs ached, his head hurt and he was dog-tired. But most of all he was fucking furious.

Then things got a whole lot worse. He arrived home to find his wife, Darlene, gone.

Every woman who marries a cop accepts there will be three in the relationship: her, him and the job. The problem for Darlene was there were four: her, him, the job and Mechanic.

Mechanic was like a mistress she could never hope to compete with. Most men who cheat on their wives tend to keep the other woman under wraps. In Lucas's case he flaunted her in front of his wife every waking minute of every day. Darlene had recognised the gradual slide into unhealthy obsession – as Lucas's physical health improved so his mental health took a dive. He thought of nothing else and certainly didn't think of her.

She stuck with him through his recuperation but was squeezed into playing a bit part in their marriage. It was ironic to think she'd come so close to losing her husband to Mechanic, nursing him back to health only to lose him all over again – to the same damn woman.

Lucas arrived home to a brief note on the dining room table. It said, 'I'm staying with Heather. Call only in an emergency. If not an emergency, don't call.'

Lucas considered the breakdown of his marriage constituted just that, so called immediately.

Neither Darlene nor Heather was impressed with his urgency, especially at one thirty in the morning. And despite his protestations to the contrary, his wife did not share Lucas's assessment that her leaving him was an emergency.

She hung up in tears.

Lucas replaced the receiver and went back to planning what to do next to catch Mechanic.

* * *

Lucas swung his car into the parking bay and bumped the front wheels against the kerb. He reached over, grabbed a brown paper bag from the front passenger seat and stepped out into the Florida mid-morning sun. He felt like shit.

Crossing the road, Lucas headed for yet another café. This time he was sure he'd find what he was looking for.

He shoved open the heavy door and the toxic atmosphere clogged the back of his throat. He put his hand up to his mouth and stifled a cough. His eyes took a while to adjust to the smoky gloom. It never ceased to amaze Lucas how many people frequented this place by choice. Their pasty faces turned to look at the stranger standing in the doorway. Harper spotted Lucas and raised his hand.

Lucas picked his way around the jumble of chairs and tables and sat next to him in the half-moon booth.

'Hey,' said Harper.

'Hey yourself.'

'Did you find anything?'

'Yes and no.'

'That sounds intriguing. You look dreadful, where the hell have you been?'

'All over.'

'I thought you'd give it one more day at most. You've been gone four days.'

'It looks like you were right. I returned to the bank several times and spoke to different people. The story was the same. No, you can't have access to our CCTV and no, we don't recall the transaction.' Lucas was drumming his fingers on the table.

'That figures.'

'I carted around the photograph but not a single person recognised Mechanic. It was as if she was never there.' Lucas continued to drum.

'Well we know she was there because she withdrew the money from the account. We even know which bank.'

'Yes, but that's a long way from her "being there" isn't it.'

'I don't get you.' Harper frowned.

'What I mean is,' he paused, 'she could have driven through Baton Rouge on the way to somewhere else, stopped off at the American Gateway Bank, withdrawn the cash and left.' The drumming on the table grew louder.

Harper nodded his head. 'Yeah, so what? I suppose she could have breezed through.'

'Only she didn't, did she,' Lucas said with a slight edge to his voice, 'because I got the letter posted from Baton Rouge containing the sugar packets. She withdrew the cash from the bank eight months ago and I received the letter three weeks ago.

So that would suggest she was in town for the best part of seven months, wouldn't it?' Lucas's fingers were drumming hard.

'Well yes I suppose it—'

Lucas cut him off.

'But not a single person recognised her photo. Not a single café, bar, supermarket, gas station or corner store has any recollection of seeing her. Seven months and not a single sighting.'

'What did you expect, man? Baton Rouge is a big place and you were stretching it if you thought you were going to get a hit.' Harper was getting annoyed with the drumming when it suddenly stopped.

'That might well be true, but it got me thinking. He reached down and picked up the paper bag. 'It got me thinking about these …' He upended the bag and hundreds of sugar packets scattered across the table and onto the floor.

'Hey, what the …'

'Take a look at them,' Lucas said holding up a handful. 'They all have print on them. Take a look.'

He scooped up a handful and thrust them at Harper, turning them over and over in his hands. They were all covered in writing, some emblazoned with the name of the establishment, some saying brown or white, some with fancy scrolling around the edges.

'See what I mean?' said Lucas holding them at eye level. 'Take a look.' He thrust them into Harper's face.

'Okay, man, I get it!' he said pushing them away. 'So they all have writing on. I get it … Jesus Christ.'

'Yes, they all have writing,' Lucas said bulldozing the entire tabletop of sugar packets into Harper's lap.

'Hey! What is wrong with you, man?'

'But they don't all have fucking writing on them, do they?'

Lucas reached across and grabbed the sugar pot from the next table and slammed it down in front of Harper. He grabbed a handful of packets and spread them out. Harper looked down at the cluster of plain white sugar packets. Lucas produced the evidence pouch from his inside pocket and slid it next to them – they matched.

'I couldn't get my head around how Mechanic knew my return-to-work date. I invented all sorts of convoluted explanations in my head and made it possible. After all, she had a direct line into your investigation and into mine, so who's to say she didn't have another link into the station. But it wasn't convoluted, it was straightforward. She didn't know when I was going back to work, cos it was you. You sent the fucking letter, didn't you? You took the sugar packets from here, sent the letter to some long-lost cousin in Baton Rouge and asked them to mail it to me.'

Lucas was shaking with rage.

Harper raised his head. 'I drove there,' he said. 'I don't have a cousin in Baton Rouge. I drove there and posted it myself.'

'You fuck!' Lucas shouted, banging his hands down and pushing himself away from the table. 'What the hell made you think that was a good idea? I've been trekking around every joint in Baton Rouge asking people if they remember a woman who probably stopped there for thirty minutes to withdraw cash.'

'You trekked around because you wanted to,' Harper snapped back. 'And you wanted to because you got your fight back. You might want revenge now but let's face it, until you received that letter you were checking out. You were ready to throw in the towel.'

'What!'

'After the first Mechanic case, I slid so far down into a black hole I couldn't crawl back out. I had every bit of fight kicked out of me and had nothing more to give. I was broken and had jack shit to live for. I stopped caring, man. Have you any idea what that feels like? When you don't care about the job, about your friends, about your family, you don't even care about yourself. I didn't care about nothing. I hit the booze hard and my life dissolved into an alcoholic mush. I didn't want the same thing to happen to you. I didn't want you to stop caring. You needed something to fight for. So I gave it to you.'

'You mean you did this …' Lucas said holding up the sugar packets, 'for my own good!'

'Yes, I suppose I did.'

'Jesus Christ.'

'I didn't want you to go the same way. I knew about the cash transaction in Baton Rouge and mailed the letter from there. Simple as that. You did the rest.'

The room was silent.

'I don't fucking believe this.' Lucas kicked the table away and left.

A dozen disappointed faces watched him storm out. After all, it's not every day you get a front-row seat to watch two guys fighting over sugar.

Chapter 14

Mechanic escorted her new boss as he created havoc in a host of casinos, though most of the time it felt less like escorting and more like chasing after.

It occurred to her that today must be can't-make-my-mind-up day. As soon as Harry got himself comfortable and started throwing chips around, he was talking about where to go next.

Mechanic advised Harry not to talk about the carjacking as the police were still investigating the case. He nodded and tapped the side of his nose, then shouted about it to anyone who would listen.

The day was uneventful. A couple of drunks took offence at Harry so Mechanic stepped in and with good humour moved them along. A fifty-dollar chip to say sorry helped them on their way. An older woman, who had dressed herself from the wardrobe of a teenager, thought it was fine to sit next to Harry and siphon chips into her purse. Mechanic pointed her out to hotel security and they took care of the rest. The chips were returned without Harry even noticing they were gone.

He was still loud and he was still brash. But, on the whole, the fact that he'd almost been killed had the effect of making Harry a nicer person, and as such there was less requirement to keep him out of harm's way. That allowed Mechanic ample time to think about Walker.

Accepting the job with Harry kept her close to him, which was essential if she was going to tidy up the loose ends. But she ran the risk that her real intentions would shine through – he might be dumb but he wasn't stupid. A casual glance or careless word in the wrong place would tip Walker off. She had to keep it clean and controlled, and convince him she was genuine.

Mechanic had not finalised her thoughts, but sticking with Walker's kidnap plan was a good option. It would also help to rebuild his confidence after things had gone so badly wrong. Mechanic needed him confident and careless.

The most difficult aspect Mechanic had to manage today was the logistics of Harry's indecision about which casino to inflict himself on.

Then all of that changed.

Harry got a phone call while in Caesars Palace and he shifted into business mode. He beckoned Mechanic over.

'I need to get back to the Hacienda – a couple of work issues need fixing,' he said, sweeping chips into her outstretched arms.

'Okay, Mr Silverton, let's get you back to base.' She nodded towards Walker who went to get the car.

Once back at the hotel, Harry shut himself away in the study and shouted down the phone. Mechanic could hear that all was not well and he was not a happy man.

That left her and Walker sitting in the lounge like a couple suffering the cold blast of silence following a quarrel. Walker edged forward with his elbows on his knees and spoke first.

'So how is this going to work?'

'Not sure yet,' she said shaking her head. 'How much were you going to take him for?'

'About two mill.'

'Wow, nice. Is he good for that much?'

'And more. He's got cash in his pockets to cover double that.'

'Would the negotiations have run smoothly or were you expecting to cut bits off him?'

'No. With me running that end of the operation it would have been a breeze.'

'Would the police be involved?'

'Definitely not. I've worked for Silverton for five years and I'm not sure everything he does would stand up to close scrutiny.

His people back in Philly are well aware his business interests are a little shady and wouldn't welcome a police presence.'

'How was the drop going to go down?'

'Keep it simple. I leave a bag of money in the trunk of a car in a disused warehouse out towards the Hoover Dam. My men come and take it, drive to the Valley of Fire State Park and switch vehicles. Then lie low.'

'And you trust these guys?'

'Yes, or at least I did until you wasted them.'

'They were second-rate, Walker.' She was unapologetic. 'Are there any more of them?'

'Yeah, there are still a couple of people I know could do the job.'

'Local?'

'Both of them.'

'Are they known to the police?'

'One's done time for aggravated burglary, the other is clean. Neither does drugs.'

'Good. Get them lined up because I want to move fast.'

'How do you see it going down?'

'Pretty much along the same lines as your screw-up but this time done properly. A carjacking followed by a ransom demand. Straightforward.'

Walker nodded his approval. He liked the fact she wanted to run with his plan.

'But with one significant difference.' She fixed Walker with an icy stare. 'This time you get kidnapped as well.'

Walker shook his head in protest. 'No, that's not—'

'If I'm going to hold your hand through this I need some added security. What's to stop you and your boys cutting me out the loop when you get the cash? If we stick with your original plan you would be in Philly conducting the negotiations and your stooges would have two mill in a bag. Then with a puff of smoke, you're all gone.' Walker made a non-committal sound which sounded like 'no we wouldn't' or 'of course we would'.

Mechanic continued, 'It's my plan or nothing. I know how to do this and your execution is piss poor. I can pull this off, you can't. When we're done you will be a damn sight richer and a hero into the bargain. But I need you where I can see you. When the hit goes down, it will be you and Silverton taken hostage. That way I know where you are.'

'But who would conduct the negotiations?'

'Come on, Walker, think it through. I saved his life, remember – he thinks I dance on water. During the initial round of contact, you issue the instruction to the estates team to hand that responsibility over to me. That way I'm in control of the money and in control of you.'

'But I could take a walk at any time.' Walker shook his head. 'You forget that my guys are calling the shots at the holding pen.'

'No, I've not forgotten. That's why I will have a little piece of added insurance of my own. One of my boys will be watching you. He's a real pro, I've seen him take out bad guys from a mile away. They never saw him and neither will you. He'll have eyes on you through the whole operation. One false move and you all die. Oh, and I will be the one to make the drop.'

'Hell no. What stops you taking the cash and doing a runner with your invisible man?'

'Nothing I suppose. But why would I put myself in that position? I've already saved Silverton from one attack so why would I expose myself like that? All I have to do is stay put and take my cut of the money. Think it through, Walker, think it through.'

'I don't like this.' Walker was not prepared for the twist in the plan.

'And the best thing about this plan is ...' Mechanic leaned forward, her voice hard and uncompromising, 'you don't have to like it. You get kidnapped along with our boss and two weeks later you're one and half mill better off.'

'One and a half, how do you figure that?'

'The other advantage of you being in the mix is the ransom goes up. You're a loyal employee and Silverton would want to secure your safe return as well as his own. So it's three mill split fifty–fifty. And before you say anything, my math is fine. You get one and a half to share with your goons and I get one and a half. And yes, I get the bigger share.'

Walker thought for a while. 'Okay. I'm in.' He extended an open hand towards Mechanic.

She looked at it and shook her head.

'This is not a second-hand car deal.'

'Have it your way.' He withdrew his hand. 'The only thing left is, where and when?'

'It needs to be soon. But as for where—' she stopped as Harry burst in waving a sheaf of papers.

'Listen up. The Vegas idiots are making a complete fuck up of this, so we'll be sticking around. Get your bunks sorted out, we're gonna be staying till it's fixed.' He turned and marched the wad of papers back into the study and slammed the door.

Mechanic looked at Walker and smiled.

'Vegas it is then.'

Chapter 15

Lucas was in an enormous sulk. The rage he felt against Mechanic had been replaced by a dark morass of frustration which penetrated him to the core. His wife was gone, he was suspended from work and his so-called friend had turned out to be a total prick. Things could hardly be worse.

He'd been in this state for three days when he got a phone call from Harper.

'What do you want?'

'Meet me at Brightwood Country Club as soon as you can.'

'Why would I do that? Do you have a whole crate of sugar for me this time?'

'Just get there.' Harper put the phone down.

'Jerk off,' Lucas said to no one.

Despite his anger Lucas had to admit Harper had a point – he had been going downhill and the envelope proved to be a wake-up call. He was firing on all cylinders now, even if they were firing in an unhealthy, morbid, obsessive kind of way. He had to acknowledge the letter had galvanised him into action, but he would never admit it to Harper.

* * *

Forty minutes later Lucas swung into a visitor's parking space at the country club and got out of the car. He waited in the sunshine as Harper crossed the grounds towards him. Harper was all business and no apology.

'There's something you need to see.'

'Have you got yourself a FedEx van now to make deliveries in person?'

Harper ignored the insult and walked to the outbuildings at the back of the club. This was the place where Mechanic had beaten Lucas half to death. If it wasn't for Harper's intervention, he would certainly be dead, that was for sure. His anxiety ratcheted up with every step.

He took Harper by the arm and pulled him back.

'Why are we going there?' He tilted his head in the direction of the block-walled building with bright red roller-shuttered doors.

'You'll see.' Harper was obviously not in the mood for chitchat.

They entered a side door into a room containing hedge-clipping tools, lawn mowers and every type of gardening equipment. A set of narrow concrete steps spiralled down to the left, leading to the basement where Mechanic had taken Lucas.

Lucas hesitated at the top, staring down at the steps as they blurred into the darkness, beads of sweat standing proud on his top lip. He grasped the handrail tight to steady himself. Harper pushed past and disappeared from view. A light flickered at the bottom and the landing below was bathed in a square of pale yellow light.

Lucas's breathing was erratic and shallow. His knuckles turned white and his whole body began to shake.

'You okay?' called Harper.

Lucas froze. He couldn't put his foot onto the first step. His heart felt like it was about to burst in his chest.

'You coming?' Harper called again.

Lucas's legs wouldn't move.

He couldn't breathe and his head swam in a collage of pain. His pulse thudded inside his head and the sound of water rushed in his ears.

He felt Harper grip his arm.

'Hey it's fine,' he said gently. 'There's no one here, it's only us. Look at me, Lucas. Look at me.'

Lucas tried to tear himself way from the images in his head. The snarling, spitting face of a killer who wanted to take his life. The sickening sound as Mechanic shattered his leg and broke his ribs. The searing pain of the cord biting into his wrists as he swung helplessly from the overhead steam pipe. The feeling of warm blood running down his arms as the rope cut deep into his flesh.

He could taste bile in his mouth. He was going to throw up.

'Look at me, Lucas. Look at me.' Harper was supporting him on the top step with his hands on his shoulders. Lucas swayed back and forth, his eyes staring straight through Harper. The whole world was swimming, his peripheral vision closing in.

'Lucas!' Harper shook him. 'She's not here. Try to focus.'

Lucas let out a rush of air and snapped back to reality. He shook his head to collect himself.

'Sorry,' he said catching his breath. 'It's just … it's flooding back.'

'It's okay,' said Harper. 'It's okay.'

Lucas's breathing slowed and the pounding in his head and chest subsided. 'I'm fine,' he said tapping both hands on Harper's shoulders. He was still a little unsteady but allowed Harper to lead him down to the basement.

He swallowed hard as the features of the room came into view. The place had been jet-washed clean and the workbenches were much less cluttered than he remembered. He felt the bile rise once more into his throat when he saw the steam pipe. The grey concrete floor below was discoloured where his blood had stained it dark red. Lucas closed his eyes and struggled to fight the rising panic.

Harper was next to him. 'You want to go on?'

'Yes.'

'I got something to show you.' Harper walked to the back of the room and turned to face Lucas. 'I'm sorry about the sugar packets. I thought I was doing the right thing.'

'You weren't.'

'I realise that now. I'm sorry.'

'You're a prick.'

Harper smiled. 'Yes, you're probably right.'

'Why are we here anyway?' Lucas was feeling a little more stable.

'It's what you said the other day.'

'What did I say?'

'That you couldn't get your head around how Mechanic would know your return-to-work date.'

'I don't remember. I only remember it wasn't her after all.'

'You said that you invented all sorts of convoluted explanations to make it fit. You convinced yourself that somehow she knew. When you figured it out, there was no complex reasoning, it was straightforward. She didn't know when you were returning to work, I did.'

'Yes, I remember. What of it?'

'You're not the only one wrestling with unanswered questions. I could never work out how Mechanic and Jo simply disappeared, the roadblocks and search zones were in place for two weeks and they vanished into thin air. How could that be?'

'I suppose she slipped through the net.'

'I don't buy it. The force threw everything at it and got nothing.'

'She's a clever bitch and somehow evaded us.'

'Yes, that's right, she is. But she's not a magician. She's a clever bitch with a working knowledge of building modifications,' said Harper rapping the back wall with his fist. He picked up a screwdriver, removed two screws from the side of the plasterboard wall and levered its flat edge against the corner. A section of the wall moved, swinging towards them like a door. Lucas held his breath.

Harper opened it wide and stepped inside. There was a flicker and the interior flooded with light.

'Take a look!' he called.

Lucas stepped around the edge of the wall and stared at the concealed room within. It was fifty-feet square with three rows of shelving running around the walls. A military field bed was in one corner and a soiled mattress in the other. He could see pots, pans and cooking equipment along with articles of clothing folded into piles. Large blue polythene drums stood against one wall and sealed white buckets were stacked against the other. Canned and dried foods sat in rows on the shelves and black plastic bags tied at the top were scattered across the floor.

'You were right.' Harper broke the silence. 'We both made the same mistake. We were looking for a complicated theory to explain how they managed to escape, when we should have been looking for the simple explanation. We couldn't find them because they never left.'

'How long do you think they were here?'

'Don't know but judging by the amount of preparation that went into this place they could have been here for weeks. While we were busy combing the basement for hair follicles, fibres and blood matches, they were here all the time.'

Lucas walked around inspecting the various items. He reached the sealed white buckets.

'Careful with them,' Harper said, 'they're full of shit.'

'Much like you.' Lucas retreated to a safe distance. 'This is incredible, it's like those people who prepare for doomsday.'

'Yeah it is,' replied Harper, 'but here's the best bit.'

Harper pointed to a stack of white boxes on the shelf.

'Medical supplies,' Harper said flipping through the boxes. 'Loads of them. Saline drips, bandages, antibiotics, adrenaline pumps, intravenous lines – you name it, it's here.'

'Are those—'

'Oxygen bottles, yes.'

'It's kitted out like a field hospital.'

'That's what I thought.' Harper knelt beside a dark patch on the floor. 'This is blood and lots of it. And take a look at this.' He stood and opened up one of the bags pulling out a dressing stained brown with old blood. 'There are sacks of used dressings and empty saline pouches. I shot one of the bitches but we don't know which one, right?'

'Right,' said Lucas.

'So let's ask ourselves a question. Which one knew how to use this stuff?'

'Not Jo, that's for sure,' replied Lucas. 'She was a backroom girl. It has to be Mechanic.'

'With her training and covert ops experience, that's what I figured. This whole room has to be down to her. It's her retreat, a place to run to when things get hot. It makes sense she would stock it with medical gear in case she was hurt and needed running repairs.'

'Agreed.'

'Mechanic wouldn't stockpile this stuff if she didn't know how to use it. And there are bags and bags of it.'

Lucas nodded and looked around him.

Harper continued, 'So now let's ask ourselves a second question—'

Lucas interrupted, 'Why would you use so much?'

The obvious answer flashed between the two men.

To keep someone alive.

Chapter 16

Staying in Vegas suited Mechanic. She was on home turf which put her at a distinct advantage over Walker. He still harboured misgivings about being taken hostage but the logic was overwhelming and the additional money was inspired. Anyway, it wasn't as if he had a choice.

Harry was spending his time either yelling at someone on the phone or holding crisis meetings with a constant stream of worried staff dressed in suits. Hitting the casinos was off the agenda, which gave Mechanic time to complete the necessary planning.

She identified the location where the kidnap was to take place and scripted the sequence of events after the vehicle was hit. The warehouse near the Hoover Dam suggested by Walker was a sound choice and she identified the ideal place for the money drop. Mechanic drew up a detailed timing plan to synchronise the play, developed a comms strategy and built a set of contingencies to cover the what-if scenarios. She took out a short-term rental on a flea-infested condo on the outskirts of the city, it was the perfect place to hold Silverton and Walker while the negotiations were in progress. The block housed around twenty apartments which were rented out by the week – different people came and went all the time and it was dirt cheap, cash only. Walker was impressed. No wonder she thought his work was shoddy.

Today Mechanic had a little surprise for Walker.

'We need to meet the others,' she said, catching him off-guard.

'But I thought I was to handle my guys?'

'I want to brief them personally. I need to look them in the eye and be sure they understand what to do. We must move quickly and with Silverton embroiled in his business now is a good time.'

'Okay, I'll contact them, they're both on standby awaiting my call. Have you figured out when we go?'

'When Silverton decides the time is right to go back on the gambling trail, that's when we strike.'

'Where do you want to meet?'

'At the warehouse – it'll be good to take another look at it anyway.'

'I'll set it up,' he said and left the room in search of the public call boxes.

* * *

In less than an hour Mechanic and Walker crunched the tyres of the limo over the dirt track and parked at the disused warehouse. It was a vast building which had once been used for grain storage but was now a derelict shell. Its location in the middle of nowhere was perfect: about three miles west of the main road to the dam, an ideal place to switch vehicles after the drop.

Walker pulled aside a section of metal sheeting and they squeezed through. The floor was a patchwork of broken concrete lit by blinding shafts of sunlight where the roof was missing.

Mechanic looked around, the place was empty.

'Where are the others? I thought you said they were here?'

She turned to find Walker holding a gun.

'There are no other guys. The same as there was never a plan to take Silverton. You played me for a fool and you lost, big time.'

'Put the gun down, Walker, and stop screwing around. We got business to attend to here. There's three million dollars at stake and I don't play games with that amount of money.'

'Drop the pretence, Jessica Hudson, or whoever the hell you are. Your acting stinks. Now take your gun out real slow and toss it over here.'

'Walker, what is this all about? You and I are working together. What are you playing at?'

'Just do it.'

'What the fuck is this about, Walker?'

'Do it now.'

Mechanic shook her head, withdrew her gun and slid it across the floor.

'The way you took out my boys you have got to be a professional. So I did a little digging and guess what? You're not ex-military or ex-police and you have no record of any weapons training. Nor do you appear on any search on close protection training. You come up as plain Jessica Hudson and that doesn't figure. By all accounts you're an office worker, well I don't buy it. You don't get that good practising on a firing range.'

'You're talking shit, Walker,' Mechanic protested. 'I got lucky with those guys, that's all. Now can we get back to business?'

'Bullshit. There was nothing lucky about what you did and you know it. No, Jessica Hudson, you're well-trained and for some reason you got a watertight cover story. And therein lies the difficulty.' He circled around Mechanic, the gun pointing at her head. 'If you're what I think you are then we both have a massive problem.'

'I don't get it. What problem? What are you talking about?'

'You figured out the kidnap plan and wasted my team, so my obvious next step is to take you out because you're a risk. You're a loose end. My problem is you'll want to strike first. This is all about loose ends, Jess, and who gets to tidy them up first.'

'Walker, where are you getting off on this?' Her voice was shaking.

'You didn't fool me for one minute with the 'we need to kidnap Silverton' routine. It was too obvious. You were playing me in order to get close enough and pull the trigger.'

'Walker, we're in this together. What happened in the past has gone. I don't like you but that doesn't mean we can't work together to get rich.' She was pleading with him.

'That's horseshit. Your only target is me, I saw through it straightaway. I have to congratulate you though on your meticulous planning. It's a work of art. Shame we won't be using it.'

'Walker, put the fucking gun down. We can work something out. I don't want to kill you, we can get rich together.'

'It's been a pleasure working with you.'

Walker squeezed the trigger.

There was a metallic click.

He pulled it again – click! He looked at his gun and flicked the safety catch on and off – click!

Mechanic put her hand to the back of her head and removed the 9mm revolver which was duck-taped in place between her shoulder blades. She blew a hole in Walker's left knee. He screamed and fell to the ground clutching his shattered leg.

'It doesn't work without this.' She reached into her pocket and held up the firing pin between her fingers. 'I did say you were sloppy.'

She picked up her gun from the floor and replaced it in its holster. Walker was writhing around in the dust with both hands on his knee trying to stop the blood.

'You should take your gun into the shower with you. Leaving it around your hotel room, you don't know who might mess with it.'

'You fucking bitch!' Walker made a grab for his right ankle where he kept his snub-nose revolver. She fired and his ankle exploded in a shower of blood and bone. The gun spun across the floor.

'You are so predictable,' she walked around him, 'very predictable. Not even you are stupid enough not to work things out. And you are pretty dumb, Walker, pretty dumb.

'I'll fucking kill you.'

'I doubt that.'

Walker was crippled on the floor and sobbing with pain, his legs covered in blood. Mechanic removed her jacket and placed both guns on the ground.

'What do you want?' hissed Walker. 'I have money, I can pay.'

'I don't want your money,' she said moving towards him. 'Money is nice but sometimes silence is better.' She drew an eight-inch serrated hunting knife from under the back of her shirt. Walker's eyes flicked between Mechanic's face and the blade as it circled in the air glinting in the light. She knelt by his side.

'But sometimes to fully appreciate the quality of silence you need to first endure some noise.' She plunged the blade into his thigh. The force of the blow lifted Walker off the floor and the point exited the other side of his leg. He screamed and squirmed on the ground clutching the handle.

Walker dragged himself across the concrete to get away from Mechanic, leaving a bloody trail in the dust. She brought her boot down hard on the back of Walker's head smashing his face into the floor. His head bounced back. She stomped again.

He cried out and rolled onto his back spitting blood and saliva into the air. Mechanic lay down next to him and cradled his head against her chest in a lover's embrace.

'There, there,' she said softly.

His nose was a bloody pulp and part of his top lip was hanging loose where his broken teeth had severed it. His right eye was closing fast and his face was swelling with purple bruises. She adjusted her position and wrapped her legs around his body, clamping him in place. Walker coughed blood onto her shirt.

'You fucking bitch, I'll—'

'Shhh, not so loud.' Her left forearm tightened across his windpipe. He struggled to pull the knife free.

'They can get a little stuck,' she said reaching down and curling her fingers around his. 'It's the serrated edge, makes it hard to get out. It needs a twist.'

She rotated the blade and yanked it free. Walker screamed as the searing pain jerked him off the floor.

Mechanic held him tight.

'They can be such tricky little bastards,' she said in his ear. Walker's cries were choked off as Mechanic crushed his windpipe.

'Now, Walker,' she whispered sliding the blade beneath the waistband of his suit. 'It would appear you have far too many body parts in place.' She forced the knife upwards slicing the front of his trousers and underwear wide open. Walker's eyes bulged from their sockets as he fought for air. His hands clawed at her arm clamped tight across his throat.

'So I need to remedy the situation.'

The blade flashed and a stream of blood and tissue spilled across the floor.

Chapter 17

Chuck Hastings scowled over the top of his half-moon glasses.

'I thought you were suspended,' he barked as he descended the last few steps into the basement.

'I was, or rather I am,' Lucas replied, not caring one way or the other.

'Then how did you dig this lot up?'

'Consider it the work of a concerned citizen, sir.'

'Give us the room,' Hastings bellowed and eight people scurried past in a blizzard of white boiler suits.

'You're fine in here,' Lucas said, 'but not in there.' He pointed past the hinged section of wall into the room beyond. 'It wouldn't be good to compromise the crime scene.'

Hastings scowled at him.

'Thanks for the unnecessary guidance. You need to have a damn good explanation for this.'

Lucas scanned the interior of the basement. 'Pretty simple. Mechanic built this as a safe room, a place to go when things got too hot and she needed to disappear for a while. Which she did.'

'How did you know it was here?'

'I didn't until an hour ago. There had to be an explanation of why we couldn't find her after the shootout with Harper. I figured we couldn't find her because she never left.'

'Where is the eternal drunk Harper?'

'Probably midway down a bottle of cheap whisky by now. Not heard from him in weeks.' Lucas had decided he had no choice but to call the discovery into the station but there was little to be gained by implicating Harper.

'What's here altogether?'

'A stash of food, cooking gear, bedding, clothes and some medical stuff. Everything you would need to hole up for a few weeks until things cooled down.'

'Let me get this clear. You had a miraculous moment of clarity and worked all this out by yourself, did you?'

'Pretty much,' said Lucas. 'Anyway the doc said it would be good therapy for me to return to the scene after what happened. You know, facing your demons and stuff like that. So I thought, why not?'

'You did good finding this place but you have to back off, Lucas.'

'I thought, if I could be of help then …?'

'Goddamit you're suspended. You need to go home, put your slippers on and reacquaint yourself with your wife and daytime television.'

'But my mind is still full of this case, sir, I can't seem to switch it off.' Lucas was toying with his boss and enjoying every moment.

'Find a way,' Hastings said firmly. 'That's a direct order. You're already in a ton of trouble, don't make life worse for yourself.'

Lucas stopped talking and stared at the floor like a schoolboy in the principal's study.

'Have you found anything out of the ordinary? Anything which gives us additional leads?' his boss asked opening the door into the room behind.

Lucas was not about to give away his prize deduction to his shit-for-brains boss. He might be a concerned citizen but he still harboured dark thoughts about killing the bitch himself.

'Not really. You might want to take a close look at those white buckets at the back.' Lucas threw him a pair of white overshoes. 'SOCO were all over them, they seemed important.'

Lucas left the basement as his boss entered the room to conduct his own forensic investigation.

* * *

Two thousand miles away Mechanic sat quietly in Silverton's hotel suite. She flicked through a newspaper with an overwhelming feeling of calm. Butchering Walker had gone completely to plan and the psycho-bitch side of her personality was very contented indeed.

She summarised her position. There were no loose ends, she had a new employer who liked her and the money was good. Unusually for Mechanic, all was well.

Killing Walker was a piece of cake, but disposing of his body had been another matter. He was a big guy and the hole in the cavity wall which she'd planned to use wasn't big enough to conceal the body. She'd contemplated cutting him up and feeding him into the recess one piece at a time but that needed tools which she didn't have. In the end she resorted to a tried and tested method, a dousing of gasoline and Walker's lighter.

It was six thirty in the evening. She had only seen Silverton briefly to say 'Hi' before he buried himself in the office with the phone grafted to his head. Then in true Broadway style he burst through the double doors, his hands held aloft in triumph.

'Nailed the bastard!' he said, crossing the room towards the drinks trolley.

'That's excellent, Mr Silverton. Does that mean we're back on the party trail?'

'Sure does, Ms Hudson, it sure does. Where the hell is Walker? I tried to get hold of him but no one has seen him.'

'Don't know, sir, he didn't say anything to me, but then I think he's still brooding a little since you took me onto the payroll.'

'He'll get over it, and I don't need him anyway, I have you.' Silverton reached into a closet and retrieved his Stetson. 'Saddle up girl, I'm feeling mighty lucky.' He galloped around the room waving his hat in the air, riding an imaginary horse.

Mechanic smiled and flinched at the 'saddle up girl' reference. She had no idea how good a businessman he was, but in his spare time Harry acted like he was in a John Wayne movie.

She glanced at her watch. 'I need to make a quick call, Mr Silverton.'

'Sure thing, take your time. Get your shit together cause it's gonna be a late one.' He belly-laughed his way through the bedroom to the shower.

Mechanic cursed under her breath. It was Thursday and she couldn't miss another visit. She reconsidered.

'Mr Silverton, sorry about this but can I take a couple of hours off? I have some personal stuff which needs my attention.'

'Sure, I can live with that. Meet me back here when you're done. Make it quick.'

Mechanic thanked him and left. She was already late.

Chapter 18

Honeydew House sat at the very outskirts of the city. It was a quaint, well-maintained property with a white picket fence set in a couple of acres of land. Its nearest neighbour was three hundred yards away and you had to drive to get anywhere.

It was as far out of town as you could go, located on the boundary of the city limits. Sitting on the front step you looked at the sprawling city of Las Vegas, and sitting on the back step you looked out across the Mojave Desert.

Mechanic pulled her car off the dirt road and steeled herself for what was coming next. No matter how many times she did this, it always tore her apart.

The house belonged to Jeb and Jenny-Jay Huxton who until four years ago were a normal married couple with a socially awkward daughter who seemed unable to date guys. But being gay in a God-fearing family was never going to be an easy option.

Jenny-Jay was a retired nurse with thirty years' clinical service. She'd worked in every department a busy hospital had to offer including midwifery, which she enjoyed the least, saying it was too damn noisy. Trauma was her speciality and the care of the terminally ill.

She was an excellent nurse and shunned the numerous opportunities for promotion which came her way. She would throw her head back and laugh at the very suggestion, saying, 'You can't do the Lord's work pushing a pen.'

She would have continued past her thirty years' service if it wasn't for a young drunk who, one cold November night, fell out of a bar and into his car. He drove five miles up the road, lost control and ploughed his vehicle headlong into another one travelling in the opposite direction. That car was driven by her daughter.

The collision propelled him through his windshield, killing him instantly. Mary-Jay Huxton was much less fortunate.

The seat belt kept her in place but couldn't prevent the steering column crushing her chest and the engine block smashing her legs. Her broken body was fixed over time but the lack of oxygen to her brain could not be healed. It left her with locked-in syndrome at the age of twenty-six.

Her mother quit her job, set up a critical care unit at home and devoted herself to nursing Mary-Jay. Her father, Jeb Huxton, set about every member of the drunk guy's family with a baseball bat when they were eating lunch one Sunday afternoon after church. He received a six month spell in jail and Jenny-Jay began her slide into depression and denial.

She didn't visit him once, instead she devoted her energies to administering to her daughter in their remote farmhouse and carrying on as though nothing had happened. After all, the events of that fateful November night were the Lord's will, and He sends trials to test the true believers. And the Huxton family were the truest of believers.

Jeb did his time and came back home to a completely different woman. To put it in non-clinical terms, she'd gone batshit crazy. She had totally lost her grasp on reality and was in full blown denial. Jeb found the best way to deal with this was to go back to work, attended church on Sundays and pretended all was well.

Medicines, dressings and personal hygiene items don't come cheap. Jeb earned enough to pay the bills but it was tough. So when the nice young woman offered to pay handsomely for Jenny-Jay's services, it was the Lord sending her a saviour. The new girl who came to stay was about the same age as her daughter and so well-mannered.

She and Mary-Jay got on like a house on fire. You couldn't stop them chatting and laughing together. They both had the same wicked sense of humour and the new girl was a great companion. After a brief trial they agreed as a family to let the new girl stay – it was a wonderful arrangement, things couldn't be better.

It was a damn shame both women were largely brain dead. Each one was locked in her own silent world and looked after by her ever-attentive nurse.

Mechanic visited every other Thursday and sat with the family as they played cards and watched television. In reality Jenny-Jay played cards on behalf of Mary-Jay and her new-found friend. The women sat in identical wheelchairs while Jeb watched his favourite game shows, shouting answers at the TV.

Jenny-Jay conducted imaginary conversations between the two women. It was like the world's worst ventriloquist act.

Mechanic stepped onto the front porch and peered around the curtain into the living room. The wheelchair women were parked in front of the TV while Jeb and his wife sat side by side on the sofa. She could barely make out the surreal conversation being conducted inside.

'Jenny-Jay said she saw some rabbits today playing out in the field. I told her it was that time of year when the bucks and the does are courting ready to get hitched and have little ones. What's that Jenny-Jay? You saw a hundred of them! Now don't you go telling tall tales in front of our guest. You are a one, Mary-Jay, isn't she Jeb?' Jenny-Jay was in a talkative mood this evening.

'Hell I knew that one! I said Duelling Banjos in the film *Deliverance*,' shouted Jeb. 'Didn't I say that, girls, didn't I just say that.'

The girls sat upright in their chairs. One was thin, her skin the colour of undercooked pastry. She wore a surgical skullcap and her eyes were open, her face completely expressionless. The other was fatter, with eyes partially closed and her mouth gaping open. Drool ran down her chin, which Jenny-Jay occasionally wiped away with a towel. A food tube ran into her open shirt, feeding tonight's liquidised dinner directly into her stomach. Both were dressed in baggy jeans and identical checked shirts. One wore blue sneakers and the other wore yellow.

'Now don't you go ribbing your father, Mary-Jay. He did say *Deliverance* – you are sassy today, missy.' She laughed and slapped Jeb's leg.

'Who fancies some homemade lemonade? Girls, are you having some? I made it special this afternoon.' Jenny-Jay sang the last few words and went to the kitchen. She emerged carrying a wicker tray with four glasses and a jug of lemonade. She set a glass down in front of each person. 'Made with fresh lemons,' she announced and began pouring.

Mechanic tore her gaze away and walked back to the porch. She knocked on the front door.

Jenny-Jay answered it.

'Hi Mrs Huxton, sorry I'm a little late,' Mechanic said cheerily.

'Well hi to you, honey child.' She shook her hand. 'Now if I told you once I told you a million times, you must call me Jenny-Jay. Come in, come in.'

Mechanic stepped inside to be met with the soft, warm aroma of fresh bread and pot roast.

Every time she came here it sliced Mechanic to the core, a graphic reminder that Lucas and Harper were still alive and they shouldn't be.

'Sit yourself down and I'll get you some lemonade. Look Jo, your sister's here.'

Chapter 19

Silverton needed to relieve himself from the stresses of his business crisis. And for him that meant running around like a teenage boy in a whorehouse.

He was a man possessed, on a personal mission to visit the entire complement of casinos and bars that Vegas had to offer, intent on sucking each one of them dry of gambling pleasure. Making up for lost time didn't quite describe it, he went berserk.

It also meant his alcohol consumption was in overdrive, along with his painfully friendly personality. The nicer side of Harry, brought on by being almost killed, had worn off and he was back to being rich, objectionable, pain-in-the-ass Harry James Silverton III.

The days blurred into one. Mechanic could barely keep up with him and had her work cut out for sure. She could no longer maintain a watching brief from a respectable distance, she was forced to stay close and shut down minor conflicts as they occurred. Of which there were many.

There was the guy who had his stack of chips knocked down every time Harry leaned forward to scatter his bet onto the table. Then there was the woman who was knocked sideways off her stool as Harry celebrated a spectacular win, which turned out to be a catastrophic loss, owing to him not having placed his bet correctly. And there was the waitress who had a full tray of drinks knocked flying from her hand, the result of another overly exuberant celebration.

Mechanic dealt with each situation with a deft hand and confident manner. The in-house security watched her and Harry like a hawk but she had it under control. Anyway Harry was splashing enough cash to make it worth the hotel turning a blind eye to his misdemeanours.

It usually resulted in Harry's pot of money being depleted by gifts of compensatory chips or 'sorry money' as Mechanic christened them. She reckoned one particularly vigorous game of blackjack must have cost him over three hundred bucks. To Harry he was still everyone's friend and extremely popular, but the truth was people were drawn to the social carnage which followed his every move. Harry was definitely a spectator sport but one to be enjoyed at a safe distance.

He occasionally had flashes of rational behaviour. 'You heard from Walker?' he asked several times. She always replied the same way. 'Nope nothing,' which seemed to suffice. Harry showed little concern for Walker's vanishing act and carried on as normal. Well, normal for him anyway.

On one occasion during the three-day bender, Silverton was at the craps table at the MGM Grand and had drawn a bigger than usual crowd. His 'drinks for everyone' tab was totalling over three and fifty bucks and the in-house security was getting twitchy. Harry was completely over the top, throwing the dice down the table with massive shows of bravado. The women loved it. They crowded around him, each one trying to outdo the other in how far their breasts could fall out of their dresses before they were asked to leave.

A red-faced guy dressed in a rhinestone shirt took a real dislike to Harry. He was very agitated and hurled abuse at every opportunity but Harry ignored it. After a while it became clear to Mechanic why the man was so worked up. One of the women preventing Harry from throwing the dice by shoving her tits in the way was supposed to be with him. But for the time being she preferred to be with Harry. It also seemed that out of all the women around the table, Harry preferred her too.

Harry announced to his entourage he needed to take a leak and fought his way to the restroom, closely followed by rhinestone guy.

There are times when being a female minder has its disadvantages and a male restroom situation does pose an etiquette issue. Mechanic stood outside and listened. Raised voices soon resonated off the marble interior and one of them was Harry's.

She entered the room to find rhinestone guy giving Harry the up-close-and-personal treatment, yelling in his face something about leaving his girl alone or else he would rip his head off. *Probably a speech he'd be better off delivering to his girl*, Mechanic thought as she walked past the line of men stood against the urinals.

She grabbed the man's right hand, shoved it up behind his back and kicked his legs from under him. He crumpled face first to the floor with a thud, her knee jammed hard between his shoulder blades. She gripped his other hand to hold him stationary.

Harry was shouting, 'What the hell are you doing, man? Have a good time and relax.' Struggling on the floor the guy was a long way from being able to do either.

The security guards rushed in and Mechanic stood up leaving rhinestone prostrate on the floor.

'Ma'am, you need to be out of here,' one of them said, putting a firm hand on her shoulder.

She pulled free from his grasp. 'I wouldn't need to be here if you had your eyes open.' She took Harry by the arm and led him out. A crowd had gathered outside. They whooped and hollered as Harry emerged, his hands held high above his head, doing a victory walk back to the table. Behind him the man dressed in his best party shirt was being led away still protesting.

Mechanic followed Harry to his spot at the table.

'Make this your last throw, Mr Silverton, it's time to move on.' He threw the dice and spun around on his heels. The women crowded in again but this time Mechanic wasn't budging.

Harry lost. He reached down for the dice but she snapped them off the green cloth.

'Come on, Mr Silverton, let's cash up and go. How about The Sands?'

'Hell yes, let's go!'

The crowd booed and called for him to stay, but the cluster of security and management gathering nearby told Mechanic the time to leave was now.

The scene was pretty much replicated wherever Harry went, a rowdy collection of new friends happy to be bought with beers and liquor plus regular donations of sorry money.

* * *

At the end of day three, Mechanic was frazzled. Harry was dozing in the back of the car as she pulled into the drop-off zone outside the Hacienda hotel reception. She got out and threw the valet parking boy the keys. She opened the passenger door and shook Harry by the shoulder.

'Sir, we're here. Time to get some rest.'

He woke and jumped from the back seat stretching and yawning. Mechanic's heart sank. Had the twenty-minute nap given him renewed energy for another foray onto the gambling floor?

'Time for some shut-eye I reckon. What do you say?' He straightened his Stetson.

'Absolutely, sir.' Mechanic breathed a sigh of relief.

They reached the hotel suite and she slid the card in the lock. There was a soft click and she opened the door for Harry to go inside.

'Call me in the morning when you're ready, sir.'

'Why don't you take a nightcap with me,' Harry said. 'You've been drinking tonic for three days straight, how about a real drink.'

Mechanic considered the invitation. 'That would be nice, Mr Silverton, thank you I will.'

She settled into the big armchair and Harry went into the other room. She heard the distinctive clink of ice striking crystal and he soon appeared with two massive tumblers full of golden liquid. He handed one to Mechanic.

'Cheers!' Harry held up his glass.

'An eventful few days,' she said chinking his glass and taking a welcome slug of whisky.

'You can say that again, it sure has been eventful.' No sooner did his ass hit the sofa than he jumped up again. 'I'll be back in a minute.' He disappeared into the other room.

Mechanic nodded and swigged the fiery liquor, it tasted so good. It warmed its way down her body and she relaxed.

After a while Silverton returned. 'Cheers!' he said raising his glass.

'Yes sir, cheers.' Mechanic went to raise her arm to return the toast but it wouldn't move. She heard a rushing sound in her head and her peripheral vision was closing in. She tried to speak but only managed to emit mumbled sounds. She tried to get out of the chair but nothing happened.

Harry leaned over and lifted the glass from her hand. Over his shoulder Mechanic could see another man entering the room, casually dressed in jeans and a T-shirt several sizes too small. His muscles bulged and he had the complexion of someone who worked in the hot sun. A rippled scar ran from the side of his face down his right arm.

She tried to get up but couldn't.

'This is Ramirez,' announced Harry. 'He's a business associate of mine who I use from time to time. He's expensive but very good.'

Mechanic fought to maintain her view of the stranger as he slipped in and out of focus. The noise in her head grew louder and her limbs felt cold. Ramirez stood next to her and placed his fingers on her neck to take her pulse.

Harry put the glasses on the table and leaned across. 'He thought, given your recent performance, using chemicals would be the safer option. You are quite the handful, Ms Hudson.'

Mechanic tilted her face to look at Harry but could no longer hold his stare. Her head slumped onto her chest and everything went black.

Chapter 20

Lucas was beginning to think Harper wasn't such a prick after all.

'That was an amazing find.' Lucas was impressed with his friend's powers of deduction and knowledge of basic building mods.

'I got lucky I suppose.' Harper was being unusually coy – he was still playing the 'unconditionally sorry' role since admitting the origin of the sugar packets.

'Bit more than luck.' Lucas slapped him on the shoulder. He'd forgiven Harper for the deception but could not quite bring himself to tell him, perhaps because that would mean having to admit to himself that Harper was right. He had been spiralling downhill. The letter had given Lucas back his drive.

The discovery had been little short of miraculous. Lucas felt small twinges of guilt for not declaring to his boss what he thought the inventory in the room truly meant. The amount of used medical gear convinced Lucas and Harper that Jo must be alive, or at least she was while they were in hiding. Anyway his boss could damn well work it out for himself after he'd finished playing with the shit buckets.

They were back in Harper's favourite café haunt, grimacing at the taste of the black liquid swilling around in the chipped mugs. The single topic of conversation for Harper and Lucas was answering the question, 'What next?'

'Why the hell do you come here?' Lucas asked.

'It's good.'

'In what way? It's dirty, the coffee is awful and there isn't even clean air to breathe.'

'You don't get it.'

'Damn right I don't.' Lucas pushed the mug away from him admitting defeat. 'Where would you go to lay low with a sister recovering from a gunshot wound to the head?'

'Depends on how ill she was. That dictates how far you can travel.'

'Let's suppose it's within a day's drive.' He spread a route map out on the table. 'That takes us—'

'Far away from here,' snapped Harper not looking at the map. 'Baton Rouge is a day's drive, so is Charleston, Atlanta, Cincinnati and a ton of places in between.'

'But not too many places have the facilities to care for someone with that type of trauma. Mechanic is not going to risk a hospital – all gunshot wounds are reported to the police. She would look for a respite or nursing home with clinical staff able to look after her. Throw in a bent owner and she has a safe place for Jo.'

Harper churned the scenario over in his head.

'Yeah, a place where Mechanic could keep her sister off the grid but close enough for her to keep an eye on things.'

'We might have a lot of territory to cover but there can't be too many places which fit the profile.'

Harper looked doubtful. 'How do we start looking?'

'Let's get a list of respite and convalescent homes on the outskirts of the six biggest cities within one day's drive.'

'That's a long list.'

'Probably as long as the number of cafés and bars in Baton Rouge.' Lucas felt the need to twist the knife now and again to keep his friend focused. 'Anyway, do you have a better idea?'

Harper shook his head and drew circles on the map with his fingers.

The bartender raised his hand. 'Hey, Harper, your guy is on the blower.'

'You have a guy?' Lucas said.

'Yes, I have several, but not like that.' Harper screwed up his face.

'Oh, but you do have a guy then?'

'He feeds me information.'

'How does he know you're here?'

'I'm always here, and when I'm not the bartender takes a message.' Harper waved at the man. 'Be there in a minute.'

'The guy serving the drinks is your router? He's your messenger boy?'

'Yes that's right.'

'So that's why we come here so damn often. Do you pay him?'

'Sometimes I bung him cash when he's a little short, but mostly I pay him by bringing new people to the café. He thinks it's good for business and is happy with that. He's a good guy.' Harper rose from the table and went to the bar.

'Shit,' said Lucas, finally realising why his so-called friend forced him to endure the life-shortening effects of this dreadful place.

Harper returned to the table and Lucas wasted no time.

'Do you mean to tell me the only reason I have to sit here breathing in smog and drinking sump oil is because—' Harper stopped him mid-flow.

'That was a journalist I know who works for Reuters. They have a nasty story which is about to break big. They've uncovered the fresh remains of a torched body on the west coast.'

'I don't see what that has to do with us.'

'The victim was set alight post-mortem. He was shot and stabbed multiple times. But none of that killed him. The cause of death was a broken neck. Snapped clean with a single twist.'

Lucas stopped talking and began to process the relevance of this new information.

'Before he died someone cut his cock and balls off. They weren't found at the scene.'

Lucas stared at Harper as the gravity of the details sank in.

'I think she's finally surfaced. Mechanic is in Las Vegas.'

Chapter 21

Mechanic was coming round, the gentle tapping on her left cheek coaxing her to consciousness. Her tongue stuck to the roof of her mouth and her head weighed a ton.

'Come on, that's it.' She was aware of a voice in the background which kept drifting in and out. 'Time to wake up.'

The tapping stopped and she felt rough hands on her face lifting her head up. Cold glass touched her lips, and water flowed into her mouth. She struggled to swallow and coughed it back out.

The hand under her chin guided her towards the rim of the glass again. She drank this time and the cool liquid flowed down her throat. The water unstuck her tongue. She opened her eyes. Everything moved in blurry pictures.

'That's it,' said the detached voice. 'Time to wake up.'

She was aware of a face in front of her but couldn't make out the features. She floated back under.

'No, no, no,' said the rasping voice. 'Come back to me.' The water flowed again and she felt it splash cold against her skin.

She kept her eyes shut trying to recall what had happened. She could remember escorting Silverton to his room, plus a faint recollection about a drink – then nothing. No, wait, there was someone else there. There was another man with Silverton. His name was Ramirez.

She flicked open her eyes and there he was. He held her head in one hand and the glass in the other.

Ramirez was in his early forties with close-cropped black hair. He wore the same T-shirt and jeans as before and she could see the rippled scar which started on the side of his face, ran down his neck, across his chest and down his arm. When he turned his head his right ear was a lump of melted flesh.

Mechanic caught his eye and recognised the look immediately. Ramirez was the real deal. She was in deep trouble.

'That's it, that's it,' he said. 'Time to wake up.' He put the glass on the floor, dipped in his fingers and splashed more water on her face. She was gaining consciousness by the second.

'What happ …' she slurred her words. 'Where …'

'Don't speak yet. Give it time. Here drink.' He poured more into her mouth, got up and stepped away. 'She's back.'

Mechanic saw another figure moving towards her. She recognised it was Silverton.

'What happened?' she said.

'Please forgive me but we had to take precautions. I need to ask you a few questions, Ms Hudson, and to be frank we couldn't take the risk of you killing us.'

Mechanic shook her head and the fuzzy outlines came into focus. She was in a dimly lit room with a single naked bulb hanging from the ceiling and concrete walls. There were no windows and she could make out the faint outline of a door in one corner. There was an overpowering stink of human faeces. She retched.

Mechanic closed her eyes, pretended to drift off again and went through a mental checklist. She was not in pain and could breathe freely, her arms and legs were fine and she was fully clothed. Her head hurt but that was from the drugs. She had limited movement but, from what she could deduce, was unharmed.

Ramirez tapped her left cheek again. 'Come on, don't go to sleep. Time to talk.'

Mechanic opened her eyes and stared at the floor. She was sitting on a chair, wrists tied together and stretched out in front of her. A thick rope joined them to a metal ring set in the floor about three feet away. A heavy leather belt looped under the seat and pulled tight round her hips. Her legs were tied to the chair by the ankles and below her knees. She was bent forward at the waist and had to strain to look up into Silverton's face. The chair was bolted to the floor.

None of this was good. This was a classic interrogation stress position.

Ramirez pulled a table along until it rested beside Mechanic. She could see the tools of his trade laid out in order: pliers, knives and plastic bottles containing various coloured liquids. A roll of barbed wire, a three-foot length of armoured electrical cable, an electric sander and a blowtorch completed the inventory. This was the kit of a serious torturer.

When he walked Ramirez crackled. Mechanic looked down at his feet to see the whole floor covered in plastic sheeting. Ramirez went out of view as Silverton stepped in front of her. She had to crane her neck to look up.

'You will notice you are lightly restrained, the ropes aren't too tight and you are still dressed. I do not want to hurt you, I really don't.' It was a chilling opener.

He continued, 'I never mix business with sentiment, but in your case I'm torn. I like you, I like you a lot. After all, you saved my life and that goes in your favour. However, we've run some background checks and you've had an array of unremarkable jobs and used to be an office worker. I have to ask myself, what type of training course does an office worker go on to acquire your type of skills?'

He knelt down beside Mechanic and placed his hand on her shoulder.

'I know you work in personal security, but that is a recent move, and you didn't learn the things you know by mail order. I watched you take down those goons like they were nothing and I recognise something special when I see it. And, Ms Hudson, I am looking at it right now.' Silverton exuded none of his usual idiotic presence. He was cold and threatening.

'I am not a squeamish man, but Ramirez here, well I've seen him do things which make even me want to look away. I haven't, mind you, but it made me feel like I should. Now you are free to keep all the secrets you want but I reckon there are some which involve me. And that won't do. As you can tell by the aroma, this place processes shit. It also processes body parts courtesy of Ramirez. All that slicing and dicing along with strong chemicals can make all sorts of things disappear. This room is encased in solid concrete so you can yell and scream till your throat is raw. Depending on how the next ten minutes goes, you might end up doing that anyway.'

Silverton paused and Mechanic could hear a metallic sheering noise behind her. She shuddered when she realised Ramirez was sharpening blades on a stone.

'This is going to be simple. I'm gonna show you some pictures and ask you some questions. The questions are straightforward – what and why.'

Silverton removed a series of photographs from an envelope and spread them on the floor in front of her.

'This is a still from the CCTV footage in the hotel car park showing you and Walker getting into the car. Time stamp is 14.03. You drive off together. This one shows you returning and getting out of the car at 17.12. No Walker. First question is, what did you do with Walker?'

Mechanic looked at the pictures then up at Silverton. She thought of Jo and the Huxtons at Honeydew House. She had to get out of this alive. There was little point in holding back, Ramirez would kill her for sure.

She swallowed hard. Her neck ached with the constant strain of looking up.

'I killed him.'

Silverton let out a sigh and flashed a knowing look at Ramirez. 'I figured you had. Next question is, why?'

Mechanic tried to keep herself calm but it freaked the hell out of her that she couldn't see Ramirez.

'The carjacking was a stunt. The real plan was to kidnap you and extort money.'

'What!' shouted Silverton. 'That's bullshit.'

She tensed her body, waiting for Ramirez to strike.

'No, it's not. It's the truth. Walker planned to hit the car and snatch you. He would conduct the negotiations and walk away with two million dollars.'

Ramirez went to the table and picked up the pliers. He knelt down grasping Mechanic's hand. She could feel the bite of the jaws as they clamped on her little finger.

'It's the truth!' she shouted, fighting to pull her hand away. 'Why would I lie? Walker knew I'd worked it out. I had to kill him before he killed me. You got to believe me.' The bite of the pliers was excruciating as Ramirez increased the pressure. 'Why the fuck would I lie? I have nothing to gain by lying!' Mechanic was fighting back the surging panic. Ramirez twisted the pliers. She screamed. All she could see was her sister in the wheelchair.

Silverton nodded and Ramirez stepped away. Mechanic let out a huge sigh as the pain subsided. She gritted her teeth and stared at Ramirez. Her look said it all – *I'll fucking kill you.*

'The little shit!' Silverton's voice echoed around the walls. 'All the things I did for him.' He'd turned an unhealthy shade of pink.

'It's the truth,' Mechanic said looking up at Silverton. 'Walker didn't plan for you to employ me during your visit. He tried to frighten me off. When I didn't play ball his only option was for his men to take me out.'

'But you were too good for them.' Silverton's colour was receding back to pasty white. 'So you killed Walker before he had the chance to kill you.'

'Yes, that's right. You had to be an idiot not to see it was a botched kidnapping. The carjacking didn't make sense. To him I was a loose end. I had to strike first.'

'I didn't work out it was a kidnapping,' Silverton said defensively.

'With all due respect, sir, that's not your line of work.'

'Where's the body?'

'In a warehouse about an hour's drive east. It's burned and concealed in a cavity wall.'

'You nasty bitch,' Silverton said with admiration in his voice. 'Are you going to kill me as well?'

Mechanic looked at him and shook her head. 'No.'

'How can I believe you?' Silverton asked.

'I have nothing to gain from killing you and if I wanted you dead … you would be.' Silverton nodded his head in agreement. She had a point. He signalled to Ramirez who stepped forward with a long hunting knife.

'No I'm telling you the truth, don't …' She let out a scream and fought against the restraints binding her to the chair as the blade slashed downwards.

The razor-sharp edge sliced through the rope and she catapulted backwards. She stared up at Ramirez. He placed the knife back in his belt with a look of genuine disappointment. He hadn't got to play with his toys today.

She looked at her bruised and bloodied finger then sideways at Ramirez. She might not kill Silverton but given half a chance she would not afford his companion the same courtesy.

Mechanic breathed deeply, arched her back and rotated her head. She could feel the bones cracking back into place as she regained her posture. Her hands hurt like hell.

'I believe you,' Silverton said as he walked around the room then returned to Mechanic.

She offered him her tied wrists.

'I presume I passed the test.'

'You did. Sorry about that.' He nodded again and Ramirez cut the cord. Blood rushed into her purple hands and pain surged into her damaged finger.

Silverton disappeared from view then returned with an envelope. He removed a further set of black and white photographs.

'My business interests in Vegas are wide and varied. One of the more lucrative is the trafficking and distribution of class A drugs for from Mexico. I run them through California and then on to Nevada. I have an active network here in Vegas which is exceptionally profitable. Normally things are pretty cool, other dealers are happy to stick to their own piece of the playground. But my operation got hit and no one on the street knows jack shit about it. I will pay you fifteen grand up front, with a twenty grand success fee.'

He placed the pictures in Mechanic's lap.

'I want the bastards that did this. I want them to have some quality time with Ramirez and I want to watch.'

She looked at the photos.

The first depicted a tall, lean guy lying on the ground in a pool of blood, his neck slashed wide open. The second showed a short, stocky guy with tattoos on his neck and chest, also lying with a dark halo of blood around his disfigured skull. The third was of a fat guy sitting on the sidewalk against a wall. His head was tilted back, eyeballs bulging at the sky, skewered in place by a giant metal cocktail stick rammed down his throat.

Mechanic rotated her head again and bones cracked in her neck.

'I got a better idea.'

Chapter 22

Lucas opened his front door to Harper standing in the rain. The streetlights spilled bouncing pools of yellow light across the sheets of water on the road.

'Hey, come in.'

Harper wiped his feet on the mat and still succeeded in leaving dirty, wet imprints on the carpet as he entered the house. Lucas watched the trail of footprints disappear into the living room. He shook his head and followed.

Harper removed his coat, dumped it in the corner of the room and made a beeline for the whisky. Any pretence of being on the waggon was long gone.

'You want one?' he said over his shoulder as Lucas picked Harper's dripping coat off the carpet and tossed it into the hall.

'Yeah, that would be good.' Lucas was used to his friend helping himself.

Harper handed him a glass with enough liquor in it to kill a horse. He dug into his jacket pocket and gave Lucas a book of tickets.

'A night flight?' Lucas said.

'Yeah, it was cheaper.'

'The Lucky 6? Never heard of it.'

'Nor me, I found it on teletext. It's a new motel on the outskirts of Vegas. They had a deal, so I called and booked us in. It was cheap.'

Lucas read the hotel details.

'The location is perfect and at twenty dollars a night that will do nicely.'

'Ten dollars.'

'What? It says here twenty bucks.'

'It does but they only had one room. So it's ten each.'

'You booked us into one room? I'm not staying with—'

'Get over yourself,' Harper interrupted before his friend could protest further. 'Like you said, it's in a great place and the room has two queen beds. It'll be fine.'

'Oh that's all right then. Two queen beds with two queens to go in them.'

'Relax. I said we were brothers.' Harper slurped his whisky.

Lucas looked at Harper, his mouth dropping open.

'It might have slipped your notice but I am several shades of skin tone darker than you. How the hell are we brothers?'

'You always look for the negatives,' Harper said. 'They were a bit edgy about letting the room to two guys, so I said we were brothers.'

'You're white, I'm black and we have different surnames.' Lucas threw his hands up and looked to the ceiling.

'It'll be fine. And we can pick up some firearms when we're there.'

'Oh no, we don't.' Lucas said shaking his head. 'The last time I was in the same room with you and a gun, you shot me.'

'Will you give it a rest with the "you shot me" routine? It's pissing me off. It was an accident, okay. You keep bringing it up and making a big thing about it.'

'Making a big thing about it? You shot me in the fucking head!'

'You're overreacting.'

'You shot me! That's why I don't want to be around you when you're packing a gun.'

'So what do you think we're gonna do when we find Mechanic? Attack her with rolled up newspapers?'

Lucas fell silent and sipped his whisky. He knew guns were inevitable.

Harper looked around the room. There were piles of clothes in the corner and dirty dishes lay beside the sofa. Used coffee cups were stacked up on the coffee table and the whole place reeked of day-old fish.

'Where's your wife?' Harper asked craning his head to look into the kitchen. Pots and pans were piled into the sink and cereal packets cluttered the countertops. The burned remnants of a battered fish dinner welded to the grill pan gave away the source of the smell.

'She's spending a couple of days with a friend,' Lucas replied casually.

'You made a shit load of mess in a couple of days.'

'Yeah well, maybe.'

'Sorry man,' said Harper.

That's the problem with having a cop for a friend. You tell them the bare minimum and they know everything.

'We'll sort it,' Lucas sighed. 'So, we got flights and accommodation. How do we find the bitch?' He got up from the chair and reached for the whisky bottle.

'I figure we need to keep a low profile, so we split up. Hire a couple of cars and cruise around, not sure there's much else we can do. If we start flashing around her mug shot she's bound to find out and then it's game over. What do you think?'

'I think that's the wrong plan.' Lucas pulled a wad of paper from the sideboard. 'If we go for Mechanic head on she'll see us coming a mile off. She'll either do a runner or kill us both, and that's if we manage to find her. She'll have a different identity and a changed appearance, we wouldn't recognise her if she served us coffee and pancakes for a week. We need to be clever about this.'

'I'm listening.'

'The chances are Mechanic has no footprint for us to track. The same cannot be said for her sister Jo. If we're right then she will be with Mechanic somewhere in Vegas. What did we say? Off the grid but close enough to keep an eye on her.'

Harper scratched his forehead. 'Are you telling me that Mechanic took her sister all the way to Vegas when she'd just been shot? How the shit would she manage that?'

'If Jo is alive, Mechanic would never leave her behind and would want to keep her close. If Mechanic has surfaced in Vegas, her sister won't be far away.'

'Hell, I don't know. How would she get her there? Jo took a shot to the head remember. She can't take a plane or train and it's a journey of two thousand miles. You couldn't drive—'

Lucas interrupted, 'Two thousand and forty-nine to be precise. Why not? We can't fall into our usual trap of making up convoluted scenarios. What's the straightforward answer here? Why not hire an RV along with a bent nurse to attend to Jo en route? The nurse gets paid over the odds for her silence and four days later they arrive on the other side of the country. I agree it's a lot to take in but how many times have we been in this position and we talk ourselves out of the obvious?'

'Yeah, we sure do a lot of that,' Harper said.

'I don't believe we'll get anywhere near her, she's too smart and we'll get burned, or worse. If we look for Mechanic, it's needle-in-a-haystack time at best and she might end up killing both of us. If we look for Jo instead, that narrows down the field significantly. Remember, we only tracked her down last time by going fishing – we set up that fake telephone line with the recorded message and Jo did the rest. She led us right to Mechanic.'

'How do you think we should play it this time?'

'There are twenty-eight care facilities in Vegas and the surrounding area. If we're right, then Jo will be in one of them.' Lucas spread the papers on the floor showing a list of twenty-eight names and addresses. 'We don't look for Mechanic. We look for Jo.'

'Then what?'

'We go fishing again, using Jo as bait.'

Chapter 23

The night flight was unremarkable. Lucas set out a detailed schedule of visits, mapping out the most effective route between the nursing homes to maximise their coverage. Harper, on the other hand, snored through the five-hour flight after quenching his late-night thirst from the American Airlines drinks trolley.

Checking into the hotel was a different matter.

While the hotel was expecting them, even at 3am, they were also expecting them to be the same colour. The receptionist took more than a little professional interest in why one of the supposed brothers was white and the other one black.

There were notes on the system to accompany their booking which now looked mighty suspicious. Harper regaled her with a rambling story about a messy divorce and how their white father remarried a black woman. This seemed to do the trick although it was patently obvious to everyone there that Lucas was the product of a black on black encounter.

Lucas conceded afterwards it would have been much easier to say they were a gay couple.

First thing in the morning they hit Lucas's list of targets. There was no point asking the homes if they had a woman staying with them in her early-thirties who required care as a result of a gunshot wound to the head. That would get them nowhere. So the game plan was simple. Lucas would request a tour of the home and discuss the possibility of placing his sister with them, who had recently suffered head trauma in a road traffic accident. Harper would drift off during the visit and see if he could spot Jo among the patients.

The plan was indeed simple but as always the devil was in the detail. Detail which neither of them had bothered to work out.

The Golden Horizon nursing home was situated in Spring Valley, about four miles south-west of the Las Vegas Strip. It was a modern building with impressive grounds adjacent to Desert Breeze Park. Lucas and Harper were keen to get started.

An officious looking woman in blue scrubs met them at reception, her nametag read Snr Nurse Janet Willow. She welcomed them to the Golden Horizon and took them to a soft seating area behind a set of free-standing dividers. Lucas introduced himself as Steve Christie.

So far, so good.

'And where is your sister now, Mr Christie?' she asked in an earnest tone.

'She's being cared for at home. We have carers who come in daily to administer to her,' Lucas said.

'And where is home, Mr Christie?'

Lucas looked at Harper who helped by raising his eyebrows.

'Not far. We have a house about a couple of miles from here.'

'And who is delivering the care at the moment?' Nurse Willow studied him over the rim of her glasses.

'Oh, um, it's a private company that comes in. They come in daily. The private company that is.'

'And what is the nature of her injuries?' She seemed to start every sentence with the word 'and'.

'My sister suffered severe head trauma which means she needs daily care.' Lucas tried hard to make it sound convincing.

'And what condition is she in now?'

Lucas flashed a second glance at Harper, it was clear his friend was not going to bail him out of this one.

'Oh, not so good.'

Harper's eyebrows went stratospheric.

'Can you be a little more specific?' Janet Willow perched herself on the edge of her seat and pursed her lips.

Lucas wanted to go away and start again.

Harper could take no more of watching Lucas drown. 'Senior Nurse Willow, my friend is struggling to fully answer your questions because he's still coming to terms with the tragic events surrounding his sister. We don't know the medical ins and outs of Chrissie's needs but we do know the family cannot give her the care and support she requires and that's why we're here. We will provide you with the necessary medical information when the time is right but not right now I'm afraid. You must understand, the family are taking baby steps and this is an enormous decision – where is the best place for Chrissie and who should deliver her long-term care. I'm sure you appreciate what they're going through.'

'And I do, Mr … er …'

Harper ignored the inferred request for his name. 'If we could take a look around, it would make a huge difference to the family and help them understand their options. This is a very difficult journey for them. We're looking for your help. We're looking for the right place for Chrissie.'

Lucas stared at Harper. *Where the hell did that come from?*

'And of course here at Golden Horizons we are always willing to help.' Nurse Willow led them to a large double door with an oversized keypad on the wall to the left. She punched a series of digits and the doors swung open with a motorised whir. 'Let me show you around.'

Harper winked at Lucas as they followed Senior Nurse Willow down the corridor.

'Chrissie Christie, really?' whispered Lucas.

'We're in, aren't we? Keep a sharp eye.'

Which both of them did, without success, for the next half hour.

Chapter 24

Mechanic watched Silverton cross the hotel suite to the room service trolley. He came back with two cups of black coffee and a sugar bowl. Ramirez was nowhere to be seen.

She heaped in two spoonsful and stirred. The steam rose from the cup, its strong aroma masking the lingering smell of shit which followed her around wherever she went. Three showers and five bottles of hotel body wash later and the stench was still lodged in her nostrils.

Silverton sat opposite, leaned back and crossed his legs. Mechanic sipped at the coffee and placed the cup onto a side table next to the photographs of Silverton's dead drug team.

'Look, Jess, it's business,' he said casually.

'It's fucking painful, that's what it is,' she said holding up her left hand with its bandaged finger.

'It's an unfortunate part of what I do – sometimes I have to use methods which are a little severe. You understand, I'm sure.' Silverton had not yet slipped back into buffoon mode.

'I get it you needed to know about Walker. You could have asked.'

'Yes maybe. And maybe you'd have blown me away as well, it was a risk I was not prepared to take. It's business, Jess, just business.'

'I have no intention of blowing you away.' She glared at him across the room. *The first chance I get, though, Ramirez is going to be picking those pliers out of his ass.*

'You said you have a better idea?'

'Yes I do. I understand you want to avenge the death of your men. That's expected, and it's about sending a clear message to the others. But there is a bigger opportunity here which you're missing. You are going to pay me a lot of money to find the people who did this.' She held up the pictures. 'That's fine, but why not take the opportunity to bring a little instability to the competition while we do that? They know you got hit and no one is coming forward with a name. Why don't you hit your competition using the same MO? Who's to say it isn't the same crew who knocked over your team. There's a golden business case here for a little destabilisation. And you can do it with impunity.'

'Are you saying, don't look for the dirtbags who did this?'

'No, do the digging because people will expect you to look. But if your eyes and ears on the street are coming up with nothing then they must be well hidden. In the meantime hit one of the competition in the same way. You can hold your hands up and say: "Not me – I already got hit by these guys. I'm trying to find them."'

'But what if they continue to target my network?'

'That will give us more to work on and we'll flush them out. Besides, hitting the other players will create confusion and whoever it is could make a mistake and give themselves away.'

'I like it. But how the hell am I gonna hire a team to do this without the word getting around?'

'I would have thought that was obvious. You already have.'

Silverton smiled and nodded his head.

Mechanic nodded back. 'Which do you want hitting first?'

* * *

Lucas and Harper visited the nursing homes on the list. Lucas divided the route map into a grid and plotted each location. 'Clustering', he called it; 'a pain in the ass' was how Harper described it. As the list of ticked-off venues grew, so did their ability to get past the reception welcoming committee and into the home.

Harper continued with his 'tugging at the heartstrings' speech while Lucas provided sketchy detail on the condition of his mythical sister. The combination seemed to work well.

The staff at the homes were all too pleased to provide a thorough tour of their facilities, which provided ample opportunity for Harper to slip away and look for Jo. They drew a blank at every visit. They were parked at the Calder Bank convalescent home discussing their latest walkabout.

'I liked that one,' said Harper. 'It had a nice feel to it.'

Lucas stopped tracing out the directions to their next location on his map.

'What?' He looked at Harper the way a family regards their mad uncle.

'I thought the staff were a little more relaxed than some of the others. A little more friendly.'

'We're not going to live there.'

'No I know. I'm only saying that was better than the others we've seen. Bit on the pricey side though.'

'Are you serious? Get real. We are looking for Jo so we can catch ourselves a serial killer – we're not conducting a suitability assessment.'

'Yes I know, but it cost quite a lot more than the others. That's all I'm saying.'

Lucas shook his head. 'You're fucking losing it.'

Harper put his head down, rereading the brochure he'd picked up from the home.

There was a rap on the driver's-side window. Harper reached for his gun and Lucas jumped in his seat. He pushed the button and the window glided down.

'Can I help you?' Lucas said.

'Sorry to bother you, but I've seen you looking around homes asking about availability.' A young man stood beside the car. He was in his late twenties, wore a two-piece boiler suit, safety shoes and a baseball cap. Emblazoned across the peak was Blue Water Medical Supplies, and across the back of his jacket was written Your Complete Solution in a Single Delivery.

Lucas and Harper both stepped out of the car. Harper stayed on the passenger side keeping his gun out of sight. The young man looked excited, like he was meeting up with two old friends.

'Hey, I deliver supplies to the homes.' He removed his cap and pointed to the logo. 'I go to every facility at least once a week and I've seen you both a couple of times. I thought if you want to know anything about the homes here in Vegas then I'm your man. I know them all.' Lucas looked across at Harper who stuffed the weapon in the back of his belt.

'I saw your van,' said Lucas pointing at the two-tone blue transit in the parking bay.

'You deliver to all the nursing homes?' asked Harper.

'Yup, and some of the hospitals as well. They don't take weekly deliveries, they do theirs on a monthly consignment basis because of volume discount and shit.'

'You must know them all pretty well then?' Lucas asked, playing him along.

'Oh, hell yes. I know them all. I don't walk around with my eyes shut, I notice things.' He seemed to have a much more exciting life taking place in his head.

'Yeah I bet you do,' said Harper. 'Do you know any of the patients?'

'Not really, but I see them coming and going. I get to stock the stores and sign off the inventory count. That means I get to walk about. I reckon I could be a doctor – that's what I want to do. My name is Gus.' He extended his hand and Lucas shook it.

'Well, Gus, a doctor eh?' Harper whistled. 'You seem like a switched-on guy, I get that. You must see a lot of stuff, I bet you notice all manner of things when you walk about.'

'Yes I do, sir. I know them all and for a small consulting fee I can give you two gentlemen the low-down.'

'Consulting fee?' Harper repeated.

'Yes, medical school is gonna cost a bundle. But I could save you guys a ton of time driving around. What do you say?'

'How much would this consulting fee be?' asked Lucas.

'Ten bucks.'

'Wow, Gus, these medical fees must be huge,' Harper said.

'You better believe it.'

Lucas looked across at Harper and shrugged his shoulders.

'Sounds good to me,' he said taking the bill from his wallet. 'This better be worth it, Gus.'

'Okay. From a purely clinical perspective I would recommend Sunny Village in Clover Heights. They have the highest staff-to-patient ratio and have some cool medical kit. It's more like a hospital than a care facility. It's not the cheapest but it looks like a really smart hotel. I'd go for that one.'

'From a clinical perspective, eh? Well that's fantastic. That will save us a whole heap of time. Thank you very much.'

'You're welcome, sir. Anything you want to know, I'm your man.'

'It sounds like you are, Gus, that's for sure,' Harper chipped in.

Lucas decided to grasp the nettle.

'We are looking to place my sister – she's in her thirties and was involved in a car accident. It left her with head injuries and she needs constant care. With your expertise can you think of a place where they already look after people like that?'

'Head injuries you say?' Gus stroked his chin. 'The majority of places take folks suffering with cancer or dementia. It's kind of end-of-life care.'

'Have any of the homes taken in a woman in her early-thirties with head trauma in the past few months?' Lucas was being dangerously direct.

'No can't think of any.'

'Hey come on, Gus,' said Harper. 'I thought you were the man. You said you wanted to be a doctor. Come on, you gotta have more than that?'

Gus assumed a theatrical pose to accentuate the fact he was thinking.

'It's not a nursing home to speak of but I do deliver to a house where they look after two women. They must be in thirty-something I suppose but it's hard to tell.'

'That might be interesting,' Harper said casually, hiding the fact that his stomach was in his mouth.

'There used to be one of them but now they look after two, and one of them has a head injury of some sort. It's not a business like this.' Gus waved his arm at the plate-glass and wooden frontage of Calder Bank. 'It's more like a family home.'

'Where would we find this place?' Lucas said.

'I don't think they take cold callers. Like I said, they're not a normal type of business. I've never seen anyone else there.'

'Yeah I understand. So, for completeness, Gus, and to make sure we don't turn up by accident, where is this place?'

'Wait here.' He ran back to his van and returned with a red folder.

Lucas and Harper held their breath.

'It's Honeydew House in Buxton Cope. The name on the docket is Huxton.'

Lucas fished around in his wallet and pulled out another ten-dollar bill. He offered it to Gus.

'We didn't have this conversation. We need to keep this to ourselves, you know like patient–doctor confidentiality.'

Gus touched the side of his nose with his finger and gave Lucas a wink.

'I was never here,' he said taking the money.

He turned and walked back to his van with the warm, fuzzy feeling that he was twenty bucks closer to med school.

Chapter 25

The answer to Mechanic's question was the Crips. They were a well-organised drug gang who controlled the south-west side of Vegas selling low-grade coke. It was cheap-end material, not in the same league as the Silverton gear. They thrived on pushing volume to compensate for the low margin and that meant there were loads of them to choose from. It didn't take long for Mechanic to select two lucky candidates.

The duo peddled their business from an out-of-town trading estate and tended to work from 6pm onwards when the shops closed for the day, though in reality it was when the shop closed – singular. The real-estate development company had grossly overestimated the volume of trade when they built the place. A four-hundred-space car park serving nine businesses was a little over the top, a ratio made even worse since eight of the business units lay empty. The only one trading was a tyre replacement workshop at the far end. For the Crips, this was perfect: no CCTV, minimal street lighting and all-round visibility.

Their trade was all drive-by customers stocking up on the evening's entertainment. They operated from the front of the unit farthest from the tyre place and used the same procedure every time. When a vehicle pulled onto the lot the two dealers would separate and stand about ten yards apart. The car pulled up to the first guy and handed over the money, he held his hands up and signalled what had been purchased and the quantity. The customer drove to the second guy to pick up the drugs. It was the narcotics equivalent of a drive-through happy meal.

The guy handling the cash was scrawny, he wore clothes two sizes too big and enough gold chains to double his body weight.

The second man was a big guy with a shaved, tattooed head and wore a long leather coat, appropriate attire for hiding a long-barrelled weapon.

Trade was brisk and most of their clients were regulars. They had been there for over twelve months selling their packets of fun without any problems. All that was about to change.

Mechanic drove the battered Dodge Sebring near to the lot and parked up. The vehicle was sprayed a putrid two-tone green with tiger seat-covers and red crushed velvet covering the dashboard. Not her usual choice of ride but it was the car of choice tonight, owing to the keys being in the ignition and no one there to prevent her taking it. She killed the engine and watched the buying and selling from a distance.

She saw the dealers dispatch another satisfied customer, and then started the car and edged towards them. The guys looked up as she rolled along the tarmac and did their usual separation routine. Scrawny guy stayed put and long-coat guy turned his back and walked away.

She slammed her right foot to the floor. The tyres screeched in protest as they gained traction and the car sped forward, accelerating fast.

The man in the long coat heard the squeal and spun around.

She reached the scrawny guy a little slower than planned but the front fender hit him about thigh height sending him bouncing onto the hood and off the windshield onto the ground. The glass splintered on impact.

Her next target was a split second away.

The big guy pulled open his coat and fumbled for his weapon. He was too slow and the impact wrapped him around the front of the car. He lay across the hood with his arms outstretched, his face a mix of terror and disbelief as Mechanic powered forward. The vehicle hurtled headlong into a parking bollard. His upper body catapulted backwards and then forward as the car came crashing to a stop. He thrashed around on the hood, pinned against the concrete pillar.

Mechanic got out and walked back to scrawny guy. He lay on the floor groaning and rolling around. She stood astride him and grasped his jaw and the back of his head. His eyes locked with hers. She smiled and with a violent twist the bones cracked as his neck broke. He went limp.

The man in the long coat was flapping around screaming and banging his hands on the hood trying to free himself. She walked over, reached into his coat and ripped free the sawn-off shotgun tossing it onto the floor. Back in the car she shoved it into reverse. Long-coat guy came along for the ride for about twelve feet then slid off the hood and onto the concrete.

Mechanic looked through the splintered windshield at the figure crumpled on the ground in front of her. He was trying to sit up. She shifted to drive and stamped the accelerator into the carpet.

There was a sickening squelch as the front grill smashed into his head and shoulders, followed by a rumbling as he passed under the car. Mechanic hit the brakes, got out and walked back to the mangled shape that only a couple of minutes ago had been selling narcotics to kids. He was unconscious but still alive.

She grabbed his coat collar, dragged him back to the car and sat him upright against the fender. Mechanic opened the trunk and retrieved what she was looking for – a two-foot-long piece of knurled metal reinforcing bar.

She bent his head back and opened his mouth.

His eyes flicked open.

Mechanic allowed herself a moment of pure indulgence as she held his gaze. She grasped his jaw and drove the bar down his throat. His body spasmed as the jagged edge tore its way into his body, blood erupted into his mouth.

Mechanic stepped back and pulled a small camera from her pocket. The tiny flash lit up the gaping face. She walked away leaving the Crips' market share more than a little destabilised.

Chapter 26

The public library located on Regents Place was particularly helpful. Lucas and Harper stared at the flickering screens as microfiche images passed before them.

Buxton Cope was a small township about twenty miles to the north of Vegas, population of 243, with sixty-one residences. Honeydew House housed three adults, family name of Huxton.

A newspaper search turned up the report of the car crash which had left Mary-Jay in a vegetative state. It also reviewed the trial of Jeb Huxton following his Sunday afternoon visit to the dead boy's home. The editorial slant vehemently disagreed with the judge who'd sent Jeb to prison. It would appear their readership thought Jeb should be made a congressman for what he'd done.

Lucas pushed his chair away from the booth and wheeled himself next to Harper.

'Doctor Gus might have given us exactly what we were looking for.'

'Yeah, and you only paid the guy twenty bucks to get him into Harvard.'

Lucas smiled. This was getting close.

'Okay, so we've confirmed Honeydew House is a real place and the Huxtons live there. They have a daughter who was injured in a car crash and the paper mentions her being in an unresponsive state.'

'I also read somewhere that the mother was a nurse,' Harper added.

'This is coming together nicely. The daughter is being looked after by the mother – Doctor Gus sounded certain there were two women being cared for at the house. Our working assumption has got to be the second one is Jo Sells.'

'It sure looks that way. Off the grid but within easy reach. I'm getting a positive feeling.'

'How do we approach this? We don't know what sort of state she's in, we need to check the place out. But we can't turn up at the front door selling life insurance or encyclopedias in case Jo recognises us. She'll alert Mechanic and then we're all in need of end-of-life care.'

'The other risk is what if Mechanic turns up, or worse still is at the property when we're there.' Both men spoke in hushed tones even though the place was deserted apart from a woman sitting behind a large counter about twenty yards away.

'Jo is less likely to recognise me,' said Harper. 'A front door approach is too risky. It makes sense if I go to the house and case the joint to see if she's there.'

Lucas was deep in thought. 'Until we've positively identified her there's nothing we can do. We need to have eyes-on confirmation and then we can work out what comes next.'

'It will be dark in a little over an hour, no time like the present.' Harper removed the microfiche tape, got up and left.

Lucas took one last look at the grainy newspaper report of the accident. The pretty face of Mary-Jay Huxton stared out of the screen. He wondered what she was staring at now.

Harper was right. Seventy-five minutes later the sun disappeared and the headlights on the rental car illuminated the sign saying Buxton Cope. Lucas slowed down and they both scoured the neighbourhood looking for the Huxtons' place. The address didn't help much as there were no street names and very little street lighting, which made for slow progress. After a while they spotted a handwritten sign pointing to a house at the end of a long unmarked dirt-track road. It said Honeydew House.

Lucas killed the lights and pulled over. The property was lit up, someone was home.

'At least I'll see anyone coming,' said Harper, popping the clip from the grip of his gun. He checked it then snapped it back in place. Lucas kept his eyes on the rear-view mirror, all was clear.

'No heroics,' he said. 'The last thing we want to do is spook them. If you can't get a clear view come away and we'll try again.'

'Got it,' said Harper flicking the switch in the roof of the car. He opened the door and the interior light stayed off. He stepped into the darkness and hurried up the road towards the house.

As he got closer he could make out the layout of the property. It looked like the Huxtons were throwing a party – every light in the house was on. He skirted around the front gate and made his way down the side of the house. Despite the light show, the place was silent. Harper placed his foot onto the veranda which ran around the house. There was a creak as his weight transferred onto the boards, and he stepped onto the whitewashed porch. He made his way to the first of four windows and peered inside.

It was a large farmhouse-style kitchen, with a big oak table and six chairs pushed under it. The wooden worktops were wiped clean and dishtowels hung against the front of the range cooker. No one was there.

Harper stayed close to the wall and ducked under the sill to the second window. This one looked into a hallway with the walls covered in paintings and photographs. Wall lamps flooded the ceiling with light and the floor was covered with rugs of various shapes and designs. No one there either.

The curtains on the third window were only partly closed. Harper bent down and looked through the gap. It was the living room, spacious with vases of fresh flowers and a random selection of soft furnishings none of which matched. He could see the back of the sofa and the dark silhouettes of two heads. One was a woman and the other a man. They were watching television.

To the side Harper saw two seated figures. He had a good line of sight to the one nearest. A withered figure of a woman in a wheelchair with a blue mask over her mouth and a skullcap which gave the impression of her being bald. He couldn't make out the second person, his view was obstructed.

He changed position but it was no use.

Harper was about to try the other window when the woman on the sofa got up. She placed both hands on the shoulders of the emaciated woman and kissed her on the forehead. She pushed her back slightly and walked towards the kitchen. Harper ducked down and held his breath.

He raised his head and peered through the curtains. The second woman was now in full view.

Her face was puffy and a neck brace held her head upright. She wore a bandage around her head with tufts of hair poking out. She stared at the TV with her jaw hanging down. Harper could only see the side of her face but there was no mistake. He was looking at Dr Jo Sells.

* * *

Moran pulled up at the out-of-town trading estate. It was dark, and the red and blue flashing lights bounced off the shopfronts. There was a buzz of activity inside the yellow taped-off area with paramedics hunched over a body on the ground. To the left there was another huddle taking high-resolution pictures of the back of a car.

She reached the tape and held up her badge.

'Detective Moran,' she said to the uniformed officer standing on guard. 'I'm here to meet Detective Chad Mills.'

'He's over there, the one in the loud shirt.'

'Thanks.' Moran couldn't miss him. If her dress sense was all about being monochrome, his was the complete opposite. He looked like a tourist who'd spent all his money at the Hawaiian market.

'Detective Mills?' She stood next to him as he checked the pockets of the man on the floor.

'Who's asking?'

'I'm Detective Moran. Despatch sent me over here.'

Mills looked up. 'Ah, the new girl.'

Moran disliked him instantly.

'I saw the new-joiners memo which said you'd be turning up sometime soon. Welcome to Vegas.' He stood up. 'What we have here is a standard drug-related hit straight out of the playbook. John Doe No.1 here looks like he was rammed by the car which broke his neck. John Doe No. 2 over there had a much tougher ride.'

They walked over to the second knot of people. The body was sitting upright against the rear of the car, illuminated by the bright white staccato flash of the camera. It gave the scene a *Friday the 13th* look.

'This vic was also run over but I don't reckon that's what killed him. He was dragged to this position from over there and died from having this rammed down his throat.' He pointed to the metal spike sticking out of the man's mouth.

Moran bent down and shone her flashlight onto the bar. It had the same knurled pattern cut into the metal as the one from the mortuary.

'I've seen this before,' she said.

'So have I, Detective, so have I.'

'No, I mean I've seen this MO before. The metal bar. I saw this on another drug relat—' She wasn't allowed to finish.

'They do this all the time. One crew grows stronger than another and moves in on the weaker gang's territory. Then they get rich and complacent and another gang moves in on them. And so it goes around and around.'

'But this is different, don't you think? No shots fired, the vics are killed by hand. The steel rod rammed down the throat. This is a high-risk strategy for someone who simply wants to take out the competition. There are three more bodies exactly like—'

'Like what exactly? Like what?' Mills was walking away.

Moran caught up with him. 'I saw this a few days ago with another gang.'

'As I said, it happens all the time. You'd better get used to it cos this is Vegas, baby, this is Vegas. I'm heading back to the station, fancy a coffee?' Mills got in his car and drove away.

This jerk was annoying as hell.

Chapter 27

Lucas and Harper were sitting in the darkest part of the darkest bar in Vegas. Lucas's vocabulary had completely deserted him.

'Fucking hell.'

'Yeah, I'm telling you it was her,' Harper replied from the gloom.

'Are you sure, are you absolutely sure?'

'It's her. I even heard the Huxton woman talking to them and she definitely said Jo.'

'I can't believe it.' Lucas finished his drink and ordered two more.

'I couldn't tell what state she was in but it didn't look good. I stayed as long as I dared and she didn't move. I mean, didn't move an inch. Nothing. The other woman, the daughter, didn't look in great shape either. She wore some sort of medical helmet and was motionless the whole time I was there.'

'Fucking hell.' His vocabulary failed again.

'Other than being in a wheelchair and unable to move, with a bandage around her head, she looked the same.'

'Mechanic brought her all this way and kept her alive,' said Lucas.

'Looks like you were right. The question is, now what do we do?'

'We need to think of a way to get to Mechanic through Jo.'

'Snatch her,' replied Harper a little too quickly.

'That's a possibility but we'll need to be able to look after her. We want her alive as bait, not dead.'

'Do we?' Harper emptied the glass in a single glug and picked up another.

'How do you mean?'

'We snatch Jo and use her to lure Mechanic into the open. She could be dead or alive, Mechanic wouldn't know. I say snatching Jo is our *only* option. We gotta use her as leverage to make Mechanic give herself up. If we keep Jo alive – fine, if we don't – fine. The result is the same.'

'I'm not sure about that.' Lucas was feeling a little squeamish. 'I want Mechanic dead more than anyone but I'm not convinced about killing Jo in the process.'

'The way to Mechanic is through Jo. We need to stop that murdering psycho bitch before she kills again, which she will. It's simply a matter of time. I shot Jo because I wanted her dead, I have no scruples about finishing the job. If she dies as a result of the snatch, so be it. If it means we get to kill Mechanic, it's worth a few sleepless nights.' He tilted back his head and another drink disappeared down his throat.

Lucas knew he was right. They stood no chance tackling Mechanic head on. The only way this could work would be if she gave herself up in return for her sister.

'There's another reason we have no choice,' said Harper.

'What?'

'Who do you think is top of Mechanic's kill list right now?'

'Yeah, I thought of that. It's you and me.'

'Exactly.'

Lucas was quiet for a while, and then offered a poorly thought through suggestion. 'We could go back to first base and inform Chuck Hastings.'

Harper looked at him in disbelief. 'You want to trust this to them? It's now a cross-jurisdiction case because it's in another state, which means the FBI will want their slice of the pie, as well as the guys from Florida and Vegas.' Harper waved his hand and ordered two more drinks. 'Let's be fair, you and I both know it's got "catastrophic screw-up" written all over it. Mechanic will slip away in the confusion and we'll be in hiding for the rest of our lives.'

Harper was on a roll. 'Besides, have you forgotten you're suspended? You drag your flabby ass to the other side of the country chasing a serial killer when you've been told to back off. You would be dead meat my friend. Dead meat.' The bartender beat a hasty retreat having overheard the last set of comments.

'Shhh!' Lucas put his finger to his lips. 'Okay, okay. I get it, that's not a good thing to do.'

'It's a stupid, bone-headed thing to do. We turn this over to the police and we lose control. You get fired for gross misconduct and I'll be done for perverting the course of justice or something. Mechanic will evaporate into thin air, and you and me will be dead men walking.'

Lucas picked up the shot glass and necked it back.

'A snatch it is then.'

Chapter 28

Mechanic showed Silverton the stark photograph depicting a long-coated man propped against the back of a car with the metal spike protruding from his mouth. He was ecstatic.

'Nice touch,' he said referring to the signature method. 'That sends a clear message. Have you turned up anything on who hit my team?'

'No nothing, Mr Silverton.'

'This goes through the accounts as a business development cost,' Silverton said throwing a paper bag across the room. It landed in her lap. Mechanic opened it and stared at fifteen thousand dollars in used notes, apparently the going rate for destabilising the drug market one gang at a time.

She was getting paid well to do something which she was doing for free anyway. Her stress levels were low and her cash reserves were high. She would soon have enough money to buy a bigger place, convert it and move Jo in. The Huxton woman could call daily to look after her as she no longer required twenty-four-hour care. Jo was stable, but nothing could be done to bring her out of her locked-in state. Drugs, bathing, toileting and feeding had become routine tasks which could be delivered at Mechanic's home equally as well as at the Huxtons. She wanted Jo to be near her.

'So who's next boss?'

* * *

Back home Mechanic put the paper bag into a holdall and stuffed it into the top of her wardrobe. She zipped up her light bomber jacket and checked her kit. The silenced .45 was holstered in place under her left arm with four spare clips, throwing knives secured to her ankles, and a hunting knife in the back of her belt. She wore black cotton trousers and gloves. The small dark rucksack at her feet contained all the necessary toys and treats if you were looking to take down a drug den. Today it was the turn of the Turks. All she needed to complete her preparation was a two-foot length of knurled metal reinforcing bar and it was time to go to work.

The Turks ran the east side, they were a small outfit and new to Vegas. What they lacked in size they made up for in bloody carnage. The territory had been previously occupied by the Cobras who were wiped out by the Turks over the course of a single weekend. On Friday the punters had bought gear from their friendly local Cobra dealer and on Monday did business with the Turks. It was clinical and brutal.

The intel and surveillance provided by Silverton was more like a military briefing dossier. Mechanic learned that the Turks operated in teams of three with one guy being a dedicated shooter for when things got rough. They peddled a wide range of drugs from crack cocaine, tina and LSD, to party poppers, and prided themselves on being a one-stop shop for all your recreational needs. Silverton had already identified the team to be hit and it wasn't going to be easy.

They worked out of a derelict house on a rundown estate. Either the developer had run out of cash or lost interest but there were around twenty part-completed homes. It had one road in and out due to the burned-out vehicles and garbage blocking the adjoining routes. The Turks occupied the property which had the sign saying Show Home.

A gunman sat in the upstairs window keeping watch, while the other two took care of business from the front garden, which was surrounded by a three-foot-high wall. Punters would place their order with one guy and leave money on the wall, the other guy would dispense their purchases, also by leaving them on the wall.

It was a non-contact transaction carried out under the watchful eye of an assault rifle sticking out of the bedroom window.

Mechanic viewed the grainy reconnaissance photographs provided by Silverton. It was a slick set-up for sure but with one tiny flaw. All the action took place at the front of the house, *who was looking after the back?*

Mechanic parked up and looked at the green digits on the dashboard. They read 11.30pm. She got out of the car, pulled the rucksack across one shoulder and approached the estate on foot. She stopped about two hundred yards out, unzipped a side pouch and took out a single lens night-sight. She twisted the ratchet and the back of the house came into focus. It looked deserted.

She crossed the ground using the other properties for cover and at fifty yards out repeated the observation. Nothing had changed. Music was playing and cackling laughter drifted towards her on the breeze. They seemed to be a happy team.

Mechanic reached the house and crouched at the back wall. She could hear the steady stream of business out front with punters revving their engines and women shrieking.

She tried the back door. It was locked – a peculiar safety measure as the window next to it contained no glass. Mechanic eased her way through the opening and dropped to the other side. She remained still, tuning into the sounds and smells of the drug den.

The place was gutted, every fitting, every worktop, every door was missing and the floor was stripped down to bare concrete. Mechanic drew her gun and crossed the kitchen into the living room. She cursed under her breath. The whole house was littered with broken glass, beer cans and pizza boxes, not easy to negotiate in silence. She picked her way through the obstacle course staying close to the inside wall. The front window was a gaping hole onto the garden and she could hear the two out front welcoming their regulars. Mechanic climbed the stairs, sticking to the edge, and as she reached the top it was easy to spot which room contained the shooter. He was in the one behind the solid metal door with no handle on the outside. She eased the thick blade of her hunting knife under the door and levered it towards her. The door was solid. Locked shut.

Mechanic surveyed her options. The doorway immediately to the right led to a bedroom. She entered and positioned herself against the front wall near the window. From her bag she fished out a small round mirror on a telescopic arm and inched it above the window ledge. Mechanic angled it and could see across the front of the building. As she watched the barrel of the assault rifle poked out into the night.

She put the mirror down and looked around the floor for something to throw. A cluster of nuts and bolts lay in one corner, the product of removing the fitted furniture during the house gutting. Mechanic gathered them up and waited.

Outside was a non-stop procession of cars with people eager to score. She would have to wait, this was not a time to be impatient.

After about an hour it all went quiet. Mechanic positioned the mirror over the ledge and the two men outside were chatting. There were no cars and no customers. This was her time.

She threw three of the bolts at the left-hand corner of the front wall. The garden guys shouted something at each other and went to investigate. Mechanic could see more of the gun barrel in the mirror as the shooter edged forward. She threw two more into the same corner. They clattered against the wall.

This time one of the two men at the front called to the shooter.

'Hey man. Did you hear that? Something's down here!'

The shooter leaned out of the window to get a better view. Mechanic threw her last bolt.

'Hey, what the hell, man?' said one of the garden men as it struck him on the back.

'Are you seeing anything?' the other called to the shooter.

He leaned out of the window, aiming his rifle into the corner. A fraction further. That's it. A little more …

The bullet hit him below his right ear and he crumpled back into the house, a muffled spit as the shell splattered blood against the brickwork. Mechanic spun her aim around and the man nearest the house took the first shot in his shoulder and the second in the head. The remaining garden guy still couldn't work out where the shots were coming from and took cover against the front wall. This was the easiest of all. Two more shots blew his head wide open.

Mechanic packed away her gear, went downstairs, through the front door and into the garden. She removed her rucksack and slid out the two-foot metal reinforcing bar.

'Now which one of you wants to be famous?'

Chapter 29

Lucas favoured the subtle approach based upon deception while Harper preferred an armoured vehicle through the front door and stun grenades. Planning the abduction of Jo Sells was proving to be a challenge.

They clashed on a minute-by-minute basis. Lucas pressed hard his opinion that a forced abduction would inevitably lead to police involvement, which was difficult to argue against. But despite this Lucas struggled to persuade Harper to ditch his Wild West option.

In order to take a well-earned break from the constant arguing they watched the house as much as they could to gain insight into Jo's condition.

The daily routine was repetitive. Jeb Huxton left the house every morning at 7am and returned at 5.45pm, dinner was on the table at quarter past six sharp. Jenny-Jay occasionally shopped for groceries but for the main part stayed in the house attending to the two women. Other than the mailman they didn't have any visitors.

During the dark hours Lucas and Harper took turns to observe the bizarre proceedings as the family sat in front of the TV, absorbing their regular diet of game shows and cop programmes. On each occasion Jo was completely inert in her wheelchair and showed no physical responses whatsoever, while Jenny-Jay busied around her. Jo was always immaculately dressed with a food tube plumbed into her stomach.

Harper persisted in championing the forced entry approach until one evening he looked through the kitchen window and saw Jeb Huxton sitting at the large oak table. He had interrupted his normal ritual of shouting at the TV to enjoy a beer and clean his guns. It was difficult to tell, but Harper estimated there were at least five different firearms laid across the table. Harper was so preoccupied trying to identify the stocks, barrels and magazines he almost missed Jenny-Jay entering the room. She sat down next to her husband and began assembling components as casually as if she were putting the blades into her Magimix.

With that amount of firepower, coupled with that amount of expertise, an approach based on deception now seemed to Harper to be the best way forward.

Lucas's plan was bold and required confidence but with a soft touch. The problem was they'd only have one shot at it and there was no plan B.

They would hire a wheelchair-accessible vehicle, wait for Jeb to go to work and simply knock on the front door. The storyline was they had come to collect Jo and take her to the Sunny Village nursing home in Clover Heights. It was a week's respite organised by Jo's sister. Harper had paid Sunny Village a visit and managed to come away with a professional glossy brochure, a current price list and a pad of letterheaded paper.

They rehearsed what they were going to say until it was word perfect and were well prepared for the 'I know nothing about this' reaction. The whole strategy hinged on them being persuasive and believable.

Once they had Jo, they needed somewhere to keep her out of sight. Lucas sourced a nursing home in a place called Victorville to the east of Los Angeles and arranged for her to be admitted for a week. The downside was it was a three-hour drive away, which made it a logistical nightmare. The upside was there was a high probability that Mechanic wouldn't be able to locate her. They briefly considered keeping Jo themselves at a motel but quickly dismissed it as a bad idea. They couldn't cope with her needs and, despite Harper's opinion to the contrary, it still seemed sensible she was kept alive.

Setting up the communications link with Mechanic was complex and high risk. If they used telephones to make contact she would inevitably figure out the call locations and come after them. Lucas had fallen foul of Mechanic's abilities to work her magic with a telecoms network before and was not about to repeat it. They had to make their demands in a way which could not be traced back. There had to be a physical cut-off between them and the messages. The solution was newspaper advertisements.

The Vegas Bulletin was a free paper, circulated daily, which printed classified ads for local businesses in the area. It also had an extensive personal section where the seedier side of Vegas touted for custom. Strip joints and massage services covered almost as many column inches as the more traditional trades. The paper accepted adverts on a daily basis over the phone and a one-off payment of a hundred bucks bought you twenty ads. You placed your ad one day for it to appear the next. Another advantage was that they accepted cash.

The sequencing of the ads was important. Lucas wanted Mechanic to receive two messages on the day they took Jo. This would maximise the shock and keep her off balance. He preordered the opening ad to go to press the day before the snatch. Lucas would place the second ad for it to be printed on the day.

During the pickup Lucas would give Jenny-Jay a sealed envelope to pass on to Mechanic. The cover story was that it contained administrative paperwork. It actually contained the personal ads page from the Bulletin with advert number one.

Once Jo was safely in the van they would to ask Jenny-Jay to put a courtesy call through to Mechanic to let her know Jo had been collected safely. They figured this would have a bombshell effect and compel Mechanic to head straight for the Huxton place. Jenny-Jay would give the envelope to Mechanic and bang! – message number one delivered. This would lead her to that day's newspaper and bang! – message number two delivered.

Once Mechanic was hooked, they would run a series of daily ads detailing how the trade was to take place and how she was to give herself up. It was far from ideal, but then when could any of this be described as ideal?

After four days of quarrelling, frantic planning and acute boredom, Lucas and Harper pulled the hired van onto the dirt track leading to Honeydew House. It felt odd to drive past their usual pull-in place, where they had previously observed the comings and goings from a safe distance. Both men were silent, both awash with nervous anxiety.

They passed through the wide front gates and killed the engine. Lucas cast a sideways glance at Harper.

'Remember, keep it light, keep it conversational and smile. Any problems and we walk away.'

Harper nodded and stepped out of the van. They were both dressed in white two-piece coveralls purchased from a DIY superstore. At least it went some way towards giving the impression of clinical care. Lucas rapped on the door.

They could hear voices from inside and Jenny-Jay opened the door.

She shielded her eyes against the morning sun. 'Yes, can I help you?'

'Good morning, ma'am, we are from the Sunny Village nursing home in Clover Heights.' Lucas smiled and consulted his clipboard. 'We are here to pick up Jo.'

Jenny-Jay Huxton furrowed her brow.

Lucas continued, 'Ma'am we have a pick up time of 10.30am. Is she ready? I believe she has a wheelchair.'

'Oh, I'm sorry but there seems to be some confusion,' said Jenny-Jay holding her hands up in a gesture of apology.

'Ma'am, Jo's sister arranged for her to stay with us at Sunny Village and we kind of assumed she would have told you. She booked Jo in for a week. It's to give you a break and for Jo to have a change of scenery.'

'No, no, no, I don't think that's right.' Jenny-Jay shook her head.

Lucas consulted his clipboard once more and handed it to her. The headed paper had their name, address and pick-up time clearly typed across it. There was no mention of Jo's surname or Mechanic's. It was the best Harper could do given the time.

'We have another guest to collect this morning, ma'am, so if we could get Jo settled into the vehicle we'll be on our way.' Harper smiled, reciting his lines perfectly.

'You don't understand, there must be some mistake,' Jenny-Jay said.

'Sorry, ma'am, but there seems to be a slight breakdown in communications here.' Lucas waved his hand at the clipboard. 'I'm sure you can sort it out later with Jo's sister. She was really excited about Jo going on this mini-break. She'll have a fabulous time with us at Sunny Village.'

Jenny-Jay looked at the paper and back to Lucas and Harper. It was not going well.

'Ma'am, if we could pick up Jo and we'll be on our way.' Harper was still manically smiling.

'But she's not here.' Jenny-Jay handed back the documentation.

'She's not?' replied Lucas.

'No, the other people came and picked her up earlier this morning.'

'The other people?' said Lucas.

'Yeah, he was from …' She disappeared inside and returned holding a piece of paper with a logo on the top. 'Forever Young. A home for the young at heart.' She offered the document to Lucas who read it and passed it to Harper.

'Jo left this morning you say?' It was Harper's turn to look confused.

'Yup. Jessica, Jo's sister, must have made two bookings or something, because a nice young man came and took Jo there this morning.'

Lucas and Harper were stuck for words. Their careful scripting had not considered this eventuality.

Jenny-Jay reached across and took the paper from Harper.

'She must have got confused somewhere along the way. She works so hard, I expect she got her wires crossed. Sorry, gentlemen, but looks like the other place got the booking and not you.'

Lucas and Harper were stunned into silence.

Jenny-Jay continued, 'Mind you, I think it's highly sensible that Sunny Village has sent two of you to collect her. The other lot weren't very well set up at all.'

'How do you mean, not well set up?' asked Lucas.

'Well I mean I had to help the poor chap. Not his fault I know and it is good that they're encouraging people back into useful work. But I mean it wasn't right.'

Lucas's sixth sense made the hairs on the back of his neck stand up.

'What wasn't right, Mrs Huxton?'

'Well I mean, fancy sending a young chap to collect someone in a wheelchair when he's only got one arm.'

Chapter 30

Moran sat in Brennan's office waiting. He was already fifteen minutes late and she was starting to understand her place in the office pecking order, a realisation which didn't sit well with her at all.

In her last workplace Moran's life in uniform was fast and furious, but for everyone else it was relatively steady and mundane. Her drive and determination was relentless and, for the people she worked with, completely exhausting. She burned with an intensity which was hard to live with. Her career was everything and she made sure people knew it.

A series of failed relationships forced her to take stock of her life. She needed to ease back a little. Work got in the way of everything and while she knew it was the major contributory factor to her still being single at thirty-one, she preferred to put that down to a bad choice of men.

Her decision to reappraise her life and modify her ambition lasted less than twenty-four hours. The very next day she put in for a transfer to Vegas. A month later and she moved into a new flat with her new job in homicide. Ease back a little? What had she been thinking …

As she sat waiting, she could feel the adrenaline coursing through her. There were inconsistencies between the latest killings and the usual turf war hits. She prided herself on spotting patterns and inconsistencies which others would overlook, and the recent killings struck her as odd.

Brennan blustered in, with no apology, and flopped down behind his desk.

'How you doing? I didn't get to have that coffee with you, did I?'

'No sir, but that's fine.'

'We must do that. Anyway, you wanted to see me.'

'Yes, it's about the bodies you sent me to look at in the mortuary and the drug-related murders from the other night.'

'Okay, what's up?'

'It's the unusual nature of the murders, sir. On the surface it looks like a turf war but the method of killing doesn't stack up. Usually when one gang goes up against another—'

'Mills is running with this, right?' he interrupted.

'Yes sir, he's the detective in charge.'

'What does he think?'

'Well he's of the opinion there's nothing out of the ordinary.'

'Then that's good, right? I mean we have this happen on a regular basis.'

'I understand that but I think this is different. I've looked at the records going back and where one gang takes out another there's a recognised formula. This doesn't follow the pattern. I've listed the inconsistencies here.' She handed him a document.

'What does Mills think?' he said scanning it.

'He says it's no different.'

'Then that's the answer, isn't it?'

'But, sir, in the past the MO is always hit them hard, hit them fast, then get the hell out of there. The first set of killings had characteristics of torture, this was anything but a drive-by shooting.'

'It's bad guys killing bad guys, there are bound to be minor differences.'

'Yes sir, I get that but this is way off the norm. This is more like—' Brennan interrupted again.

'Have you spoken to Mills about this? Have you shared your observations with him?'

'Yes sir, I have. He says "This is Vegas".'

'Look, Mills is a good cop. He can be a little off at times, but then can't we all? He's seen this kind of thing time and time again. I'll talk to him if you like. Thanks for this.' He placed her work on top of a huge pile of papers.

It looked as if the conversation was over.

'Thank you, sir,' was all she could think to say, other than, *Fucking listen to me!* which she kept firmly in her head.

Chapter 31

Lucas and Harper were back at their black hole of a bar. It was 1.30pm but the ambient lighting made it feel more like three in the morning. The bar glowed with a red and white fluorescent haze from the Budweiser signs on the wall. Harper sat at a small round table in the corner. A narrow cone of light illuminated two glasses of soda and a stack of sandwiches piled up on a plate.

Lucas appeared out of the gloom to join him.

'Well?' asked Harper devouring his lunch.

'Spoke to his father and he says he's been on a "discover yourself" kind of road trip. Seems he's a lot better and this is all part of the getting himself back together. He wouldn't give me any specifics and doesn't know where he is now. He's been gone around two weeks and hasn't left any forwarding address.' Lucas pulled a well-filled sandwich from the pile.

They were both numb following the events of the morning.

'I went to Forever Young and they've not received any new patients and they don't have anyone on their staff with one arm. It has to be him. It has to be Bassano. It's too much of a coincidence.' Harper slurped the soda through a straw.

'I can't get my head around it. Why the hell would Bassano want to take Jo Sells?'

'The same reason you do.' The voice came out of the shadows.

It was Chris Bassano.

He reached the table and pulled up a chair. In the poor light there appeared nothing amiss with the tall dark-haired Italian dressed in jeans and a long-sleeved shirt. He sat down with his elbows on the table.

'Afternoon, boss,' he said nodding towards Lucas. 'Nice to see you both again.'

He edged the chair forward and the cone of light caught his face. It was much improved from the last time Lucas saw him, the deep purple scars had faded into a thin cobweb of red lines which ran across his face. The dentist had done a good job replacing the missing teeth and his nose looked normal as opposed to the flattened pulp Lucas had witnessed at the hospital. There were slight bald patches in his hairline where the skin grafts had taken, but on the whole he looked in good order. His hands were clasped in front of him, or more accurately one hand and a metallic hook. The three men stared at one another, no one spoke. Then delayed reaction kicked in.

'How the hell …' Lucas stood up, half a sandwich hanging from his mouth. Harper choked on his soda.

'Do you have her?' Harper blurted out the sixty-four-thousand-dollar question, spitting droplets of soda onto the table.

'Yup,' Bassano said nodding his head.

'Where is she?' Lucas said.

'At my motel. I rented another room and she's there.'

'Jesus Christ.' Harper looked at the ceiling.

'What … How …?' Lucas was struggling with his mouth full of meat and bread.

'I did the same thing you were thinking, I guess. Snatch Jo Sells and use her to get to her psycho sister.'

'How did you know where she was? How did you know she was still alive?' asked Lucas, the questions tumbling out.

'I didn't. The boys down at the station tipped me off about the concealed room and about you being involved. It was a big topic of conversation because the big boss man got covered in shit or something. Anyway, I figured it was time to get back in the game and this seemed like a good time.'

'Yes, but how did you know about Vegas?' asked Harper.

'I didn't, I followed you.'

'What!'

'I used to be a detective, remember, and you guys leave a trail so wide a kid could follow. I came down to Florida to pick up where we left off and found you two up to your asses in tracking Mechanic. I figured you wouldn't react kindly to dragging along a cripple, so I sat back and let you get on with it. Joining the dots, I ended up here in Vegas. I figured this must be where Mechanic was hanging out and then discovered the unexpected bonus, her sister Jo.'

'But how did you find out about Jo?' asked Harper.

'I followed you to the Huxton place. It wasn't difficult.'

'Did you go to Baton Rouge as well?' asked Lucas.

'Hell no, I heard about that but there was definitely something odd about that letter. I mean why would Mechanic give herself away like that, when essentially she'd slipped the net. It made no sense. No, Baton Rouge wasn't worth the effort.'

Lucas smarted at the blunt analysis.

'So how did you decide to …' Harper didn't finish his sentence.

'I took Jo when I had the chance with a cover story that I was from a nursing home taking Jo for a break. The Huxton woman bought it.'

Lucas looked at Harper and closed his eyes.

'That was our plan. We turned up shortly after you, looking like fucking lemons.'

'Well we have her now.' Bassano shrugged his shoulders.

'Tell me again,' asked Harper. 'Why have you snatched Jo?'

'Two reasons. The first is to kill the bastard that done this.' Bassano held up his right arm and waved the hook in the air.

'And the second?' asked Lucas.

'To prove to you two that I still got it.'

'You didn't need to do that.' Lucas leaned over and put his hand on Bassano's shoulder. 'It's good to see you. I was worried. You wouldn't return my calls or letters.'

'I was in a bad place and feeling sorry for myself. There was a rage inside me and I no longer had the tools to do anything about it. It ground me to a standstill.'

'You were in a shocking state, and when your folks decided you could no longer cope, that was it. You disappeared,' Lucas said.

'I was clinically depressed and got prescribed a shit load of meds which helped. But it was pretty bleak.'

'What changed?' asked Harper.

'I felt a little better and decided to enrol on a recovery camp. It's one of those places where people with serious life-changing injuries go to get their confidence back. It encourages you to do things which ordinarily you can't do, or rather you don't believe you can do, like abseiling, scuba diving, climbing, living in the wild, that type of thing. It's about challenging yourself mentally as well as physically, making you realise what you *can* achieve rather than focusing on what you can't.'

'So these physical challenges gave you back your self-belief and motivation,' Lucas said eventually.

'Fuck no. Turns out the women there were more interested in trying out the Italian love stick. I'd completely gone off the boil but those three weeks certainly got the motor running hot again.'

'You pulled women on the course?' Lucas asked.

'Yup.'

'But you weren't exactly in working order, you were still recovering? I mean your arm and your face?' Harper chipped in.

'Turns out women like a bit of imperfection.'

'Bit of imperfection!' Harper choked again on his soda. 'You have one arm and a face Peter Cushing would run from.'

'Correction, I have one and a half arms, my face is on the mend, but there's nothing wrong with the pork sword.' Bassano smiled broadly and grasped his crotch with his good hand.

'Let me get this straight. You went to a retreat and women with similar conditions hit on you?' Harper obviously needed further clarification.

'Not exclusively. The able-bodied chicks fancied a go as well.'

'I don't believe this.' Harper thought of his monthly expenditure on hookers and wondered if he would save money if he chopped his arm off.

'Anyway it did the trick?' Lucas was keen to bring this lurid conversation to an end.

'Yes, sure did. Three weeks of screwing myself to a standstill was exactly what the doctor ordered. As I said, I feel ready to get back in the game. So I lifted Jo.'

'What's next in your plan?' asked Harper.

'This is it. Snatch Jo and find you guys.'

'That's it!' Lucas was beginning to remember some of the more frustrating elements about working with Bassano.

'Yup. I figured you guys were working along the same lines. So I saved you the trouble of taking her.'

'We need to move fast or this will quickly unravel.' Lucas's head shifted into cop mode. 'We've arranged for Jo to spend some time at a nursing home in Victorville. It's a hell of a drive but we need to ensure she's out of Mechanic's reach. We have to get her there before she runs into health complications. Harper, you go to the motel with Bassano, pick her up and drive her there.'

Harper nodded.

'You want me to go along too?' asked Bassano.

'No. You need to go back to the Huxton place and tell the mother to call Jess and let her know her sister has been collected safely. When you're there, give her a letter to pass on to Mechanic. Tell Jenny-Jay it's the paperwork which you should have dropped off earlier. It contains a newspaper advertisement for Mechanic, I'll explain later.'

'What about you?' asked Harper.

'I'll contact the paper and place our second ad. It needs to be in before two thirty to make tomorrow's run.'

'What's it gonna say?'

'Not sure yet.'

They sat in silence each one racking their brains for something suitable.

Bassano chipped in.

'How about, "You're a dead woman".'

Chapter 32

Mechanic was riding on a permanent high. Silverton had the look of a teenage boy thumbing through a porn mag when she showed him the photographs from the hit. He flicked back and forth through the images on the camera.

'Hell girl, when you say you're gonna to do a job, you sure as hell do a job. This will piss on their picnic.' He slapped his thigh and crowed like a banshee.

'Have you had any contact with the other gang leaders?' asked Mechanic.

'No, complete radio silence. Though I figure after this latest little incident my boys will get a call.'

He opened a desk drawer, pulled out a plain paper bag and tossed it to Mechanic. She didn't bother opening it. From the look and feel she knew it was another fifteen thousand bucks cash deposit for the top of her wardrobe.

'Where do we go next, Mr Silverton?'

'The Wild Crew. They run the central east side in the Winchester township of Vegas. They're the oldest gang around and consider themselves part of the establishment. They have some top-ranking officials in their pocket and so tend to get away with murder. Often literally I might add.'

'Any particular reason why they're next?'

'Yes, I don't fucking like them.' He handed Mechanic a large envelope.

'Thanks. I'll do some additional surveillance this time if that's okay, Mr Silverton. The intel and photos you provide are fine but it's no substitute for eyes on.'

'Yup, play it as you wish. Keep me posted and let me know when it's going down. I want to be sure my team are fully occupied.' She got up and left the room a much richer woman.

* * *

Forty minutes later Mechanic was opening the front door to her house. She crossed the hallway into the kitchen and flicked on the coffee maker. The answerphone message blinked red requiring attention. She hit the play button.

'Hi Jessica, this is Jenny-Jay.' Mechanic smiled and busied herself making coffee. 'It's a quick call to let you know Jo got picked up safely this morning. She was so excited about going on her mini-break she wouldn't shut up about it. Anyway talk to you soon, bye for now. Oh, before I forget, they left paperwork for you. You can pick it up on your next visit. See you soon. Byeee!'

Mechanic froze.

She held a cup in one hand and a carton of milk in the other. Very slowly she returned the cup back in the cupboard and again pushed play. Mrs Huxton's voice was light and airy, unaware of the cataclysmic shock she was creating at the other end. Mechanic replaced the milk in the fridge, hit play once more and steadied herself with both hands on the worktop. The message played a third time. She could feel the fury boiling through her body. She began to shake.

Mechanic forced herself to move, she opened the compartment on the phone, removed the cassette tape and shoved it in her pocket. She ran to the bedroom, rammed the brown paper bag into the wardrobe and picked up the black rucksack, holstering her weapon. Fifty minutes later she stood outside the Huxtons' front door and knocked, not sure what was about to happen next.

The shaking was gone, replaced by cold, hard aggression. She was cool and calm. Completely focused and prepared for anything.

Mrs Huxton opened the door.

'Hello, Jessica, this is a nice surprise. I didn't expect to see you so soon. Come in, come in. Look Mary-Jay, Jessica has come to see us, isn't that great?'

'Is there anyone else here, Jenny-Jay?' asked Mechanic.

'No it's only the two of us, Jeb is at work. We are so pleased to see you.' She stepped away from the door allowing Mechanic into the house.

'I got your message, Jenny-Jay,' Mechanic said.

'Oh, that's okay. No worries. Do you want coffee? We were settling down for a nice game of cards. Do you want to join us?'

'Coffee would be good thanks, but I'll pass on the cards.'

'Coffee it is then. Look Mary-Jay, look who's come to visit.' She fussed around her daughter and then disappeared into the kitchen. Mechanic followed her.

'So, Jo got picked up okay then, Mrs Huxton?' Mechanic asked casually.

'Please, Jessica, it's Jenny-Jay,' she scolded her playfully. 'Yes she was collected this morning for her break at Forever Young. I think it's a great idea, she'll really enjoy herself there. I know a little about the place, it's lovely.'

'Yes, well I thought it was a good choice. When did they pick her up?'

'Called at around half nine, I guess. Then what do you think happened?'

'What?'

'The other men turned up. That was a bit of a mix up.' She slapped the worktop to emphasise the pantomime nature of the muddle.

'Mix up?' asked Mechanic.

'The Forever Young guy turned up first, then before you knew it two other men from Sunny Village nursing home in Clover Heights were standing on my doorstep. They looked extremely put out when I told them Jo wasn't here.'

'Yes, that is a mix up. I spoke to a number of homes and I suppose it all got a little confused. I'm sorry about that.'

Jenny-Jay pushed a coffee and the sugar bowl in front of Mechanic.

'That's fine, my dear, no harm done. The Forever Young chap left you this.' She handed over the envelope. Mechanic was not about to open it in front of Jenny-Jay.

'Did I hear Mary-Jay then?' Mechanic said looking over her shoulder.

'Maybe. She's been acting up since Jo went on her little break. She misses her I think.' Jenny-Jay scurried off into the living room.

Mechanic ripped open the envelope and removed the contents. She opened up the torn newspaper page, one of the adverts was ringed in thick red pen. It read:

YOUR PRECIOUS POSSESSION IS SAFE
IT WILL BE RETURNED IN EXCHANGE FOR YOU
BUY THIS PAPER AND AWAIT INSTRUCTION

She closed her eyes and gritted her teeth.

Her head raced with possibilities.

Was this revenge for hitting the drug teams? Was it Silverton giving himself an insurance policy? Who would want to take Jo? And who in hell's name knew she was here? Mechanic's thoughts spun in ever-decreasing circles.

Whoever took Jo must have looked genuine or Huxton would have called the police. Mechanic had to play for time, she had no choice but to go along with the charade. This was not good. Not good at all.

Jenny-Jay came back and Mechanic stuffed the paper into the envelope. She put three spoonsful of sugar into the cup and stirred vigorously.

Jenny-Jay was waxing lyrical about how her daughter was being sassy and answering back. Mechanic wasn't listening. Her head was running amok with scenarios and possibilities. She snapped back to reality.

'I want to thank the guys for picking up Jo. Did you get any names?' she asked.

'No, I didn't.'

'What sort of vehicles did they have?'

'Oh I don't pay no heed to things like that,' Jenny-Jay replied pouring herself a coffee. 'Good idea for you to talk to them though because those people at Forever Young could do with some constructive feedback.'

'In what way?'

'They sent a young man to collect her who only had one arm. I had to help load her into the van. It wasn't right to be honest.'

'One arm?'

'Yes, he was a tall dark-haired chap with a lot of scarring on his face. And he only had one arm. I think it's great that they're helping people back into work but to be honest it wasn't right.'

'What about the other two?'

'Older gentlemen, both in their fifties. The one was very charming and the other looked a bit sour-faced.'

'These guys were from Sunny Village?'

'Yes that's right. The nice man was black and the miserable one was white.' Jenny-Jay sipped from her cup.

'Did they leave anything for me?'

'No nothing. They went on their way looking very confused. Fancy a top-up?'

Mechanic looked at her cup, it was full to the brim. 'No thanks, Jenny-Jay. I have to go unfortunately.' She tapped her watch.

'Please let us know how Jo is getting on, Mary-Jay is dying to know what she's up to.' Jenny-Jay rose from the table to see her out. Mechanic said her goodbyes and headed back to her car.

She needed to get to a phone fast.

Back at home Mechanic called all the nursing homes around the Vegas area, starting with the two Huxton told her about. Predictably, they both came up blank. She worked her way through the directory and got the same response each time.

Mechanic looked at her watch, she'd been on the phone for two hours.

She was dialling the next number when she jumped up, snatching the envelope which Jenny-Jay had given her from the table. She spread the torn page flat on the surface.

'Shit!' she said racing out the front door.

It was dated the previous day.

Mechanic needed to buy a newspaper.

Chapter 33

Mechanic sat in her car tearing through the classified ads section of the Bulletin. There were hundreds of them. She turned the pages one by one tracing her finger down the printed columns.

'Damn it,' she exploded and grabbed the torn one from the envelope. Mechanic tried to collect herself and breathe deeply. The red-ringed ad was in the personal section, page twenty-two. She flipped through the pages and tried again.

There, on page twenty-four, was what she was looking for:

MECHANIC WANTED IN EXCHANGE FOR PRECIOUS
POSSESSION
REFUSAL WILL REDUCE THE QUALITY OF THE
POSSESSION
ACKNOWLEDGE RECEIPT

Mechanic shut her eyes and banged her head against the steering wheel. Tears rolled down her face and onto the paper. She stared blurry eyed out of the windshield.

'Who the hell would do this?' she yelled.

Then she laughed and rubbed her eyes. It was a dumb-ass question, the list of candidates for that honour was too long to count.

Mechanic stared at the ad and for the next thirty minutes sat in her car, running through every possibility in her head.

Then it all fell into place.

A charming black guy and a sour-faced white man.

A tall dark-haired guy with one arm. Not sure how the guy is even alive, but it all makes sense.

Piece by piece the picture came together.

There was only one set of people who matched those criteria and who wanted to inflict damage on her and Jo. The option posed a morass of unanswered questions for sure, and it was a long shot, but the jigsaw fitted together perfectly.

She knew who she was up against and if she was right it changed the game completely.

The time for emotional indulgence was over.

It was time to go to work.

Chapter 34

Mechanic needed to buy herself time and find a way to somehow hit the brakes. It was a high-risk strategy but if both she and Jo were to survive she had to slow things down. Twenty-four hours would do it.

She knew Lucas would be hellbent on ratcheting up the pressure and accelerating the pace. It was crucial for him to maintain the upper hand and do everything he could to dominate the timescale and events. If she allowed that to happen she was a dead woman for sure.

Mechanic was taking an enormous gamble – that Lucas would not harm Jo.

She surmised he probably had her at a nursing home or hospital, or was supplying the nursing support himself, but that was unlikely.

Lucas would have done a thorough job placing Jo well out of harm's way and Mechanic could spend days on the phone and never find her. She needed a different tack and for that she needed time.

It always amazed Mechanic the number of favours she could call on when needed. It struck her that for a sadistic serial killer she must come over as quite a nice person. By five thirty she had what she needed. She phoned Silverton and requested a meeting.

They met at his suite at the Hacienda.

Mechanic held three pictures in her hand and waved them at Silverton.

'I have a strong suspicion these are the men who carried out the hit on your operation.'

'Who are they? Do I know the bastards?'

'Unlikely. The reason why you couldn't turn anything up was that you were looking in the wrong place. These boys are not from a gang or a drug cartel, they think of themselves as what you might term Good Samaritans.'

'I don't get it.'

'Your men are looking for a new crew or a gang with an axe to grind. These guys are neither. They come from Florida and share one thing in common.'

'What?'

'They've all lost someone close to them because of drugs and they all used to be cops.'

Mechanic spread the mug shots on the table. The faces of Lucas, Harper and Bassano stared out of the photographs.

'Cops? Why us and why here?' Silverton was not expecting this.

'Why anywhere, I suppose, Mr Silverton. These people roam around the country hitting drug gangs. They have nothing against you or your operation other than the fact you distribute and sell narcotics.'

Silverton picked up the pictures and stared at each one.

'How did you find them?'

'Now that I can't say.'

'What do you mean, you can't say?'

'Do you trust me, Mr Silverton?'

'I pay you well enough, don't I?'

'I agree, but do you trust me?'

'I trust you with my life and my business, what more can I say?'

'Then you need to trust me when I say these are the ones. They took out your team and I want to deal with them my way. These are not your normal meatheads, they are sharp and very dangerous and if they get the slightest inclination you are moving in, they'll be gone.'

'I want these jerks hanging from fucking spikes.'

'And you will, but only if we do things my way.'

'So what do we do?'

'Circulate the mugshots to your boys on the ground, someone must have seen them. When they're found I want complete hands-off from your team, that's the only way this will work. I want the order to come direct from you. If anyone spots them and makes a move, I will fucking blow their heads off. Is that clear?'

'Do you have previous with these guys? Because this sounds personal.'

'You need to trust me, Mr Silverton. I will deliver these men's heads to you on a silver platter, but first I need to know where they are. Can you make that happen?'

'Leave it with me,' he said gathering up the pictures. 'And the message is very clear to my guys – leave well alone or you'll blow their fucking heads off. Sounds a little strong but okay.'

Silverton went into the other room to make his calls.

Mechanic left to prepare for war.

Chapter 35

Next day Lucas was up and out of the motel the early. He'd had a dreadful night tossing and turning while Harper slept the sleep of the dead and snored non-stop. Getting a separate room had to be a priority for today.

He pushed open the Perspex front on the news-stand and removed a copy of the Bulletin. Walking back to the hotel he felt energised and on top of his game. This was what he'd been dreaming of for so long. For the entire time of his convalescence, during his therapy sessions, and even during his disastrous meeting with his boss, his head was only ever full of one thing: catching the bitch and making her suffer. This was his day.

He sat with a coffee and opened the paper, flicking through the pages, scanning down the personal columns. Nothing. He moved to a table with better light and repeated his search. Absolutely nothing. He flipped over to the front section to see if her response had been misprinted in the business section. No, there was nothing.

He checked the date on the top. Sure enough it was today's edition. Where was Mechanic's acknowledgement?

He left his coffee and returned to the room. Harper was cleaning his teeth while peeing in the toilet.

'There's nothing here.' He threw the paper onto the bed.

'Have you checked them all?' He said showering the wall with toothpaste.

'Yes, I've checked them all.'

'Let me see.' Harper emerged from the bathroom, picked up the paper and donned his glasses. Several minutes later he folded the paper and placed it to one side.

'You're right, nothing there.'

'Why would Mechanic not acknowledge?'

'Maybe she missed the deadline for the ad.'

Lucas sat on the bed deep in thought.

'Yes, that's probably it. She missed today's edition.'

'Relax Lucas. Focus on what we've achieved. We have Jo in a place where Mechanic can't reach her. We've made first contact and she's going to be flapping around not knowing which way is up. Her sister's gone and she's on the rack. She'll be in complete turmoil, man, and not thinking straight. That's what we want isn't it?'

'Yes, I suppose so.'

'We want her crumbling under the pressure. Right?'

'Yes, you're right.'

'Let's pick up Bassano and get some breakfast. We got an exchange to plan.'

* * *

Across the city in a luxury suite Mechanic was far from crumbling. She was nowhere near a state of turmoil or flapping. Mechanic knew exactly what to do.

Silverton's men had worked wonders overnight.

'No one has made contact?' she asked looking at the scribbled note in her hand.

'No. It's as you requested.'

'I'm impressed, Mr Silverton.'

He bowed his head in mock acceptance of the compliment.

'Apparently though, these guys may not be as hot as you made out. They weren't exactly keeping a low profile when my men eyeballed them. They were having dinner at Hooters.'

'You're sure they didn't clock your boys?' Mechanic asked.

'I'm positive, but then I told them you'd blow their heads off if they did.'

'Thank you.'

'When are you going to make a move?'

'Already started.'

Chapter 36

It was pitch black when Mechanic pulled into the car park. There was no moon and the courtesy lighting spilled a watery glow across the front of the building. She stepped out of the car and made her way along the walkway in front of the ground-floor motel rooms.

She glanced through each window as she went. Nothing took her interest. Then she passed a room with a semi-clothed man lying on the bed watching TV, a beer bottle resting on his belly. The woman sat at the dressing table brushing her hair. They were both early twenties and were probably taking advantage of a dirty few days in Vegas. Room G46 fitted the brief perfectly. Mechanic returned to her car and settled down for a long wait.

After an hour the light went out in the room but the dancing flicker of the TV screen still played across the partially closed curtains. Forty-five minutes later the room went dark.

A further hour and the clock on the dash said 01.34am. It was time to move.

Mechanic staggered and swayed along the walkway with her head bowed, bumping into the wall and tripping over her feet. When she reached G46 she knelt down to tie her shoe and unzipped a flat, rectangular pouch. She laid it on the floor and removed two thin metal implements. Mechanic slid the slender tension pick into the lock followed by the Bogota rake. There was a faint metallic scratching as she pulled the rake back and forth, setting the pins inside the lock. Mechanic felt a soft click as it disengaged. She withdrew the tools and replaced them in the wallet.

She twisted the handle and pushed open the door. Cool air hit her face as the noisy buzz of the air-conditioning unit provided useful cover. She stepped inside and closed the door.

The sallow glow from outside seeped through the tatty curtains and partially lit the room. The couple were sound asleep. The bedspread moved up and down in time with their breathing. The woman lay on her side with her back to him, he was curled around her with his left arm draped across her shoulder. Mechanic watched them from across the room.

How cute, she thought.

She removed the gun from the side of her belt and walked slowly to the bed. The newly carpeted floor made her footfall completely silent. Mechanic's usual preference would be to have some fun, but on this occasion it was strictly business.

She levelled the silenced weapon and blew a neat hole in the guy's temple. The woman stirred as her boyfriend's body jolted under the impact of the bullet. Mechanic reached across the man's body and popped the next shell into her brain.

Mechanic went to the bathroom, picked a hand towel off the floor and returned to the bodies still hugging each other in bed. She rolled each one onto their back, opened their mouths and unwrapped an object from her pocket. The clinical steel of the scalpel glinted in the dark.

Taking the towel she grasped the tip of the man's tongue, pulling it out towards her. The blade cleaved through the muscle and she sliced it off. The woman was next. Mechanic opened her mouth and carved out her tongue.

Blood pooled in the depressions of the pillows and ran onto the floor. A ground-floor room had to be the target. No risk of scaring the folks below when the claret seeped through ceiling.

Mechanic held the woman's tongue and dipped it into the blood.

'Let's see how the fuckers like this.'

Ten minutes later Mechanic left.

Her advert in tomorrow's Bulletin would now make perfect sense.

Chapter 37

The hotel finally came up with a cancellation, which Lucas jumped at. A room on his own was hugely preferable to one with Harper in it. The privacy gave him the opportunity to call his wife. It was late and he lay on his bed in the dark watching the digits click over on the clock. He hated the way their previous conversation had ended and wanted to make it right.

Lucas lifted the phone and dialled his house. The phone rang but there was no answer. He flicked through his billfold, pulled out a scrap of paper and punched in the numbers.

'Hi Heather, sorry it's late.'

'Come on, Edmund, it's God knows what time here. I thought Darlene was clear the last time you two spoke, she doesn't want to talk to you.'

Lucas tightened his grip on the receiver. Heather was making far too much of her guard-dog role.

'I need five minutes, Heather. That's all. Please tell her I'm on the line.'

'She knows.' There was mumbling in the background as Heather handed over the phone.

'Hi.' It was Darlene.

'Hi.'

'What do you want?'

'I needed to hear your voice.'

'Is it something important? Because if not I'm hanging up.'

'I miss you. I needed to talk.'

'Really? Well here's what I need.' Darlene choked back the tears. 'I need you to come home to me. And that's not the same as you showing up at the house, sticking your key in the lock and hollering "Hey honey, I'm home". I need you to come back to *me*. But instead you sit in the living room and I know your head is in Baton Rouge or Vegas or wherever the hell you think she is. I can't do that anymore.' The flood gates opened and she began to sob.

'I love you, honey, but I have to do this.'

'I know you do, and you need to understand that I need to do *this*. I can't be with you until you want to be with me. Why can't you be like other men and screw around with hookers, or spend your nights at the titty bar? I'd know how to deal with that. I could fight that. But I can't fight a woman who occupies your head twenty-four hours a day, I can't win.'

His eyes were moist and his throat was dry.

'We've got a strong lead and I gotta take it. This could bring the whole fiasco to an end.'

'It's already ended.'

Darlene hung up.

* * *

Lucas slept very little and woke way before his alarm. He lay in bed turning the conversation with his wife over in his head. It certainly hadn't gone the way he intended. At least now he had a room to himself. No heavy breathing, no snoring or early morning farting. This was a welcome relief. He could try Darlene again later.

It was 7am and he couldn't wait to get his copy of the Bulletin. Despite Harper's reassurances it bothered him that Mechanic hadn't posted an acknowledgement. He understood the logic behind Harper's explanation but couldn't shake the underlying feeling that something wasn't right.

He got out of bed, dressed, and made his way to the news-stand down the street. On his return he sat in the motel reception skimming through the columns of the personal section.

Midway down on the left was a short message. It jolted him upright in his seat. It was for him, no mistake.

LUCAS
WHAT COMES NEXT IS IN YOUR NAME

He crumpled the paper in his fist and dashed to Harper's room, stopping only to make a call to Bassano to get his ass over here now.

Twenty minutes later Lucas sat with both of them trying to make sense of what was happening.

'What the hell …' Harper said a little too loudly. 'What does that mean?'

'I don't know,' said Lucas reading it out loud for the hundredth time. 'I don't get it'

'Okay, let's step through this logically,' said Harper. 'How does Mechanic know it's you?'

'It must be from talking to the Huxton woman,' said Bassano. 'She probably described us, and Mechanic pieced it together from there.'

'Shit!' Lucas paced around the room with the paper in his hand.

'I'm not sure this changes anything. So she knows it's us, so what?' Harper was still trying to be logical. 'It doesn't change what we do. Let's not forget, we still have her sister and that's our big advantage. That's our leverage.'

Lucas and Bassano considered the analysis.

'She knows it's us and she knows we're in Vegas. Those two points are definitely not in our favour.' Lucas was rattled.

'We need to be extra vigilant in where we go and what we do. Travel separately and not be seen together, that sort of shit.' Harper was determined to pursue his glass half-full approach. 'We need to—'

A woman screamed outside. It was not the type of scream which said 'I've stubbed my toe', it said 'I'm going to die'.

Lucas opened the door to see what was happening. A couple of people were running to a maid who had collapsed on the walkway near her trolley. A man reached her and called for help while another shouted to call 911.

'Call the cops, someone call the cops.' The woman was hysterical.

Lucas gestured to the other two. 'Wait here.' He made his way over to the commotion.

He saw a man come out of a doorway and vomit on the floor. The maid was still screaming for the cops and pointing at the room. Lucas skirted around her, creaked open the door and looked inside.

A young couple lay dead in bed with bullet wounds to the head. The sheets were sodden with blood. On the bedside cabinet lay two pieces of purple flesh and above the headboard was written in bold block capitals:

IN YOUR NAME

The scrawled letters were streaked red where crimson rivulets had run down the wall. It was written in blood.

Chapter 38

Moran eased her car into the Lucky 6 motel. The previous day had not ended well. She'd been expertly sidelined by Mills and was kicking herself – after all it wasn't as if she hadn't encountered this before. Being the smartest in the class doesn't come without its downside.

Her boss had taken time out of his 'running around like a headless chicken' diary to speak to Mills, which resulted in her being dropped from the case. Mills even gave her back her page of inconsistencies and across it he'd written 'That's Vegas, baby'. What a dick.

She was angry and resented being ignored, but Captain Brennan wasn't interested, he was too busy. She had resigned herself to smouldering at her desk for the rest of the day but snapped out of it when Despatch told her to attend a murder at the Lucky 6. She leapt from her seat, the adrenaline was pumping once more.

Moran pushed her way through the pack of chattering onlookers. The uniform boys had set up a yellow taped cordon around room G46 and were holding back those looking for a thrill. The inside of the hotel room flashed bright white with exploding camera flashes. She lifted the tape, waved her badge and stepped inside. She was flying solo on this one.

The bloody mess lying naked on the bed stopped her in her tracks.

'Detective Moran.' She screwed her face up and introduced herself to the medical officer. 'What have we got?'

'A particularly nasty one,' he replied looking up from his notebook. 'James Kelly and Kathy Spink, aged twenty-four and twenty-three respectively, both from Layton, Utah. Both shot once in the head, with no sign of a struggle. Looking at the blood patterns they were probably asleep. I estimate the time of death around two this morning. They were due to check out early today and the maid discovered them when she came to clean the room.'

Moran studied the letters daubed on the wall. She took out a pen and poked the purple lumps of flesh on the bedside table. 'Is this what I think it is?'

'That depends. If you think it's a human tongue, then you'd be right. The killer removed them from the vics, probably post-mortem, and if I'm right used them to do this.' He waved his arm at the writing daubed across the wall above the bed. 'Like some grotesque magic marker.'

'Seen anything like it before?' Moran asked.

'No. This is a new one on me.'

'Any idea what the message means?'

'Your guess is as good as mine. Do you need me for anything else?'

'No thank you, I'll take it from here.' Moran put on a pair of thin latex gloves and picked her way through the contents of the room. She called to one of the uniformed officers by the door. 'Can you get me the hotel manager and tell him to bring the guest list.' The officer nodded and shot off in the direction of reception.

The SOCO team were still snapping away ensuring every inch of the room appeared in one photo or another. 'Can we remove the bodies now, ma'am?' asked one of them.

'Yes, that's fine. I'll be with the manager, if you find anything out of the ordinary let me know.' As if two dead people with their tongues removed and a bloody message on the wall wasn't out of the ordinary enough. Moran marched across the car park to the door marked reception.

* * *

Lucas, Harper and Bassano were sitting together in one room. The atmosphere was tense, no one made eye contact, each one staring into the distance.

'She knows we're here,' said Lucas. 'In your name. That's what she wrote in the paper and that's what's written on that fucking wall.'

'If she knows we're here, then why isn't it us with bullets in our heads?' asked Bassano.

'Because that's not the game. If she wanted us dead, we would be,' answered Lucas.

'The game? What game? I don't get it. We have her sister. We're the ones in control. I don't understand what Mechanic's playing at.' Bassano got to his feet and made his way to the window. Blue flashing lights and people in uniform filled the car park outside.

Harper was equally struggling to get a grip on events.

'Mechanic doesn't know where her sister is being held. Her goal has to be her safe return, right? She could take one of us, torture him half to death and extract the location. Why do this? Why kill two innocent people instead?'

'Because it's a game.' Lucas put his head in his hands.

'What game?' Bassano was not catching on.

'Think it through. Mechanic knows there's an easy option to locate her sister but she's chosen not to take it. She wants us to know she could kill us. Mechanic wants us to know that two people are dead because of us. She's playing a game.'

'What do you think her next move will be?' asked Harper.

'She's shifting the power towards herself. I think she will kill again and keep killing until we return Jo.'

'What! Like there's going to be more of these?' Bassano waved his hand at the commotion outside. 'More people are going to die? But we have her sister, doesn't that count?'

'She's put the pressure back on us. We either roll over or more people die,' said Lucas.

'So it's kind of, like, we took Jo, so we need to return her.' Harper was finally getting it.

'Exactly,' said Lucas.

'What's our next move?' asked Bassano.

'She's gambling heavily on us not hurting Jo,' said Harper. 'So I guess we need to up our game, increase the pressure. I don't think she'll kill again. I reckon this is a one-off. It's a frightener to scare us.'

'She's done a pretty good fucking job.' Bassano turned from the window and sat on the bed.

'We can't allow ourselves to get diverted,' Harper continued. 'We have to press ahead with our plans for the exchange and extract some leverage from Jo. We took her for a reason, we need to use it.'

'I don't like it,' said Lucas. 'I'm telling you Mechanic will kill again and keep killing until we return her sister.'

'You don't know that for sure. Mechanic will be expecting us to run for the hills. We need to stay strong. We need to stick to the plan.' Harper was on his feet.

The phone on the side table rang.

Harper picked up. 'Yes.'

The voice on the other end was brief and he replaced the receiver.

'The police want to speak to everyone at the hotel. Looks like they're starting with you.' He nodded towards Lucas.

'Shit, that's all we need.'

'Look, man, it's standard procedure you know that.' Harper was trying to be reassuring.

'I know but we got a ton of things to do.'

'Go see them and get it over with. We have our cover story and it will be my turn at some point. Me and Bassano will get things moving on the exchange. We need to stay focused and keep our eyes on the prize.'

He got up and patted his friend on the shoulder.

'This is a typical Mechanic tactic, believe me. We need to stick to the plan.'

Lucas headed for reception not at all sure that's what they should do.

Chapter 39

'I swear they get them straight out of high school these days.' Harper had been interviewed by Detective Moran and was less than impressed. 'She looked about twelve years of age.'

Lucas was quiet.

'She kept asking the same things over and over,' Harper continued as he threw himself onto the bed. 'It was a joke, man, a sorry waste of time.'

Both men had experienced a particularly painful day. Moran had interviewed everyone in turn, with the uniform guys doing the paperwork. The problem was it took for ever. Lucas was one of the first to go and Harper one of the last. Bassano thought it best not to hang around and retreated back to his hotel to plan the exchange.

'Isn't that what she's supposed to do?' Lucas replied.

'Yes, but I mean, where do they get these kids from?' Harper was letting his prejudice show.

'I didn't like it. She's trouble that one.'

'Trouble? She's just out of pigtails. Come on, man, get a grip.'

'I'm telling you, Harper, she's trouble.'

'Get over yourself.' Harper slammed his hand down hard on the bedside table. 'She's pedalling around on her pink LVPD bike with the trainer wheels still on. Get real.'

There was a knock on the door. Lucas opened it expecting Bassano, instead it was Moran.

'Hello again, Mr Lucas, can I come in?'

'Yes, of course.' He flashed a sideways glance at Harper. 'How can I help?'

Moran stepped inside. 'Ah, Mr Harper, good to see you again. I'm glad I have you both together, I have a couple of follow-up questions, that's all.'

Harper snorted and picked up the morning paper.

'Yep, fire away.' Lucas was working hard to hide his anxiety. Harper was working hard to show his disdain.

'Mr Lucas, when we spoke this morning why didn't you tell me you were a serving police officer? A lieutenant out of FPD.'

If Lucas had been eating something he'd have choked. 'I didn't think it relevant. You wanted to know my whereabouts around the time the couple were murdered. That was all.'

'He answered your questions, Detective. If you didn't ask the right ones, then ...' Harper smouldered behind his paper.

Moran ignored him. 'You also didn't tell me that you are currently suspended from duty. No doubt that wasn't relevant either.'

'I was keen to tell you where I was when the killings took place. That's all.'

'Mr Harper, you also didn't think it relevant to mention that you were a ranked police officer, now retired. That is the case isn't it?'

Harper put down his paper and fixed Moran with his best intimidating stare.

'You seem to have all the answers, Detective, so I must have.'

Moran held his gaze, Harper's stare wasn't working.

Lucas said nothing.

Moran tapped the side of her head. 'You see, I asked you where you were at the time of the killings. I also asked you a set of background questions. If it were me, and forgive me for being frank here, I would have said I was a cop, or in your case, Mr Harper, an ex-cop. Because I think it is relevant.'

'I'm here with Harper to forget the fact I'm a damn cop. I'm currently being investigated and that's doesn't feel good. So we will have to differ on the point of relevance.' Lucas marched across the room to the door.

'Okay, gentlemen, I wanted to clear that up.'

'So if that's it, Detective?' Lucas opened the door to show her out.

'Yup I suppose so.' Moran got up to leave. 'Let's be clear, sir. I realise you are a shitload of ranks higher than me, but on the point of relevance it's me who says what's relevant and what's not. Have a good day both of you.'

Lucas banged the door shut and turned to face Harper.

'I said she was trouble.'

'Why the hell did you say you were being investigated?'

'I wanted to get her off our backs.'

'Okay what's done is done. We gotta stick to the plan and keep our eyes on the prize. Moran's a mild irritant and nothing more.'

'We need to watch her, I'm telling you.'

'Then you should go to the mall and watch her buy fucking Barbie gear. We got work to do.'

Lucas felt sick.

Chapter 40

Bassano had been a busy boy. While Lucas and Harper were doing their level best to piss off a certain detective, he'd been putting the final touches to the exchange plan.

The venue of choice was Centennial Hills Park. It was much like many other municipal green space in Vegas but with one significant difference, it had an amphitheatre with grass seating for three thousand people.

All three sat in the bar stuffing their faces with tacos and beer. Bassano cleared the table and laid out an assortment of condiments.

'It's critical we take Mechanic when she's out in the open. She needs to be isolated and accessible. This …' he said placing his napkin in the centre of the table, '… is the performance area. It's surrounded on three sides by grassy hills where the spectators sit. Lucas, you're here at the top on lookout. There's a tree line which will provide you with cover.' Bassano positioned a saltshaker on the table. 'Harper, you're here. There's a wooden bench where you have a clear line of sight to the centre of the amphitheatre.' He stabbed a finger into the table and marked it with a vinegar bottle.

'That's good,' said Harper. 'We have high ground and three-sixty-degree vision.'

Lucas liked it so far.

'I'm in the van parked here in a small car park.' Bassano placed another marker on the table. 'It's about one hundred and fifty yards away. I'll be waiting for your signal. When I get the go-ahead, I'll drive to the pickup point, here.' He marked the middle of the napkin with a sachet of sauce.

'I got three-way walkie-talkies with earpieces and enough range. We'll be in constant contact with each other, no problem. When she reaches the van we need to immobilise her. Not sure the best way to do that. It means getting close and we all know what happens when we get too close.'

'Don't worry about that,' Harper said. 'I've kitted us out. There's a holdall in the car with three handguns and a selection of cuffs, ropes, a hood and a baseball bat. The van we hired has eye bolts in the floor for transporting pallets, we can secure her to those. When we get to that point, she's all mine.'

'What happens after we take her?' asked Lucas.

'We drive to the Mojave Desert, or to be more precise Red Rock Canyon. It's twenty miles west of the Strip. Eight miles into the canyon there's a dirt road leading to an outcrop of rocks about a mile off the main drag. That's where I've dug a hole, that's big enough for the bitch to flop right into.' Bassano had looked forward to this for so long, even the hardship of digging the arid ground with one arm had been worth every aching muscle.

'Sounds good,' said Harper touching the items on the table. 'When do we do it?'

Lucas picked up the napkin and wiped his mouth. 'I'll place the advert tomorrow, she reads it the next day and we go the day after that. I would have liked it sooner but these damn interviews today screwed with our timings.'

'No worries, keep your eyes on the prize. That gives us two clear days to make the plan really slick.' Harper was raring to go.

'What time of day?' asked Lucas.

'I figure 7am sharp. The park will only have joggers and dog walkers at that time, so less opportunity for any passer-by disruption.' Bassano had obviously been thinking as well as digging.

'Then we're good to go, guys,' Lucas said. 'Explain to me again why we don't simply shoot her when she turns up in the park?'

Bassano moved in close.

'Because she gave me this,' he said holding up his metal hook. 'And I want her to feel it before she dies.'

Chapter 41

The next two days were like waiting for Christmas to arrive. They had plenty to do but it felt as if they were marking time until the main event. Lucas placed the advert in the paper. It read:

MECHANIC TO ATTEND CENTENNIAL PARK
AMPHITHEATRE
THURSDAY, 7AM SHARP
PRECIOUS POSSESSION IS SAFE
COMPLY TO AVOID DAMAGE

There had been no further contact with Mechanic. At every opportunity Harper made the case that the killings at the hotel were a one-off tactic designed to knock them off balance. The more he said it, the more convincing it became.

Keeping their eyes on the prize was their operational mantra. They would take Mechanic down the following day.

Lucas was keen to utilise the time productively and keep everyone busy. They ran through the plan until it was second nature. The amphitheatre had never been so popular out of season, as the three of them practised over and over. They assumed their positions, relayed instructions to each other via the walkie-talkies, rehearsed getting into the van and driving to Red Rock, only to reappear an hour later and repeat the whole thing over again.

Harper was right at home, it felt like Korea.

* * *

It was late evening. Lucas lay on his bed running through the sequence of events in his head but all he could think about was Darlene. It was the time of night he hated most. He knew he shouldn't but he picked up the phone anyway.

'Hello.' It was the attack dog.

'Hi Heather, can I speak to Darlene.'

He heard a hand cup the mouthpiece and the sound of raised voices.

'She said no.' The line went dead.

Lucas shoved the phone off the side table and it clattered to the floor. Not the best preparation when you want a good night's sleep.

* * *

The morning came and all three had slept badly. They were wide awake and ready to go by 5am. Harper tucked into a cold cheeseburger from a vending machine and encouraged the others to do the same.

'You need to keep your energy levels up,' he said taking a huge bite from the soggy mess.

'I know,' replied Bassano sipping black coffee. 'But I don't think I can keep anything down.'

There was a nervous sense of high expectation, each one awash with adrenaline.

Lucas drained his cup. 'Let's make a move. We're better off waiting at Centennial than sitting here looking at each other.'

'Agreed, are we ready?' said Harper.

'Let's go.'

The time for rehearsal was over.

* * *

Centennial Park was as Bassano had predicted, the occasional jogger and dog walker, but other than that deserted.

Lucas stood a yard inside the tree line at the top of the amphitheatre. He scanned the park through a small pair of red-lensed binoculars and could see Harper sitting on the bench about two hundred yards to his left. Bassano was in the van. The time was 6.05am.

As the time ticked towards the hour the anxiety grew. Bassano was the worst. He was stuck in the vehicle unable to walk about, at least Lucas and Harper could move around and change position. He was hunkered down below the window ledge in case Mechanic arrived in the car park.

Lucas and Harper were in constant communication, vetting anyone who passed by. They had no idea what Mechanic would look like, so everyone entering the park had to be considered a potential sighting.

Harper held a newspaper in front of him and wore a baseball cap pulled so far down that he could barely see out.

'Dog walker approaching from the left, one hundred yards and closing. Looks male,' Lucas said into his handset.

'I see him, he's turned away and headed to the car park.'

'Stand by. Lone woman approaching from your right. Wearing a suit and carrying a briefcase.'

'Yup, got her. Nothing doing, she walked straight by.'

It was 6.40am.

The running commentary continued with every visitor. And with every visitor the tension went up a notch. It was unbearable.

Lucas could hear his heart thumping away the seconds while Bassano squirmed in his seat trying to make himself comfortable. Harper kept a cool eye on the expanse of green in front of him, every few minutes checking the gun which was tucked into the back of his belt. He glanced at his watch. The digits flicked over to 7.00am.

Across the park a figure in a long dark trench coat and wide-brimmed hat came into view. A black rucksack was slung over one shoulder.

Lucas nearly dropped his walkie-talkie.

'Person coming from your left, about eighty yards out, heading straight towards you. Can't tell if it's male or female.'

Harper turned slightly, peered over his paper and clocked the figure – even from this distance it was a terrifying sight. The person was medium height, lean and walked with a purposeful stride. Head down, the wide-brimmed hat covering the face, long black coat flapping open in the early morning breeze.

Harper breathed deeply to steady himself and put his right hand at the back of his waistband to grip his gun. Lucas and Bassano were simultaneously doing the same.

'Steady,' said Lucas. 'Target heading for the amphitheatre.'

'Shit,' Bassano joined in blindly, sitting bolt upright.

The person in the billowing coat passed Harper without looking up. Harper whispered into the mouthpiece.

'Confirm female, repeat, confirm female.'

'Is it her?' Bassano asked.

'Can't see her face.' Replied Harper.

Lucas moved out from the cover of the trees, his hand tucked under his jacket, gripping his gun for dear life.

The woman reached the centre of the amphitheatre and dropped the rucksack on the ground. Harper turned to face her and waited for Lucas to get closer.

'Can you confirm target.' Lucas was already out of breath.

'Negative.'

She bent down and unzipped the bag.

Lucas's heart leapt into his mouth.

Harper jumped up, removed his gun and walked towards her.

'Close in,' he whispered.

'Is it her?' Bassano asked again.

Lucas hobbled down the grass bank and positioned himself about fifteen feet from the woman. Harper approached from the other side.

'Negative, her face is covered,'

Lucas could see Harper's gun.

The woman bent down, fished around in the bag and brought out a long, black metal barrel.

Harper sprang into action.

'Drop it!' he shouted levelling his pistol. 'Drop the weapon. Do it now!'

The woman shrieked and threw the metal object to the ground.

'Step away!' Lucas shouted. 'Bassano, we have contact.'

The woman held her hands in the air and screamed, spinning on the spot, looking first at Harper then Lucas.

'What are you doing?' she yelled.

'On your knees. Hands behind your head.' Harper reached the woman and twisted her arm behind her back.

'Don't shoot, don't shoot.' She dropped to her knees.

Harper's right boot hit her between the shoulder blades sending her sprawling onto the grass, her hat went flying.

He kicked away the bag.

Lucas watched it skid across the ground scattering paints and brushes onto the grass.

Harper knelt on the woman's back and clicked the cuffs in place.

Lucas stared at the metal object on the floor, it was a telescopic easel.

Harper was roughly patting her over when Lucas reached down and turned her face towards him.

The terrified woman stared back with eyes the size of dinner plates.

'Take my money. There's money in the bag. Take it.'

The sound of an over-revved engine hurtled towards them. She snapped her head sideways away from his grip and stared in horror at the van. 'No don't. Take my money. Don't kill me.' She was pleading, tears running down her face.

Lucas cursed through gritted teeth. 'Shit, it's not her.'

He pulled Harper away from the woman.

'It's not her. It's not Mechanic.'

'Fuck.' Harper slapped his hand hard against his thigh.

'Abort, abort,' Lucas said into his walkie-talkie. The transit skidded to a standstill on the wet grass. Bassano could clearly be seen through the windshield, his mouth wide open and a 'What the fuck?' look on his face.

Harper scurried away across the park.

Lucas limped as fast as he could up the hill to the tree line.

Bassano swung the van into reverse and disappeared in the direction of the car park.

The woman lay on the ground, her face buried in the dirt screaming, 'Don't shoot, don't shoot.'

Harper trudged his way through the wet grass. With every step he uttered the word 'fuck'.

Chapter 42

Harper and Bassano were pacing around Lucas's room shouting at each other.

'How the hell did Mechanic not show?' Harper was not a happy man. 'We need to get over to Victorville and start slicing bits off her sister.'

'I don't know. Maybe she didn't get the paper or something.' Bassano was trying to defuse Harper's rage.

'She got it alright. We need to teach that bitch a lesson.'

'Let's talk it through with Lucas when he gets back.'

The door burst open and Lucas threw the latest edition of the Bulletin onto the bed.

'Read it,' he said bluntly.

Harper picked it up and flicked over the pages. There in the personal section was an ad meant only for them. It was short and to the point:

LUCAS
PUT HER BACK

He passed it to Bassano, who read it and flung the paper onto the floor.

'She's playing us,' Lucas said. 'Mechanic was never going to show. She doesn't believe we'll hurt Jo.'

'It's like you said, boss. We took her, so we have to return her. That's the game.'

'We got to seize back the initiative.' Harper was stomping around, furious with the events of the morning. 'We need to go to Victorville and make Jo pay for her sister's actions.'

Lucas shook his head.

'How are we going to achieve that? Check her out of the nursing home, hack a couple of fingers off and put her back? That doesn't work.'

'We don't have to hack anything off,' said Bassano.

'Yes we do,' shouted Harper. 'Mechanic has to know we're not fucking around. She needs to learn a lesson. She needs to know we mean business.'

'Yes she does. I agree. But we only have to tell Mechanic we've chopped her fingers off. She has no way of knowing if we have or not.'

'Go on,' said Lucas.

'We place an ad stating that because Mechanic didn't show this morning we've taken it out on her sister. She has no way of verifying it.'

'What do you think?' Lucas looked at Harper.

'I think we should go to Victorville, remove her fucking head and mail it to Mechanic.'

'That's plain stupid. Bassano's right, we can fake it. We can make it look as though we've retaliated.' Lucas was beginning to think rationally at last. 'We place another ad and set up a second exchange.'

Lucas left the room to get some coffee while the others continued to argue. He needed time to think and the place was filled with a heady mix of confusion and rage, neither of which helped him work out what to do next.

The hotel reception contained a large line of people checking out. Like most hotels in Vegas the management had not yet figured out the inverse relationship between the length of the line and the number of reception checkout staff.

Most of the queuing tourists looked exhausted, broke and happy. Pretty standard for people leaving Vegas.

Detective Moran sat at a table drinking tea.

Lucas spotted her and tried to backtrack. She called him over.

'Morning, Mr Lucas, how are you today?'

'Good thanks. Yes, I'm good.' Lucas wanted to run for the nearest exit.

'Enjoying your break?'

'Yes, it's fine thanks. Who wouldn't enjoy themselves in Vegas.'

'Glad I've bumped into you, I was meaning to have a little chat. Do you have a couple of minutes, I wouldn't mind running something past you?' She had accidently bumped into Lucas only because she'd been waiting for forty-five minutes for him to show up for his morning coffee.

Moran patted the seat next to her. Lucas complied.

'I wouldn't mind getting your advice, in a professional capacity.' Her tone was soft and gentle.

'A professional capacity? I'm not sure that's quite ethical given my circumstances.'

'Don't worry it'll be fine.'

'How can I help, Detective?'

'I have a problem and you might be able to provide some insight.'

'Okay, what is it?'

'You see, Lucas, I've recently moved into a new place, and like most people who move into a new property, I'm constantly seeing things that need fixing. The bathroom needs re-tiling, the kitchen worktops could do with changing, you know, that kind of thing.'

Lucas nodded but had no idea where this was going. He wanted to get the hell away from this woman.

Moran sipped her tea and continued. 'Now I'm not what you might call a DIY type of girl. I work long hours and the last thing I want to be doing when I finally knock off work is to be on the business end of a circular saw. So I figure I need to find some local tradesmen who can do that for me.'

Lucas interrupted. 'Detective Moran, I'm sure you and I have more important things to do than discuss home improvements.' He got up to leave, every sinew in his body screamed 'run'. She put her hand firmly on his arm for him to sit back down.

'Stick with me on this one, Mr Lucas, I think this is important.'

'I don't see how?'

'I've been reading this local paper where businesses advertise that sort of work. It's fantastic, there's all sorts in there, it's called the Bulletin. Looks like whatever I want to do there's a guy who can do it.' Lucas flinched.

'I got bored looking through the classifieds and started to look through the personals. There's a lot of busy girls in Vegas that's for sure.' She laughed and gave him a theatrical wink still holding his forearm tight. 'I came across this one advert and it stood out from the others because it wasn't really advertising anything. I notice things like that. I notice when things look out of place. Take a look, Mr Lucas. It's a little odd, right?'

She pushed the paper in front of him. Midway down on the left, circled in red marker pen, he read:

LUCAS
WHAT COMES NEXT IS IN YOUR NAME

'What do you think, Mr Lucas?'

'I don't know. I've never seen this before.' Lucas wanted the ground to swallow him up.

'That's strange because when I came back to your room the other day and we had our little disagreement about what was relevant, I saw the same newspaper. Your friend Harper was reading it.'

Lucas shrugged his shoulders.

'So here's where I need your help. Can you tell me how your name appears in a newspaper and underneath are the very words which are written in blood above the bed of a murdered couple? A couple who are killed in the very same hotel that you're staying at. How does that happen?'

'I don't know.'

'You don't know about which part?' She let go of his arm. Lucas was going nowhere now.

'Any of it. I can't give you an explanation for any of it.'

'I know we had problems with relevance last time. Do we have a problem with coincidences this time?'

'I have no idea what the advert means and I have no idea who the shot couple were. Harper got the paper because he wants to include a little female attention during our stay. You have an over-active imagination, Detective.' He made a half-hearted attempt at a laugh.

'Yes I do, Mr Lucas. It helps me join dots up where others don't see it.'

'But I'm afraid that's what it is, Detective, an unfortunate coincidence. There must be hundreds of people in Vegas called Lucas. I have no idea where this came from, or what it's about.'

'I contacted the paper and they don't know who placed the ad. Items for print are placed over the phone so they couldn't help. That's why I wondered if you could shed any light on it.'

'I understand your concern and you've done the right thing discussing it with me, but as I've already said, Detective, I know nothing about this. It's an unfortunate set of coincidences. Have you got any leads on who might have killed that poor couple?' Lucas tried to deflect the conversation.

'No we're still digging.' Moran recognised the change in direction in the same way she recognised his facial twitching and rapid eye movement. Lucas was a poor liar.

'It's a difficult one, I'm sure.' He got up to leave, successfully this time. 'Sorry I couldn't be of more help, Detective.'

'Thank you for your time, Mr Lucas.'

'That's fine. I'm glad you felt you could come to me and talk. You did the right thing. See you around.'

Detective Moran watched Lucas scurry back through reception.

I'm so pleased you think I'm doing the right thing, she thought to herself.

Lucas returned to the room without coffees. He was about to impart the news that life had just become a lot more complex.

Chapter 43

Mechanic lay on the sofa listening to the strains of Pachelbel's Canon in D through the headphones as she visualised her next move. This was a game she loved. The exquisite feeling of wrong-footing your opponent was almost as satisfying as crushing them to dust.

She envisaged the mayhem caused by her non-appearance at Centennial Hills. Harper crashing around, Lucas quaking in a corner and the one-armed wonder boy ... well, he should be dead anyway.

It was a huge gamble but that was the point – take away the potency of their trump card, and the balance of power shifts. They weren't going to hurt Jo, they wouldn't do it.

She glanced at the clock, 8.35pm.

Mechanic smiled to herself thinking of the hapless trio flailing around in a state of chaos. They were amateurs playing a professional game and completely out of their depth.

She savoured the feeling a little longer, then went to shower. The ad was placed and there was work to be done.

* * *

It was 11.05pm when Mechanic pushed the column shift into park and turned off the engine. Thirty yards away was the Crimson Lake motel. It didn't have much going for it, with threadbare towels, Styrofoam cups and dirty carpets. It was very much at the budget end of the scale, but its most attractive feature was its location. It was next door to the Lucky 6.

Mechanic crossed the street and strolled onto the parking lot near reception. She was parked directly opposite, at a closed-down fast food joint, and needed to find a suitable room facing the road.

The motel was on two levels, decorated in an odd patchwork of blue and beige, which suggested an acquisition of cheap paint rather than a carefully designed colour scheme. The ground-floor rooms had parking bays directly outside, which made it easy to see which were occupied and which were not. The outside lighting was virtually non-existent.

Mechanic veered off left and walked along the front, hands in pockets, head down, glancing through windows.

About halfway along she spotted what she was looking for, a couple lying on the bed watching HBO and drinking beer. She stopped and bent down to adjust her shoe. They were both in their thirties with a pack of ten beers on the side table. Mechanic returned to her car and waited with her eyes firmly fixed on room 112.

Ideally she would have paid the Lucky 6 another visit, but because the investigation was ongoing, there was still the occasional police presence outside room G46. That was a shame but the Crimson Lake would do just fine. It was far enough away not to give Mechanic any unnecessary complications but close enough to make the point.

Back in the car Mechanic sipped water from a bottle and watched the lights go out in 112. The clock on the dashboard said 1am. The movie must have finished, along with the beer.

At 1.50 she was kneeling down outside the room pushing the picks into the lock. The occupants were sound asleep as the lock disengaged and Mechanic slipped inside, closing the door. She watched the couple as they slept. The guy was sprawled naked on his front while the woman had rolled herself up in the covers, hugging the edge of the bed. The room stank of smoke and bottles were stacked up on the floor beside the bed. Mechanic was tempted to shake the headboard to see which one woke first but she snapped out of it. This was business, not pleasure.

Mechanic drew her gun.

The Lucky 6 would have been better but the Crimson Lake will do just fine.

* * *

Lucas woke with a start as the sunlight poured through the drapes. It was gone eight o'clock and he needed to get to the news-stand. He'd tossed and turned all night unable to sleep, the troubles of the day playing on his mind. He'd last looked at the clock at 4.20am and then must have dropped off – shit, he was late.

He threw on some clothes and dashed from his room as fast as his dodgy leg and stick would carry him.

The Bulletin was dispensed from a standalone box located about one hundred and fifty yards away at the side of the road. Lucas made his way out of the hotel and along the sidewalk. He was eager to see his latest ad, keen to get things back on track.

He reached the stand and pulled a copy from the pile flicking through the pages looking for the personals.

As he scanned through the columns, a siren whooped and an ambulance swung into the road about sixty yards ahead. Lucas looked up and could see the red and blue lights through the trees. He was torn between searching for his ad and looking at the lights. After a frantic scrabble with the pages he found what he was looking for:

PRECIOUS POSSESSION BROKEN
MECHANIC URGENTLY REQUIRED TO PREVENT
FURTHER DAMAGE
CENTENNIAL PARK AMPHITHEATRE
TOMORROW 7AM

Lucas read the advert over and over with a renewed sense of determination. This would shake Mechanic up for sure. He folded the paper under his arm and walked back to the hotel.

A second ambulance whooped and pulled onto the road behind him.

A chill ran through his body.

He turned and watched the vehicle disappear in the distance and his stomach sank to his boots. *It can't be, not again.*

Lucas walked to where the ambulance had emerged and came to the Crimson Lake motel. In the car park were two police cars and a crowd of people talking excitedly. He pulled his jacket collar around his face and walked towards them.

He arrived at the taped-off area.

'What's going on?' he asked the woman next to him, desperately trying to get a better look.

'Don't know for sure, but it looks like someone's been shot.'

The man on his other side wanted to get in on the act.

'I heard someone say it was two people.'

'Oh my,' said the woman straining on tiptoes for a better view.

Lucas fought to stay calm. He needed to know.

Pushing his way to the front he could see into the room through the partly opened door. Figures dressed in white moved around inside but that was all he could make out. Then there was a bright flash of light from inside the room. There was no mistake.

Through the window Lucas could clearly make out the words written on the wall:

IN YOUR NAME

His head spun and he needed to get away. He turned and elbowed his way through the tight knot of people. He had to get back to the hotel.

'Lucas,' a familiar voice called after him.

He turned to see Detective Moran getting out of her car.

'Is that today's copy of the Bulletin under your arm?'

Chapter 44

'Are you sure?' asked Harper. 'Are you absolutely sure?'

'I saw it, I tell you. It was written on the wall. I said she'd kill again, I knew it.' Lucas was stomping around banging the ball of his fist against the furniture.

'We gotta hand her back,' Bassano said.

'Let's not get ahead of ourselves. We have Jo and that's our main advantage. The new ad in the paper tells Mechanic we've done Jo some damage. That's gotta make her see sense.'

'You don't get it do you, Harper? It's over. We have hand Jo back and make this stop.' Bassano sounded desperate.

'We can't risk any more killings and that girl-guide detective is constantly sniffing around. She called me over at the crime scene. I say we give Jo back and get the hell out of here,' said Lucas.

'No, no, no. We stick to the plan,' Harper said wagging his finger. 'We're so close to nailing that bitch we can't jack it in now.'

'We're not close to anything. We're no closer to her now than if we'd stayed in Florida.'

'We stick to the plan!' Harper punched the table.

'Damn it, we have no plan,' Lucas shouted back thrusting the crumpled pages of the Bulletin into Harper's chest. 'Read it, damn you, read it.'

Harper didn't have to read it.

In the personal column was written:

LUCAS
IN YOUR NAME

'We don't have a choice. It's finished. We need to get her back to the Huxtons today.' Lucas got up and made for the door. He needed space.

'Where are you going?' called Harper.

'Out.' He slammed the door behind him.

* * *

The bar was empty as Lucas lifted himself onto a stool and ordered a whisky.

'It's a little early for that isn't it?' Came a voice behind him, it was Moran.

'You stalking me, Detective?'

'I could say the same about you, Lieutenant. Everywhere I go, you seem to be there.'

Lucas huffed. His drink arrived and he took a large gulp.

'This is getting out of hand. What were you doing at Crimson Lake this morning?'

'I told you at the time, I was out for a walk and being curious.'

Moran shook her head and gestured to the barman, 'Two more please.'

Lucas scowled and went to leave.

'This is about Mechanic, right?'

Lucas stopped and reached for the remainder of his drink. 'You don't know what you're talking about.'

'I think I do, Lucas.'

'No you don't, Detective. Mechanic is gone, probably dead. You can read it in the case notes.'

Moran reached down and swung a heavy bag onto the bar. It contained several buff-coloured folders.

'I have,' she said.

Lucas stared at the files as new drinks were slid in front of them on paper coasters.

'I spoke with your boss, Hastings.' She dropped the sentence like a grenade in his lap.

'You did what?'

'Yup, he sure likes to talk. I told him we could use his help because we might have a copycat killer similar to Mechanic. His office sent me a whole load of useful material.' She patted the bag and smiled.

Lucas gulped hard on his second drink.

'This is outrageous, I'll have you—'

'Yes, I'm sure you will. Then there are these.'

Moran pulled a wad of newspapers from a second bag and thumped them down in front of Lucas. Certain pages were marked with yellow Post-its. Moran flicked them over.

'So here's the first ad: MECHANIC WANTED IN EXCHANGE FOR PRECIOUS POSSESSION. Then another: MECHANIC TO ATTEND CENTENNIAL PARK, PRECIOUS POSSESSION IS SAFE, COMPLY TO AVOID DAMAGE. Then PRECIOUS POSSESSION IS BROKEN. And so on and so on. Do I need to read them all?'

'So what?' Lucas stared into the middle distance slurping his drink.

'That's what I thought until I found this one.' She folded the paper over so only the ad was visible.

YOUR PRECIOUS POSSESSION IS SAFE
IT WILL BE RETURNED IN EXCHANGE FOR YOU
BUY THIS PAPER AND AWAIT INSTRUCTION

Moran stabbed her finger at the advert.

'Then it all began to make sense.'

'I don't know why you're showing me this shit.'

Moran allowed the silence to drift between them.

'Do you know what the key to all this is?' She waved her hand across the files and the papers.

Lucas said nothing.

'The precious possession. Now what do you think that could be, Lucas?'

'I don't know what you're talking about.' His standard response was wearing thin.

'If I put all this together,' she patted the stacks of newspapers and files, 'and throw you, Harper and Bassano into the mix, I come to one conclusion.'

Lucas waited, his stomach churning.

'The precious possession is Dr Jo Sells and you have her held somewhere.'

'That's absolute horseshit and you know it.'

'I don't think it is, Lucas. You snatched Jo in order to flush Mechanic out into the open. Only she didn't play ball did she? And that's why we are stacking up the bodies in the morgue. "In Your Name", Lucas, that's what it says. It's written here in the newspapers and scrawled on the walls in blood. And here is the clincher. If I follow the chronology I reckon Mechanic posted this ad in the paper after you took her sister.' Moran forced the page under Lucas's nose. It read:

PUT HER BACK

'That's right isn't it? You snatched Jo, and Mechanic started her latest killing spree until you return her sister. *"Put her back or I continue filling body bags in your name."* That's what she's telling you. Those poor people are on a slab because of you.'

Lucas stared into his drink, unable to respond.

'I can't figure how you knew Mechanic was in Vegas. But then in the scheme of things it doesn't matter. You're here, Mechanic is here and her sister Jo is here, somewhere.'

Lucas drained his glass.

'Are you going to talk to me, Lucas?'

'I still don't know what you mean. This is crap and you know it. You're overreaching yourself, Detective, and it's beginning to piss me off.' He had no option but to go on the offensive.

'Save the bullshit for your disciplinary hearing.'

'This is circumstantial crap. It proves nothing. It's nothing but a bunch of adverts which happen to include my name and the name of a probably dead serial killer, plus some writing on a hotel wall. None of this would stand up, none of it.' Even as he said it Lucas had to admit it was a shitload of circumstantial.

Moran leaned forward and beckoned Lucas to do the same.

'I'm going make this really simple. Here's the deal. I keep this off the grid and in return you give me Mechanic. If I declare this to my chief, I'll be taken off the case as fast as you can say new starter. I'm three streets smarter than anyone else I work with and this one is mine.'

Lucas started to make another lame protest, but Moran put her hand up and stopped him.

'The alternative is I go to my chief and see what he makes of it all. Maybe he doesn't share my vivid imagination and it will all blow over, or maybe he'll put two and two together and haul your sorry asses into the station. What do you think?'

Lucas looked at the stack of paper and back at Moran.

'You give me Mechanic and I give you a way out. Otherwise I sink you so deep they won't even bother with your disciplinary.'

Even for a black guy Lucas was beginning to look a little pale.

'The first thing to do is give her back before more people die,' Moran said.

Lucas spun his empty glass on the bar.

'I need to talk to some people,' he replied.

'Yes you do, Lucas. But remember we don't have much time if we are to avoid another early morning wake-up call with ambulances.'

Chapter 45

Bassano pressed the button on the tail lift and the wheelchair lowered to the ground. Jo sat bolt upright staring straight ahead.

The drive to Victorville had been easy with very little traffic. Lucas went with him to share the driving, however, the seven-hour round trip had taken its toll on both of them. Most of the journey they sat in silence – after all they only had one topic of conversation and that one had been talked to death. The key thing now was to pick up Jo and return her to the Huxtons.

The nursing home was put out by the unexpected nature of Lucas's call. They normally required twenty-four hours' notice to discharge a patient early and were pretty shitty when Lucas said he was not prepared to pay the cancellation fee for the remaining days. He would be there in three hours and they better have her ready to go.

They took the precaution of dropping Lucas off before they got to the home. It was Bassano who took her there so it should be him doing the collection. Similarly, Lucas went back to the hotel when they reached Vegas because Bassano needed to do the Huxton trip on his own.

The gravel crunched under the weight of the chair as Bassano approached the house and Jenny-Jay Huxton spotted them through the living room window.

'Oh my goodness, oh my goodness,' she chanted as she ran to them. 'I didn't think you'd be back for a little while yet. What a lovely surprise.'

Bassano retrieved a clipboard from the front seat to make himself look official.

'How come you're back so early?' Bassano was going to respond then realised she was talking to Jo.

'Did you have a lovely time? We missed you while you were gone,' Jenny-Jay continued chatting to Jo. 'Mary-Jay has not shut up since you left. She'll be delighted you're back.' Bassano needed to get out of there fast.

'Mrs Huxton, our apologies for not calling ahead. I hope bringing Jo back is convenient for you?'

'Yes, of course. We've missed her and we're so pleased she's back. She's looking so well, it's done her the world of good. Hasn't it, Jo?' She patted Jo's arm.

'Is there anyone else at home?'

'Me and Mary-Jay, that's all.'

'Okay, if we can get Jo into the house I'll be on my way.'

'I won't hear of it, young man, I have some pink lemonade made special. You come inside and take a drink with us.'

'Actually, Mrs Huxton, I need to get back.'

'Nonsense, I won't take no for an answer. Do I need to phone your boss and tell him you refused my lemonade?'

Bassano considered his options. He couldn't risk a call to the nursing home as they would deny all knowledge of him or Jo, after all, she was supposed to be taking a break in a local rest home not one in Victorville. He needed to placate Jenny-Jay and get the hell out of there.

'Lemonade would be great, Mrs Huxton.' Before he knew it he was perched on the sofa looking at the two women in wheelchairs sitting side by side.

'They don't shut up their chatter, do they?' Jenny-Jay called from the kitchen.

Bassano raised his eyes and shook his head.

Jenny-Jay arrived with four glasses of pink fizz.

'So how come she's back early?' This time the question was directed at Bassano. It took him by surprise as he wasn't expecting to have to join in the conversation.

'Er, she said she missed you and wanted to come back.'

'Ah that's nice. Did you lose your arm in a car accident too? Only Mary-Jay has been dying to ask.'

Bassano couldn't believe this was happening.

* * *

By the time Bassano returned to the hotel it was 6.30pm, he was hungry and the experience had left him shell-shocked. He'd endured the Huxtons' peculiar sense of hospitality for far longer than expected and was feeling all the worse for it.

All three of them sat in the bar.

'You said what?' Harper asked.

'It was the first thing that came into my head.'

'You came back because a woman with locked-in syndrome said she'd like to go home early?'

'Yeah, pretty much. Anyway, the important thing is she bought it.'

'No, the important thing is, did you deliver the message?' Lucas was less concerned with the surreal aspects of Bassano's visit to the Huxtons.

'Yup, I told her to call Jess to let her know her sister was back. I told her it was really urgent.'

'Good.'

'I tried to get her to phone there and then but she was too preoccupied catching up on Jo's adventures and coping with her daughter's overexcitement, despite the fact both women were totally fucking inert.'

'Okay, so now we sit and wait and hope Mechanic hasn't gone hunting.'

'We could work out what to do with this?' Bassano pulled a scrap of paper from his back pocket and handed it to Lucas. When we weren't having one-way conversations, me and Jenny-Jay did get to talk a little. 'So I took a chance.'

'And?' Lucas unfolded the paper.

'It's Mechanic's phone number.'

* * *

Across the city Pachelbel's Canon in D played through the headphones as Mechanic lay on the sofa mentally enacting the chain of events which would take place at the Bossanova motel later that night.

She'd hoped Lucas would have caved in by now and returned Jo to the Huxtons. But as yet it looked like he was holding out.

The phone rang.

Mechanic looked at the dial details in the small LED window, it was the Huxtons' number. She picked up.

Jenny-Jay rambled on about how Jo had enjoyed her mini-break and how Mary-Jay was delighted to have her friend back.

'Is she okay, Mrs Huxton?' asked Mechanic.

'Oh yes, honey, she's fine. She's so pleased to be home and Mary-Jay is over the moon.'

'Did the man with one arm bring her back?'

'Yes, he was ever so nice. He came in for lemonade and we had a nice chat.'

They talked a little longer and Mechanic hung up.

A wave of relief swept through her entire body. Jo was safe and back where she belonged. She closed her eyes and breathed deeply.

When she opened them they were hard and cold.

She went to the closet, took out several bags and started packing.

Now the fun could begin.

Chapter 46

Lucas strolled into an ice-cream parlour at the north end of the Strip. It was late evening. He pushed open the door to be met by the sickly sweet smell of sugar and essences which coated the back of his throat.

The place was clean and bright with red candy-cane striped walls and a huge array of ice creams in a refrigerated display cabinet that ran the entire length of the shop. The tabletops were bright red, along with the mock leather upholstery on the chairs. The smiling people behind the counter wore paper hats and crisp shirts with the same candy stripe and when they moved around it made Lucas's eyes go funny. Harper would hate it.

Moran sat in a corner booth with a bowl of multi-coloured ice cream in front of her the size of her head. She was dressed in her usual all black attire looking completely out of place amongst the knickerbocker-glory décor. Lucas squeezed in beside her.

'I thought this was a good place to meet. Somewhere we wouldn't accidently bump into Harper or Bassano.' She spooned a heap of toffee-coloured loveliness into her mouth.

'You got that right,' Lucas said looking around him.

'So, are we going to be woken by the sound of ambulances tomorrow morning?'

'No she's back. We don't know for sure that the Huxton woman made the call to Mechanic, but it's a safe bet.'

'Good.' She shovelled in another load. 'We need to think through our next steps.'

Lucas pushed the slip of paper in front of her with Mechanic's number on it. Moran picked it up.

'Is this what I think it is?'

'It's the number the Huxton woman uses to contact Mechanic. Bassano got it when he delivered Jo.'

'Clever boy,' Moran said scraping her spoon around the sides of the glass. 'I'll trace it, see what comes up.' She put the paper in her pocket.

'We need to be careful. Mechanic is a tricky son of a bitch and we can't risk taking her head on.'

'Well firstly she's a tricky *daughter* of a bitch and secondly now we have the advantage.'

'How do you make that out?'

'She knows you three. She played you to perfection which tells me she's got you guys all worked out.'

Lucas had to acknowledge that was probably true.

'She doesn't know about me and that gives us an edge.'

'I want to kill the murdering bitch and I have two others who want it just as bad. We're willing to do anything to make that happen.'

'The deal is you give Mechanic to me in exchange for me not going to the chief, or have you forgotten that?'

Lucas was silent.

Moran waved the spoon at him. 'You and I need to be clear on this or nothing doing.'

Lucas thought for a minute. 'How do you want this to play out?'

'Mechanic is going to be coming after you three. Returning Jo is one thing but if I'm right she's going to want to make you pay. She's gonna want her pound of flesh.'

'Yes I know. That's why we're going to go back to Florida to hide out a while.'

'That's exactly what she'll be expecting you to do. If you lie low, she'll pick you off one at a time and you can't hide forever. You need to stay here and force her hand.'

'With what? Are you suggesting we snatch Jo again?'

'No, I'm suggesting we try a different bait.'

'What's that?'

'You.'

* * *

The phone on the bedside table rang.

'Hello.' Moran was groggy and rubbed her eyes. The clock said 4.13am.

'It's the station, ma'am, I'm patching you through.'

She heard clicking on the line, then a voice she wasn't expecting.

'Hey Moran, it's Mills.'

'Mills, what can I do for you?'

'There's been another shooting. It's a similar MO to the ones you've been looking at.'

'The 'in your name' cases?'

'Yeah that's right only this one's different. We need to get over there.'

'Okay, where are you? I'll meet you.'

'I'm outside your front door. We can go together.' The line went dead.

Moran got out of bed and ran her fingers through her hair. She looked like a character from a Bruce Lee movie in her black pyjamas.

She unlocked the front door and allowed it to swing open. Mills stepped inside as she shuffled back into the living room.

'I'll be two minutes,' she said.

'Hey, nice place you have here.'

Moran ignored the comment. 'How come this has bounced your way?' she called from the bedroom.

'There's nothing doing with those turf-war killings, so the chief said I should get involved in the hotel murders.'

Moran cursed under her breath as she pulled a sweater over her head.

'He thought it would be good if you and I kissed and made up.'

She returned to the lounge holstering her gun. 'Not literally I hope.'

Mills shrugged his shoulders. 'The drug-related murders were bad guys killing bad guys. I mean, you know how it is.'

Moran flashed him a sideways glance which conveyed the simple message of 'No I don't.'

'Ready,' she said clipping her badge to her belt.

'You always wear black?' Mills asked.

'You always look like you've been paintballing?'

The drive took no more than twenty minutes. Mills briefed Moran that the 911 had come in from a guest in the hotel who'd heard strange noises coming from the room below. The whole city was jumpy, and the station control centre was taking about a hundred calls an hour from hotel guests concerned about strange noises. In this case the motel was located about half a block from the Lucky 6 and Crimson Lake so they responded straightaway. An officer investigated and sure enough found two people shot dead.

Mills slung the car into a parking space and Moran got out of the car first ducking under the yellow tape strung across the ground-floor room. She wanted to get there ahead of Mills before he started telling her what she was looking at. She showed her badge to the officer and pushed open the door.

Moran flicked on her flashlight and surveyed the all too familiar scene. A man and woman lay naked in a king-size bed shot through the head. The white bed linen and beige carpet shone dark red under the cone of white light. Unlike the other two crime scenes, this one reeked. Moran shook a handkerchief from her pocket and held it to her nose and mouth. The unmistakeable smell of corroded copper filled the room. Moran noticed the air-conditioning unit was switched off, which explained the overwhelming stench of blood.

On the side table lay two chunks of purple flesh. She didn't bother poking them with a pen this time, it was evident what they were.

A plaque hung above the bed saying 'Welcome to the Bossanova'. Written below it in dripping block capitals was daubed:

PAY THE PENANCE

Chapter 47

The morning sun poured into the ice-cream parlour making the interior even brighter than before. Families lined up at the counter with screaming kids demanding an unhealthy breakfast. Lucas sipped his coffee.

Moran careered through the door making straight for Lucas.

'How did you get on with the number?' he asked.

She shook her head. 'Nowhere. We got a problem.'

'Nowhere? Then what have you been doing?'

Moran removed a set of photographs from her bag and spread them on the table.

'This.'

'Oh my God.' Lucas looked at the images lying stark against the red tabletop.

'Yes, that's what I thought.'

'When was this?'

'Last night, I got a call at 4am.'

'Could it be a copycat?'

'That's unlikely. There are details which we haven't released. It's her all right. Mechanic did this.'

'But why would she continue killing? She's got Jo back. I don't get it.'

'That's what we need to work out.' Moran stuffed the photos in her bag.

'What the hell does 'penance' mean? Isn't it something to do with the church?'

'Yes it is. Penance means a punishment you have to endure after you've repented your sins – you know the way it works: first you confess your sins to the priest, then he gives you a punishment and that's it, you're forgiven.'

'But how does that apply to Mechanic?'

'Not sure, however I found another definition. An act of penance is also a voluntary self-punishment to atone for a sin.'

'So it's like you hurt yourself to say sorry?'

'Yeah. It's a punishment which you inflict on yourself to show how sorry you are for something you've done wrong. The important thing is it has to be done willingly. It can't be forced on you by someone else.'

'I still don't get it. What does that have to do with Mechanic? We returned Jo to the Huxtons, that's what she wanted.'

'Yes but Mechanic made you do it, she forced you to put her back.'

'So this is directed at us?'

'No. I think it's directed at you.'

'Me? Why me?'

'Because the other messages were for you and I think this one is as well.'

'How do I pay a penance? And why kill two more people?'

'I don't know. But what I do know is she's sending you a message.'

Lucas looked up at the ceiling as if seeking divine intervention.

'I'll run the telephone number when I get back to the station.' Moran slid from the bench seat to leave.

'We need to work this out fast,' Lucas said. 'She's going to kill again.'

* * *

'I want heads on spikes.' Silverton was letting his impatience show.

Mechanic drove the limo away from the Hacienda and headed for Fremont Street. She'd been expecting this.

'I want those shits to pay for what they did to my guys. We had an agreement and I don't see any results.'

Mechanic looked in the rear-view mirror. Her boss was changing colour.

'I can't rush this, sir. These people are professionals – if they get one sniff that we're onto them, they'll be gone.'

'We could have taken them out days ago, but you said to hold fire. I don't understand why we don't waste them now.'

'If I take out one, the other two will bolt and I thought you wanted all three to meet Ramirez.'

Silverton considered the comment. 'I do, but I want it done.'

'Then that will take time. You want all three and that takes planning. Don't worry, Mr Silverton, I'm onto it. Anyway, we are seeing results, this meeting at Fremont Street is a direct result of what we've achieved. Don't you think, sir?'

Silverton had to admit she was right.

Despite his flare of frustration Harry was in a buoyant mood. The meeting was a gathering of the Vegas drug barons in response to the recent spate of killings. Two of the gangs were significantly weakened by the hits and the objective was to call a truce. However, in Silverton's mind it was an opportunity to negotiate a wider turf. He was looking forward to it immensely.

The meeting was called by Enzo Bonelli, head of the Camorra firm which worked downtown Las Vegas. He was suave, sophisticated and totally ruthless, with a passion for oysters and champagne. There were two strict stipulations for the meet – hand over all weapons on entry and only one minder per delegate. This was perfectly acceptable to Silverton who was eager to get down to business. Mechanic was less certain this was a good idea.

Mechanic swept the car into the half-moon drop-off zone outside the Park Piazza hotel and casino. The overhead canopy was ablaze with thousands of tiny lights which reflected off the polished paintwork of the limo. A bellhop opened her door and she climbed out. Silverton did the same and straightened his Stetson.

Inside, the casino hall was much less grand. It was dark and smoky with a tired, shabby décor, much like the clientele, who were definitely more motor home trailer park than Park Piazza. To the left was a staircase leading to the upper floor. A thick red rope hung across the entrance with a sign saying Private Function. The rope and sign would not normally prevent the marauding punters from the trailer park marching up the stairs but the two men the size of fridges standing at the bottom certainly did.

They acknowledged Silverton, unhooked the rope and allowed them to pass. At the top were two more guys bursting out of their tuxedos.

'Good afternoon, Mr Silverton,' said one of them. 'Your weapons please.' The second guy held out a tray and Mechanic removed her gun and handed it over. The first guy then ran a wand over them both and gestured for them to enter. Mechanic watched as the man with the tray deposited her weapon behind the counter.

Mechanic looked around, it was a total contrast to the casino below. A row of high stools lined the marble bar, their cream push-button leather upholstery matching the semi-circular booths cut into the walls. Behind the bar was a bewildering array of spirits with crystal glasses sitting on polished chrome shelves, and the spotlights above sent shards of reflected light cascading across the room. A middle-aged man in a white suit and trilby hat sat at a baby grand piano playing old time jazz. This was an oasis of sheer opulence.

A tall man in a charcoal grey suit came over and shook Silverton's hand.

'Please come and join us.' He spoke with a soft Italian accent. He was in his mid-fifties with slicked-back hair and a tanned complexion, Mechanic recognised him from Silverton's description, it was Enzo Bonelli. He showed them to a large oval table.

Four gangland heads turned to face them as they approached, each one flanked by his minder. Silverton nodded and took his place at the table. Mechanic took up her position behind him and studied the faces of the other guests. The personal traits were easy to recognise: there was the ambitious one, the one who had seen all this before, the bored one, and the one that nobody trusted.

She allowed herself a little smile, it was much like any other corporate board meeting.

Bonelli opened the session. 'Well now this is an unprecedented gathering indeed.' The men nodded at each other. 'Welcome to the Park Piazza.' He clicked his fingers and two waiters appeared with trays of glasses and bottles of Dom Perignon champagne. The corks popped loudly and the glasses overflowed with the bubbling liquid.

'To a successful meeting, gentlemen.' Bonelli raised his glass and the others followed suit. 'For the next hour we need to put aside our differences and resolve an issue which is hurting all of us, some more than others.' He downed half his glass.

'Harry, your crew were hit first, closely followed by the Crips and then the Turks. All of them were taken out with a distinct calling card, a metal spike rammed down the throat. The strange thing is, no one knows a thing, which I'm sure you will agree with me, gentlemen, is a little odd.'

A short, stocky man with piggy eyes and a stubbled chin interjected, 'I think it's an outside crew, Enzo. There's not a single word on the street. It's like whoever did this don't exist.'

'Yes, it's a mystery. What do you think, Harry?' asked Bonelli.

'As you said, Enzo, we were hit first, and we still can't find jack shit on who did it.'

'It is a mystery, that's for sure.' Enzo nodded, finally joining his guests at the table. 'Only I don't truly believe in mysteries. There is usually an answer to everything if you look in the right place.'

Mechanic shifted uncomfortably behind Silverton.

Harry chipped in, 'Is this a good opportunity to look at the boundaries? I mean some of you, like me, have territories which have died off. When a team gets hit the people look elsewhere for gear so it makes sense if we rejig things.' This was Harry's play.

Mechanic's senses were in overdrive. She looked at the faces of the men around the table and something wasn't right. The two sitting opposite were staring into the middle distance as though they were bored with the proceedings.

Silverton was in full flow. He was playing the statesman role, describing the mutual benefits of shifting the boundary lines and supporting each other until whoever did this was caught.

Bonelli let him finish. 'Harry, that sounds a sensible way forward but I'm still hung up on the mystery.'

You could hear a pin drop.

Bonelli continued, 'You see, a tried and tested method for resolving a difficult problem is to look for inconsistencies, identify what's changed. And when I look at what's different I find the majority of things have stayed the same. That is except for you, Harry.'

Silverton gave his best attempt at looking confused.

Mechanic tensed. Then it struck her, the two guys opposite weren't bored, they were waiting.

'You get hit first. Then you hire your new girl here, who blows away a couple of carjackers in spectacular fashion, and Walker disappears.'

Sweat was seeping through Silverton's shirt.

Mechanic scanned the room looking for possible exits. The two men opposite weren't looking at Bonelli they were staring at Silverton.

Bonelli continued, 'that's heavy shit, my friend. So I think to myself, who does Harry Silverton call upon when things go wrong?' He snapped his fingers again, but instead of more champagne, the two gorillas in tuxedos dragged Ramirez into the room and dropped him on the floor. The men opposite pulled guns from beneath the table and levelled them at Harry and Mechanic.

Ramirez was tightly shackled with chains around his naked torso, his hands behind his back. His left eye was closed and his right cheek protruded about two inches from his face. His hair was matted with blood and his body was covered in angry purple stripes which stood out from his flesh. Mechanic recognised the biting wounds of armoured electrical cable.

'What the fuck!' Silverton exploded and went to get up but Mechanic put her hands on his shoulders.

They were seriously screwed.

'You will be pleased to know that no matter how hard we beat him he remained silent. But he sang like a bird when we played this.' Bonelli slid a camcorder across the table towards Silverton. 'Press play.'

Silverton fumbled with the buttons and the small screen flickered into life. It showed a woman with her arms wrapped around three children shouting in Spanish at whoever was taking the video.

'Mi marido va a matar a todos ustedes,' she screamed, as the kids burrowed into her, crying.

'Ramirez has a family, which proved much more persuasive than we could ever be and now the mystery is solved.'

Bonelli made a slight hand gesture and one of the men in tuxedos made a grab for Mechanic. She twisted sharply and elbowed him full in the face, then kicked his legs from under him. The second tuxedo man came in low and hard. Mechanic stepped to one side and cracked his head on the table. Silverton slid from his chair onto the floor.

The place erupted with people shouting and guns being waved in the air. Mechanic knew she had to get a weapon if they were to survive this, and ran to the bar, hurling bottles of champagne from the table as she went. She could see the guns on a shelf.

A metal stool cracked into the back of her head and she slumped down.

It would appear that the bartender was capable of delivering more than a tray of expensive drinks.

Chapter 48

Moran was parked in a side street a block away from Lucas's hotel. She was staring ahead, deep in thought. Lucas opened the door and sat in the passenger seat, he was clutching a newspaper and was clearly agitated.

'I don't like you calling the office,' Moran said angrily. 'It's too risky.'

'It's important.'

'So is keeping this off the grid as far as my boss and dickhead of a partner is concerned.'

Lucas accepted his scolding.

'Do you have an address? We need to stop her fast.'

'It's apartment 3C, Welbourne Chase.'

'That's good. I'll get Bassano and Harper and head over there now.'

'I've already been to the place and it's empty. I spoke to one of the neighbours and no one has been there for the past two days.'

'She's done a runner.'

'Yeah, looks that way.'

'Shit. That was our best lead.' Lucas slumped back in the seat. 'The Huxton woman must have told Mechanic she'd given her number to Bassano.'

'That's what I figured. At least we have a name for her now, Jessica Hudson. I got it from the rental agreement. Are we meeting so you can get an update?'

'No, you need to see this.' Lucas handed Moran the paper, carefully folded to show an ad in the personal column.

Moran read the advert:

PAY THE PENANCE
THE OLD MAN OR THE ONE-ARMED BANDIT
YOU CHOOSE
YOU HAVE SEVEN DAYS

'If you're right, then my penance is to choose,' he said. 'Choose between Bassano and Harper. If I fail to make a choice, presumably there will be another dead couple in seven days' time.'

And what happens to the one you select?' Moran asked the question but already knew the answer.

'I think she's going to kill him.'

* * *

Mechanic couldn't tell how long she'd been chained to the wall. She was hungry, thirsty and cold.

The room was a concrete box with no windows. The only light came from around the badly fitting door, leaving Mechanic in semi-darkness. She had explored the confines of her cell as much as the chain would allow and had located the walls with her feet. She could reach two sides but not the back. She was shivering and her joints were seizing up.

She could hear distant voices occasionally, but the rest of the time it was silent. Her guess was she was being held underground somewhere. Despite her predicament, Mechanic remained calm and positive. After all, whoever had chained her to the wall were amateurs. They had made two fundamental mistakes.

She estimated she'd been there two days when she heard the sound of voices and footsteps getting closer. She strained to hear and could make out the conversational tones of two men. A bolt slid across the door and it swung open, a shaft of light spilled across the floor.

Mechanic was blinded. She hid her face in her forearm to protect her eyes. The men were standing close, she could make out their boots through her watery vision. Slowly she opened her eyes and tried to focus.

'Ramirez said it was your idea to kill the other gang members using the same MO. Clever, I like it.'

Mechanic recognised the voice of Enzo Bonelli and kept her head down, allowing her eyes to grow accustomed to the light.

'He also said you killed Walker because you rumbled his kidnap plan. That's a smart move as well. And your boss, Mr Silverton, confirms everything. Actually I think he would have confirmed anything we wanted, as we were hammering roofing nails into the tops of his fingers at the time. He held out well for a pen-pusher, but then we got bored and fed him into a meat grinder.'

Mechanic looked up into Bonelli's face for the first time. He was smiling as if he'd won on the horses. It must have been an enjoyable couple of days. A tall beefy man stood behind him.

'Now the question is, what to do with you? I think you're an asset and have proved yourself worth keeping alive. Under normal circumstances I would want you to work for me, but unfortunately it's not solely my decision. You upset a lot of people and they are not happy. So with regret we're going to kill you with a good old-fashioned public execution, because that way everyone gets the chance to enjoy it.' He nodded his head and the other man pulled a set of keys from his pocket and reached for the lock connecting the chain to the wall.

He fiddled around and the lock snapped open.

The fundamental mistakes of Mechanic's incarceration were twofold. First, they had secured her hands at the front rather than behind her back and second they hadn't swept the cell before putting her in it. During her restricted walkabout Mechanic had found an empty Coke can in the corner. She'd bent it in the middle and repeatedly worked it back and forth until it split in two. The ragged aluminium edges would be put to good use when the time was right.

When she heard the click of the lock, Mechanic struck.

She reached under her leg, brought out one half of the Coke can and slashed the razored edge deep into beefy man's neck. A shower of blood splattered across his shirt and his hands grasped at his lacerated throat. Blood spurted through his fingers as his severed jugular pumped him dry.

Mechanic unclipped the chain and swung it hard as Bonelli was making a dash for the door. The heavy links smashed into his face, knocking him off his feet. He rolled on the floor screaming in pain. Mechanic leapt on his back and wrestled him onto his front. She wound the chain around his neck and leant back with all the strength she had left.

Bonelli gurgled and choked as the links cut deep into his flesh. His hands clawed at the metal. Mechanic glanced across to see beefy guy keel over as blood pulsed onto the floor. Bonelli's eyes were bursting from their sockets as the chain crushed his windpipe. His head was blowing up with the increased pressure and his flesh was bright purple. Mechanic heaved with all her might and eventually his flailing body went limp and his hands dropped away.

She slumped forward, exhausted, and unwound the chain. To her amazement, Bonelli let out a low groan and she could feel his lungs fill with air. He was moving below her.

She leaned across his back to raise his head and stretched the chain tight across his forehead. Gripping it with both hands Mechanic leaned right back. There was a loud crack as Bonelli's neck broke.

Mechanic struggled to stand and fell to the ground. She unlocked the cuffs and took the gun from beefy guy's belt. She went over to Bonelli and frisked him. *No gun, schoolboy error*, she thought.

The corridor outside was long and featureless with a door at the end. Mechanic reached it and placed her ear to the wood. She twisted the handle and it opened up onto a concrete stairwell. She climbed the steps and tried to control her breathing. At the top was another door with a window in it. She peered through.

On the other side she could see an office with a female cleaner busying herself with polish and a duster. Mechanic slid the gun into the back of her waistband and stepped inside.

The woman jumped as Mechanic came in.

'Sorry, didn't mean to startle you,' she said in a husky voice.

Mechanic started opening and closing desk drawers while the cleaner looked on with her mouth open and duster poised. In the fourth drawer she found her wallet and gun and stuffed them into her pockets.

Outside the office was a trolley stacked with plates of curled-up sandwiches, the remnants of a lunch meeting. Mechanic grabbed a handful as she went by, along with a bottle of water. Leftover food never tasted so good.

Through a few more doors and up a flight of stairs and she was outside in the warm Vegas air. She collapsed with her back against the wall to gather her strength. She was dehydrated and starving. The last of the food disappeared, washed down with the water. The sun warmed her face. Mechanic got to her feet, followed the road around the block and eventually recognised the bottom of Fremont Street.

All her instincts screamed to go back into the Park Piazza and blow the rest of Bonelli's men away, but she was in no fit state. Anyway she had more important things to take care of and a free newspaper to collect.

Chapter 49

It's disturbing to think of Las Vegas crawling with bad people, even worse to think they are all looking for you.

Mechanic made it back to her newly acquired digs, a one-bedroom condo on a short-term rent. She missed her comfortable apartment but that was strictly off limits since the Huxton woman had given away her phone number to the one-armed idiot boy.

She shouldered open the front door and stepped inside with her heavy bags. A quick trip to the supermarket while the taxi kept the meter running had been an urgent necessity. The bags contained food and isotonic drinks to replace the nutrients and salts her body so badly needed, along with a selection of silk and woven scarves, cheap children's bracelets, hair dye, false tan and a veritable jumble sale of odd accessories.

She went to work in the bathroom while the kettle boiled, emerging forty-five minutes later sporting jet black hair and eyebrows with a thin layer of fake tan on her face and neck. In two hours' time she would repeat the process.

Mechanic ate like she hadn't seen food before and downed several bottled drinks. She lay on the sofa and drifted off. Thirty minutes later her alarm went off, she didn't have time for deep sleep but needed to have some rest. She got up and began to assemble her new look.

After twenty minutes of wrapping herself in scarves and pinning her new clothes in place, she was ready. Mechanic left the flat wearing a hijab and long skirts. She walked with a slightly lopsided gait and steadied herself with the aid of a brightly coloured hiking pole. Her skin was a little too pale for her ethnicity but that would develop later, it was the best she could do given the time. She carried a small rucksack slung over one shoulder and hailed a cab.

The taxi dropped her off outside the Hacienda. Mechanic tipped the driver and said something incomprehensible to the bellhop who offered to take her bag. She ambled through reception to the lifts and hit the button for the twenty-first floor. The key to suite 8123 slid into the lock. Mechanic drew her gun and opened the door. She was amazed to find Silverton's room untouched.

How had the goons from Fremont Street missed this? They wouldn't have done a fingertip search, they were far more likely to have torn the place apart looking for information. The condition of the room suggested no one had been there.

Mechanic headed straight for Silverton's office and as expected the drawers in the oversized desk were locked. She put down the gun and retrieved a combat knife from inside her wraps. Seconds later the first drawer slid open. Mechanic rifled through the contents looking for anything with her details on it. Similarly, with the next, and the one after that, until all the drawers were busted open. Nothing.

She found a briefcase and prized open the locks. This too contained business documentation but nothing linking her to Harry. Mechanic opened a cupboard and inside was a safe with the buttons 0–9 illuminated with a pale green light. She unzipped her bag and removed a small spray can, flipped the top off and sprayed a fine mist onto the keypad. The chemicals in the spray reacted with the residue of oils and sweat left by Silverton's fingertips and four of the buttons turned purple. Mechanic noted the digits: 0,1,3,6. Shit, it was a six-digit code and the permutations were too many to try.

In frustration she twisted the handle and the safe opened. Silverton had forgotten to re-set the code in his excitement to get to the Fremont meeting. Mechanic pulled out neatly stacked bundles of bank notes and pushed them into her bag, there was nothing else of interest so she closed the door and wiped the keypad clean. The cash would come in useful.

She made her way to the ornate writing desk and set about the drawers with her knife. They were all empty. She cursed under her breath.

Mechanic then noticed the books in the bookcase weren't in line, the ones on the left of the top shelf were sticking out about an inch proud of the others. Mechanic pulled them free and found what she was looking for, a plastic wallet containing a wad of paper. She immediately saw her passport-sized picture and a raft of personal details relating to her. Mechanic placed this in her bag and removed more books. She uncovered the photographs of Lucas, Harper and Bassano which she had given to Harry.

Behind her she heard the metallic click of the lock and the suite door opened. Mechanic rolled across the floor and hid behind the desk. She reached out and slowly pulled her bag towards her out of sight. Two men entered the room, one much taller than the other. The tall one went into the living room and the other into the bedroom. Mechanic picked up her gun from the table and went to grab the photos from the bookcase. The taller man walked across the doorway forcing her to duck back behind the desk. She was trapped.

One man called to the other and she saw him cross the doorway once again. This was her chance. Mechanic moved towards the bookcase.

She stopped in her tracks as the man reappeared in the doorway with his back to her, she could see the long silenced barrel of his gun. Mechanic changed direction and hid behind the open door as both men entered the room.

'Hey take a look at this,' one said in a deep southern drawl. 'Someone's forced open the drawers.'

The desk was at the far side of the room. Mechanic peeked around the door. Both men were sifting through the paperwork.

'There's a safe,' one said.

Both of them knelt down, peering into the cupboard at the safe.

'Try and force it.'

Mechanic made her move and dashed out into the hallway. She opened the front door and ran down the corridor. The sound of the handle turning made both men look around but all they saw was the door closing.

Mechanic heard them burst out of the hotel suite, footsteps running, but she was already hurtling down the fire escape. Her robes flowing behind her as she fled. She opened a door to the eighteenth floor and mingled with the tourists entering the elevator. No one followed her.

The elevator pinged open at the ground floor. Mechanic kept in the middle of the group and pulled her scarf tight across her face as they spilled out into the lobby. She crossed the floor, weaving her way through the melee of tourists and stepped outside. The two men bundled their way out of a second elevator and were frantically scanning the crowds of people. Mechanic put her head down, hunched her shoulders and ambled off towards the Strip.

She cursed and gritted her teeth.

That was too close for comfort and a major screw-up.

The money and the documents were a good result but leaving the photographs behind presented her with a massive problem.

Chapter 50

'How in hell's name am I supposed to choose?' Lucas was in a bad way.

'Because that's what you have to do,' Moran replied. 'If you don't, more people will die and we've had enough body bags with your name on them to last a lifetime.'

'Is that supposed to help?'

'No. It's what you must do.'

'I have another suggestion.'

'Go on.'

'I share the dilemma with Harper and Bassano. Tell them about the penance and explain what Mechanic is demanding. We can use it to lure her into the open, she thinks she's hunting us when actually we're hunting her.'

'That's horseshit. Not a chance,' Moran said. 'What if neither of them goes for it? What if they say no? After all, you're effectively asking one of them to volunteer to be the sacrificial lamb in the vague hope that you get to her first. I don't think that works.'

'But I can't choose one of them to be slaughtered by Mechanic either.'

Moran thought for a moment. 'There may be a way of doing both.'

'How?'

'By running with the hare and the hounds.'

'Don't talk in riddles, I'm not in the mood.'

'We play it both ways. Mechanic wants you to offer up either Harper or Bassano or she will kill again. The assumption on our part is that whoever you select she will kill. So you choose one.'

'But that's the very thing I can't do. This is going nowhere.'

'Hear me out. We concoct a story that encourages one of them to put themselves up as bait to draw Mechanic into the open – then we take her out. We know she does things up close and personal and we'll be ready for it.'

Lucas considered the plan. 'What would be the cover story?'

'Don't know, we need to think of something convincing.'

Lucas and Moran sat in silence.

Then Lucas kicked into gear. 'There is a way to do both, but it will only work with an additional piece in place.'

'What's that?'

'You.'

* * *

Two hours later, Lucas, Harper and Bassano were sitting in a backstreet car park drinking take-out coffee. It was dark and the Vegas night air was hot. Not the best environment for three men in a car. They sat with the windows down.

'What are we doing here?' Bassano asked.

'You'll see,' Lucas replied.

'See what?' Harper asked. 'I don't see jack shit.'

'You will. In fact, here she is now.'

Another car trundled along the road and parked next to them.

'Oh no, not her again,' Harper called out, loud enough for Moran to hear.

'That's why I didn't say anything, you wouldn't have stuck around.'

Moran ignored Harper's outburst and climbed into the back seat next to him.

'What the hell?' said Bassano.

'Shut it,' Lucas said. 'I've asked Detective Moran to join us because we have a mutual interest.'

'Oh yeah,' Harper said giving her a sideways glance. 'What is it, playing jump rope?'

'Cool it, guys. She's here to help.' Lucas was determined to keep control.

'Help with what?' Bassano was challenging hard.

'Killing Mechanic.' Moran let the words land with their full weight. The car fell silent and all eyes were on her.

'She worked out our sorry bunch of shit but instead of turning us in she came to me,' Lucas said.

'What do you mean, worked out?' asked Bassano.

'Everything, tracking Mechanic to Vegas, taking Jo, the ads in the Bulletin and the motel killings. The full shebang. So I think you both need to shut up and let her speak.'

'I want to be the person who takes Mechanic down, but I can't do that on my own, I need your help,' Moran said.

'What for, when you have the whole of LVPD's finest at your disposal?' Harper asked.

'I believe we have a leak in the department. We've been on Mechanic's tail since she landed in Vegas but she's always one step ahead. Those guys are spinning in circles to capture her and she slips straight through, every time. I'm the new girl and to me there's only one logical explanation. Someone is tipping her off.'

'We know how that feels,' Harper said with almost a hint of sympathy.

'That's why I came to Lucas. You guys have done what entire police forces have failed to do, you had a shot at her. You got close.'

'What would we have to do?' Bassano asked.

Lucas continued, 'There's one thing guaranteed to make Mechanic break cover, and that's her sister. Moran puts out a story that one of you is about to cut a deal with the cops and hand Jo over in return for protection. Mechanic won't be able to stop herself, she will do anything to protect her sister.'

'And that's what we're counting on,' Moran said. 'I'll leak the meeting place where you are going to do the deal and Mechanic is bound to show up. And when she does, we take her out.'

No one spoke. The gravity of the situation was sinking in.

'It's asking a lot but the alternative is we spend the rest of our lives looking over our shoulders wondering when the hammer will fall,' Lucas said.

'How do we know she'll take the bait?' Harper asked.

'We don't,' Moran replied. 'But one thing is for sure, whatever the cops know, Mechanic knows as well.'

'When do we do it?' Bassano asked.

'The sooner we get the story out there the better,' Moran said.

'I have a question.' Bassano sounded pensive. 'Why does it need to be me or Harper?'

'If it was me, Mechanic would see through it right away. She knows me inside out, I would never cut and run leaving you guys to face her alone,' Lucas said.

'What makes you think I would?' Bassano replied.

'I'll do it,' Harper said without a moment's hesitation.

Chapter 51

Mills was making a complete hash of the motel murders and Moran was not about to put that right. She watched from the sidelines as he strutted around in spray-painted shirts, bluffing his way through the investigation, meticulously collating evidence and analysing it to death then failing to make any real headway, which suited Moran fine.

The more Mills bogged the team down, the happier she was. Moran needed time and the way Mills was performing she had all time in the world. In fact, when she thought about it she had hardly seen him the past couple of days, he'd been hiding away in meetings. This gave her ample opportunity to park the case in the slow lane and concentrate on catching Mechanic.

Moran had to be seen to make some progress with motel murders. It was a tough juggling act, especially as the Mechanic work had to be done under wraps. It meant working long hours, which for most people it would be an exhausting schedule, but for Moran it was energising and exciting.

Her goal was clear. She wanted to be known as Detective Moran, the woman who finally brought one of America's most notorious serial killers to justice. She pictured the day when the Las Vegas chief of police would shake her by the hand and pin a commendation medal on her chest. Brennan would listen to her then. She could almost taste it.

It was 10pm and the station was quiet. Moran was completely engrossed in her work, so engrossed she didn't realise the Mechanic folder was open on her desk.

'What the hell has she done now?' A man with a quiff of hair walked by and pointed at the photograph of Mechanic pinned to the cover. Moran jumped. It was one of the team she had met on her second day but couldn't recall his name.

'Er what? Nothing, I was checking some old cases.' She shuffled the pages together and closed the folder.

'Sorry to interrupt. I saw her mug shot and thought she'd been causing trouble again.' He started to walk away.

'What trouble? You know this woman?' Moran asked after him.

'Yes, she blew away a couple of local hoods who tried to carjack her boss. She was working as his personal security and shot them both dead.'

'When was this?'

'About a week ago, I guess. She was a piece of work that one, cool as you like. We tried to rattle her but nothing doing.'

'Why did you do that? Didn't she have the right permits and paperwork?'

'All that was fine. We tried to rattle her because she worked for Harry Silverton, an obnoxious piece of shit who blows into town now and again throwing his cash around. He has an oil drilling and distribution business based out of Philadelphia, and spends a fair amount of time in Vegas. He's a real pain in the ass. We've never been able to prove it but we reckon he's dirty.'

'In what way?'

'Drugs. The word is he traffics narcotics into Vegas and pushes them onto the street through his network. He's a sharp operator, very slick and very careful. The details are on the system, search under Silverton. It's a big file.'

Moran's head was in overdrive.

How the hell did she not know this? But the more she thought it over, the more she convinced herself it didn't matter. So what if Mechanic worked for a shady oil guy who dabbled in drugs? Her focus was getting Lucas to offer up Harper to Mechanic and prevent any more deaths, then use it to trap her.

'Hey, Moran, got a minute?' Mills poked his head around the office door. What was he doing here at this time?

She placed the folder in her desk drawer and followed him out.

He disappeared into the conference room opposite and started pacing around. The walls were full of pictures and handwritten notes. Coloured string connected items together like a giant subway map.

'I need to bounce something off you,' he announced.

'Yeah, fine, what is it?' She was distracted by the worst shirt yet, it looked like a toddler had thrown their dinner at him.

'I'm turning myself inside out but the motel murders are going nowhere. The bullets and the pick marks on the locks all match. The handwriting expert says the same person wrote all three messages. But that's it, that's the end of the good news. The rest is a big fat nothing.'

Moran agreed with his assessment.

'So I got to thinking about what you said,' he continued.

'What did I say?'

'You said this was about patterns and inconsistencies.' Mills waved his arm at a second evidence board, this one covered with the pictures taken at the drug-related murder sites. Moran recognised each of the victims as they stared lifelessly from the wall, especially the three with metal spikes protruding from their faces.

'The motel murders and the drug killings are totally different, but in other ways they're similar.' Mills wasn't making too much sense.

'They look completely different to me,' Moran said shaking her head. 'These are gangland hits probably driven by a turf war, and this is the work of a serial killer who targets couples in motels. I can't see any similarities.' Her mind was racing, trying to fathom where this was leading.

'At face value I completely agree. But I come back to what you said—'

'I was out of line,' she interrupted. 'I wanted to make an impact and went about it all the wrong way.' For Moran, this was pride-swallowing on a gigantic scale, but she needed to keep the peace with Mills. She wanted him happy and useless.

'But I think you had something, you said it was about patterns and inconsistencies.'

'I said a lot of things, I was trying to make a point and I was wrong.' She held her hands up in mock apology.

'Hear me out. The connection is that both are styled as executions and both send a message.' Mills pointed at the three men impaled with the metal bar. 'This sends a message saying, "I did this, and when I take out the next crew I'll do it again. It's my calling card." The same with the writing on the walls, that's a calling card as well.'

Moran allowed him to jabber on.

'And then there's the chronology.' Mills was on a roll. 'The drug killings started and the motel murders followed shortly afterwards. What if both sets of killings are drug related?' Moran was desperately trying to determine if this new-found enthusiasm from Mills was a problem or not.

He continued, 'What if these are tit-for-tat murders? What if the motel crimes are in retaliation for the hits on the drug teams?'

'Wow, that's a huge leap.' Moran considered the implications. 'There is nothing connecting the motel victims.'

'But I'm not sure we've looked hard enough. 'In your name' suggests the killings are targeted at hurting someone. Penance is a form of retribution, right? The writing on the wall is a message, the iron bar is a message. These could all be connected, we simply haven't found out how.'

Moran's mind was fizzing. If Mills were seriously considering linking the two investigations that would mean his already stretched resources would be even less effective. The more Moran could slow down the motel cases the better. It was time to be supportive.

'Yes, I see it now. You might have a point. If we understand more about the drug killings it might help us with the motel murders.' This was seriously screwed up thinking, which from Moran's perspective should only be encouraged.

'That's right. I think there's a connection, we haven't dug hard enough.'

'So what's the next move, do we widen the investigation?'

'Yes, I guess that's the way forward.'

'Maybe we can divert people from the motel killings to look more closely into the gang murders.'

'Yes, I think we'll have to.' This was perfect, Moran felt a warm glow of satisfaction.

Mills flicked through his notebook and stabbed a finger into a cluster of photos on the wall.

'Get a pad and note these down, we can get cracking in the morning.'

Moran did as she was told and waited like an expectant secretary.

'These are the Turks run by a guy called Mehmet Hassan, they control the east side.' He moved onto a second cluster. 'These are the Crips headed up by Billy Crosier, they have the west. And the first team to be hit were Asylum run by ...' he flicked over more pages, '... a man named Harry Silverton, they run most of the Strip.'

Moran stopped writing when she heard the name. In fact, her whole world stopped when she heard the name Harry Silverton.

* * *

Lucas sat in his hotel room battling the usual demons. He stared at the phone, it was fast becoming his enemy. Every encounter with it left him angry and frustrated. He picked up and dialled home.

'Hello.' It was Darlene.

'Darlene, honey, it's me. Don't hang up, please.' For once he'd managed to avoid the horror that was Heather. The line was silent, but not dead.

'You're home, that's great.'

'I needed to collect a few things.'

'This will all be over soon,' Lucas said. 'I've been thinking about what you said about me not being there for you and you're right. This will end in the next few days and I'll come home. I promise I'll come home to you.'

'I've heard this all before.'

'No you haven't. I've never acknowledged it before. I understand now and I can't stand the thought of losing you.'

'But that's the point. It's me that's lost you. You're always somewhere else, thinking about that damn woman. And I know what she did, and I know how it hurt you, but at some point you have to let it go. It's destroying you, it's destroying us and you're allowing her to win all over again.'

'I know that now. I need a few more days, that's all, and I'll be home. Whatever the outcome, I'll come home to you.' There was a long pause.

'Take care.' Darlene hung up, not believing a word of it.

Chapter 52

Mechanic looked at the neat bundles of one hundred dollar bills wrapped in Clingfilm on the table. It was the money taken from Silverton's suite, she didn't consider it stealing, more like severance pay.

There was enough cash there to keep Jo looked after for another eighteen months but she was acutely aware that might be a little over optimistic so she had included an extra three thousand dollars for funeral expenses. She stuffed the money into a padded FedEx envelope and peeled away the cover on the adhesive strip. The Huxtons' address was on the front.

Mechanic was torn. All her instincts told her to avoid the Huxtons' place, it was bound to be under surveillance, she would be taking a huge risk if she returned. But her heart screamed to see her sister one last time.

Once the penance was paid, Mechanic knew her time in Vegas would be over. Bonelli's men wouldn't stop until they had her cut into little pieces and fed to the sewer rats. She had to hit the eject button and get out, however painful that would be.

She sealed the envelope and noticed the backs of her hands. They were tanned the same colour as her face, a deep walnut brown. A bright blue silk scarf covered her head and the long flowing dress swept the floor when she walked. The disguise was a bad caricature, but she'd achieved her objective – she looked starkly different.

Mechanic now felt physically better following her ordeal at Fremont Street. She had slept and eaten more than usual to regain her strength, along with some gentle exercises to get her joints and muscles back in working order.

She had given Lucas seven days and by her reckoning this was day three. The preparations were in full flow, this had to be planned and executed with absolute precision. The clock was ticking.

There was a rap on the door and Mechanic opened it to see a young man in a dark blue shirt and shorts waiting patiently on the front step. She shielded her eyes from the morning sun.

'Morning, ma'am, FedEx collection, I'm here to pick up a package.'

Mechanic paused holding the envelope and turned it over in her hands.

'Ma'am, I'm here to pick up a package?'

'Oh I'm sorry,' Mechanic said still not looking up. 'It's not ready to go yet, can I call your office again for it to be picked up?'

'Yes, ma'am, that's fine.' He was already halfway to his van.

Mechanic had made up her mind.

She could hand-deliver it to the Huxtons when she visited her sister for the very last time.

* * *

Alonso Bonelli was much less polished than his older brother, he hated oysters and was teetotal. While Enzo had looked after the front-of-house side of the business, Alonso took care of the less palatable aspects of running a drug cartel. He was the enforcer and kept regimental order amongst his foot soldiers, while inflicting catastrophic damage on those who deserved it.

Enzo's sudden death catapulted him to head of the firm and he wasn't entirely sure what to do. He was, however, clear about one thing, that silver-haired bitch of a bodyguard needed to have her tits removed with a rusty blade.

A man with spiky hair wearing ripped jeans and a vest stood in front of him not looking forward to what was about to come next.

'Have you found her?' Alonso asked in a low voice.

'No sir. Her place is deserted and we have everyone looking for her.'

'And are people being cooperative?'

'Yes sir. The other firms have their guys out on the street looking too.'

'Then where the fuck is she?' He slammed both hands down on the table and spiky-haired man almost shit his pants.

'Sir, we've got everyone out on the streets, she can't hide for long.'

'I want that woman wrapped in barbed wire, with her guts hanging out, pleading with me to kill her. Do I make myself clear?'

'Yes, boss, we have everyone on it. We'll have her soon, I promise.'

'Let's hope so.' Alonso's low tone had returned, which sounded more chilling than his outburst.

He looked at the three photographs on the table.

'You found these at Silverton's place?'

'Yes sir, they were half-hidden in a bookcase. Someone had already gone through the hotel suite before we got there. The drawers were prised open and it was difficult to tell what had been taken.' Spiky-haired man thought it best not to mention that the person in question was still on the premises at the time. Probably a wise decision.

'Do we know who they are?'

'We know one.' He handed Alonso a sheet of paper which he read in silence.

'Now what would Harry Silverton be doing with a picture of an ex-cop in his possession? Anything on the other two?'

'Not yet, our pet police officer got himself distracted.'

'Then make sure he's focused, I want to know who these people are.' Bonelli pushed the photos across the table. 'Do we have any intel?'

'We checked the hotels and flight manifests and turns out our man is here in Vegas. We got a search underway as we speak, sir.'

'As we can hardly ask Harry Silverton why these pictures are important enough to hide, we'll have to ask him, so go find the son of a bitch.'

'Yes sir.' The guy collected up the photos and marched out.

Alonso didn't have time to grieve the loss of his brother, he was too busy seeking vengeance.

* * *

Harper was partial to taking a mid-morning stroll around the Strip, or at least that's what he told Lucas and Bassano.

'I know it's twenty-eight degrees outside but it keeps me fit,' Harper told them whenever he went on his constitutional. No one wanted to join him in the sweltering Vegas heat, which was precisely what he banked on.

The Hooters bar was located three blocks from their hotel, a place where Harper could while away a pleasant hour doing the two things he liked the best – drinking beer and looking at pretty women. He had to be careful not to return drunk, which on occasion was a bit of a struggle.

He opened the glass door to be met with a rush of cold air. It wasn't the smoky, claggy atmosphere he was used to, but then it did have a parade of spectacularly tight T-shirts to compensate.

Harper sat at the bar and checked out the scenery. The beers and solitude helped him to think. Putting himself forward to be a target for Mechanic was either a brave move or a really stupid one, he couldn't decide. One thing was for sure, he needed closure and being so close to catching Mechanic only made him want it more.

The beers flowed nicely as did the procession of T-shirts. Harper read the paper, watched some sport and, for a glorious fifty minutes, completely forgot about everything.

He checked his watch and paid his bill, leaving a sizeable tip. The women called 'Thank you' after him as he walked outside into the Vegas heat. Harper pulled his baseball cap down to shield his eyes and made his way back down the Strip.

A car pulled up next to him at the kerb with its hazards flashing, and the passenger window slid down.

'Hey, buddy, can you tell me the way to the Hacienda?' Harper looked at the lone well-dressed driver with a street plan in his lap. 'I know it's round here somewhere but I can't seem to find the damn place.'

Harper approached the car. 'You need to carry on about three blocks then hang a left—'

From behind him a man stuck the muzzle of a gun in the side of Harper's neck.

'Get in old man.' He reached around, opened the door and shoved him into the passenger seat. The back door slammed shut and Harper once more felt the gun cold against the back of his neck. The driver turned off his hazards and eased out into the flow of traffic.

Chapter 53

The landscape changed from urban sprawl to barren desert as Harper was driven away from the Strip. The two men in the car said nothing despite Harper's constant stream of questions. After about fifteen minutes he gave up.

Harper compiled a mental log of every detail: the roads they used, the type of car, what the guys were wearing, distinguishing marks, anything that might help him once this was over. He was desperately trying to work out who the hell they could be. The problem was the list of scumbags with a grudge against him was as long as his arm. The man sitting behind him, dressed in jeans and a jacket, pressed his gun hard into the back of Harper's seat, the muzzle digging into his spine as a constant reminder.

The farther they drove away from the city the more Harper could feel a knot of panic growing inside him. This was not looking good. He was isolated, with no weapon and no idea what was in store for him. Harper normally remained cool under pressure but even he was beginning to crack.

The sun blazed through the windshield as they cruised across the Mojave wasteland. The driver slowed down and swung hard right onto a dirt track. He flicked the air-conditioning to off but that did little to stop the dust from blowing through the air vents.

'Can I open a window?' Harper asked, buzzing it down to allow some fresh air into the car. Bad idea, the dust nearly choked him.

After a couple of miles the car skidded to a halt. The driver switched off the engine, removed the keys and both the men got out. They stretched their legs and the man from the back seat lit up two cigarettes. He handed one over.

Harper was left sitting in the car. He was unsure if he was to stay in the vehicle or not. He elected for not.

He got out and patted himself down trying to shake out the red dust. The sun was blistering hot. His two captors sat on the hood of the car casually chatting, not paying any attention to him. Harper looked around at the flat, featureless terrain. He could run but to where? There was nowhere to hide. He was stranded.

'Hey, can I have one of those?' He called to the two guys smoking. The well-dressed one looked over, then turned back to continue his conversation. 'I suppose that's a no then,' Harper said to no one in particular.

* * *

Harper checked his watch. They had been in the middle of nowhere for forty-five minutes. He sat on the ground in the shade with his back against the car, while the two guys still chatted about who knew what. Then he became aware of the distant sound of engines and tyres on dirt.

Harper got to his feet, shaded his eyes and looked towards the noise. Two vehicles approached sending a column of dust spiralling behind them. He could feel his heart pounding in his chest.

The cars came to a halt about twenty feet away, the doors opened and four powerfully built men in white shirts stepped out. Harper's captors wandered over and were slapped on the back by the new arrivals. Obviously for a job well done. He could hear the buzz of conversation. Two of the white-shirted men broke off from the group and walked towards him.

'Dick Harper, ex-cop, thrown out of the force for threatening to punch his boss.' It was Alonso Bonelli.

'And you are?' Harper tried his best to sound hard.

'Fucking angry.'

Harper held his ground as Bonelli came closer.

'Is that because you can't get laid?' Harper sneered.

'Ha, so you're a tough guy.'

'Maybe. I notice you've brought your girlfriends with you for protection.'

'You are a funny guy, Mr Harper, but it is not wise to tell jokes to an angry man.'

'Then tell one of your girls to get down and blow your dick. You know, release a bit of tension.'

Bonelli pulled his gun and pointed it at Harper.

'Good idea, on your knees.'

Harper sank down, putting his hands on his head. Bonelli circled around him.

'How do you know Harry Silverton?'

The question took Harper by surprise. 'I don't, never heard of him.'

Bonelli stopped directly in front of him, the gun levelled at his head.

'Try again.'

'I don't know a Harry Silverton. That's the truth.' Harper's bravado was evaporating.

'Then how does he know you?'

'I don't know him, I swear I don't.' Harper tried to look Bonelli in the face but the sun blinded him.

Bonelli took a photograph from his pocket and dropped it on the ground in front of Harper.

'Then why did we find this in his hotel room?'

Harper bent forward and picked it up. It was a picture of him.

Bonelli's stare bored holes into Harper.

'So I ask you again, how do you know Harry Silverton?'

'And I tell you again, I've never heard of him.' Harper gritted his teeth. 'I have no idea why he would have my picture, maybe he's someone I put away in the past and he wants revenge. I don't know.'

Bonelli walked behind Harper and jammed the revolver against the back of his head. Harper recoiled from the weapon. 'I never heard of Harry Silverton and I have no idea why he would have my picture. Please don't, please—'

Bonelli fired the gun.

Chapter 54

Moran rubbed the tiredness from her eyes and gazed at the collage of gory pictures on the wall. She was still reeling from her discussion with Mills.

What the hell had made him suddenly decide the two sets of crimes were connected was beyond her. And what had looked like an ideal scenario to divert the investigation away from Mechanic had bitten her squarely in the ass. The last thing she wanted was cops rummaging through Silverton's business arrangements – Moran had to keep Mechanic out of the spotlight if she was going to deliver her head on a plate.

The other members of the team filed into the case room confused as to why they all had to attend an impromptu meeting. Mills marched in wearing a plain blue shirt and a smart suit.

'Okay, guys, listen up, I want to brief you on our latest thinking regarding the gangland hits and the motel murders.' He introduced both by waving his hand at the photos pinned to the wall.

'This has all the trademarks of a turf war with a distinctive calling card.' He pointed out the metal spike. 'These murders, on the other hand, look like the work of a serial killer or killers, again with a very clear calling card.' He pointed to the messages daubed in blood on the walls. 'I think these are tit-for-tat murders ...'

Mills droned on about how investigating the drug-related killings would shed light on the motel murders. It was total crap, and Moran waited patiently to make her move.

'... so we need to find out more about the drug cases. Any questions?' Mills eventually came to a stop.

'I'll take Silverton,' said Moran before anyone could say a word, patently ignoring the fact it was not a question. 'I went to the mortuary when his guys came in and I've already done some work on this.'

'Okay, sounds good. Anyone else?' Mills asked.

Moran had bagged her prize. Now all she needed to do was to make her enquiries last longer than three days.

The evidence file on Silverton was indeed big. Moran spent the next few hours trawling through the documentation looking for angles of attack. It was a difficult tightrope to walk, she had to be seen to be making progress while at the same time steering away from items related to Mechanic. The most telling piece related to the failed carjacking. It contained the documentation and transcripts of the interviews with Silverton, Walker and Mechanic or Jessica Hudson as she was referred to in the notes. It listed her address and permit details, which seemed like a good place to start because Moran knew that they would lead nowhere.

* * *

The next three hours flew by. Mills pulled the team together again to get an initial view on what they had uncovered and agree the next steps. Moran overstated the insight she had gleaned from the files and suggested paying a visit to Jessica Hudson and Silverton. Mills agreed enthusiastically and dismissed her.

Moran went through the motions at Mechanic's apartment and filed for a search warrant, which she knew would take days to be sanctioned. She then headed over to see Lucas.

'We got a problem,' they said in unison.

'Go on, you first,' said Lucas.

'There's been another set of gangland murders involving drugs.'

'I heard something about that on the news. There have been three now, haven't there?'

'Yeah that's right. My partner has a bee in his bonnet about these being linked to the motel killings and he's directing the investigation to focus on the drugs.'

'But that's okay it doesn't affect us.'

'It does. One of the gangs is run by a man named Harry Silverton and guess who his bodyguard is?'

There was a moment of silence.

'Shit,' said Lucas.

'Exactly. Mechanic has been working for him since he came to Vegas. The way this is moving she's bound to be taken in for questioning at some time, and if Mills is trying to find links between drug gangs and the motel murders, there's one right there.'

'Can you slow it down?'

'I'm heading up the Silverton part of the investigation, so at least I can control the flow of information.'

'Can you hold out long enough?'

'I can try, but Mills has really got a stick up his ass about this, and he's pushing hard.'

Lucas passed Moran a piece of paper. On it was written:

MECHANIC
OLD MAN SELECTED

'I posted it this morning, it will appear in tomorrow's edition.'

Moran nodded her approval.

'I'm not sure what will happen next,' said Lucas. 'Mechanic might print another ad with instructions or try to take Harper out without warning. We need to be ready for both.'

Moran nodded again. 'You said we had a problem?' she asked.

Lucas scratched his head.

'Yes, it's probably nothing, but we can't find Harper.'

Chapter 55

The bullet thudded into the ground sending a shower of red sand into the air. Harper let out an involuntary scream.

'You bastard!'

'You were very rude.'

'Shit man!' Harper shouted getting to his feet, his right ear ringing from the blast.

Bonelli shoved him back down and he landed on his knees in the dirt.

'I might not be so kind with the next one.'

'I told you, man, I don't know anyone called Silverton. I have no idea why he would have my picture.'

'You said that already.'

'And you must believe me since I'm still breathing.'

Bonelli walked around Harper staring intently at his prey. He pulled something from his pocket and threw two more photos onto the floor in front of Harper.

'Look at them.'

Harper glanced down at the mug shots.

'You don't know Silverton. Do you know these two?'

Harper swallowed hard and tried desperately not to react. The pictures in the sand were of Lucas and Bassano.

He leaned forward and straightened up the photos, playing for time.

Harper shook his head. 'No, never seen these before.'

Bonelli observed him carefully.

'You sure about that?'

Harper picked up one of the photos, shook his head and dropped the picture back onto the floor.

'Yup I'm sure. Were these in Silverton's place as well?'

Bonelli didn't answer. Harper's mind was a blur trying to figure out what his game was.

'Look at them again.' Harper felt the cold of the gun pressing into the back of his neck.

He picked up the photos and flipped them over and over in his hands.

'Look, man, I don't know who Silverton is and I don't know who these guys are either.' He turned to look at Bonelli.

The butt of the gun cracked against the side of his head. Harper was out cold before he hit the sand.

'You're lying.'

* * *

Mechanic parked her car half a mile from the Huxton place. The night air felt cool on her face as she walked along with the moon flitting between the clouds turning the landscape to greyscale. She was dressed head to foot in black with a rucksack over one shoulder and a baseball cap on her head. The houses quickly ran out and Mechanic saw Honeydew House standing alone. As usual every light in the place was on.

One last hug with her sister was not going to happen, however much she wanted it. Mechanic was already fighting with the risk she was taking going to the Huxtons' in the first place. This was not a sensible thing to do, but she couldn't leave without saying goodbye, even if it was from a distance.

Mechanic crouched down at the open-link fence surrounding the property and took the night-sight from her bag. She placed it to her eye and scanned the area, the distant house shone bright in the grainy green image. Nothing moved.

She approached the property, stopping every twenty yards to check all was clear. The mailbox was located at the entrance of the driveway. She took the FedEx parcel and dropped it into the box, then made her way to the porch. The floorboards creaked as she crept around the house peering through the windows.

The kitchen was a shambles with dishes and pots strewn across the worktops, Jenny-Jay was seriously slipping. The curtains in the lounge were open a crack, and Mechanic looked through. No one there either.

The TV was off and the lounge was empty. The coffee table was a mess of cups, plates and half-full glasses. Mechanic moved to the back of the house where the bedrooms were located. The first room contained a single bed with a hoist above it. The walls were painted clinical white and it was sparsely furnished. It was empty. The second had frosted glass and the third had the curtains closed. Shit, this was proving more difficult than she'd planned.

Mechanic could hear sobbing coming from inside. She crouched under the window ledge and listened. There was a flash of light and the curtains parted slightly as someone brushed past them. Mechanic held her breath.

Standing up she peered through the slit. The room had the same all-white appearance with Jeb busying himself around the bed moving chairs and tucking in the bedclothes. Jenny-Jay sat facing Mechanic on the opposite side of the room with her face buried in her hands. On the bed Mechanic could see a figure draped in a white sheet. Her heart stopped when she saw the sheet covered the person's face.

Jeb moved across the room and slipped out of sight. Jenny-Jay looked up and dabbed her eyes with a handkerchief shaking her head.

'Oh Jeb, what are we going to do?' She burst into floods of tears. 'I've called so many times but she's not at home.'

'I don't know, honey. I honestly don't know,' he replied his voice breaking with emotion.

'We have to let her know.'

Mechanic shifted to get a different view but could see very little. She stared at the body laid out on the bed.

Suddenly Jeb crossed the room pushing a wheelchair and parked it at the foot of the bed. He put his arm around his wife.

'How are we going to cope?' she wailed turning and pressing her face into him.

Mechanic looked at the woman in the wheelchair. Her emaciated body sat bolt upright. She wore a blue mask over her mouth and a surgical skullcap.

It was Mary-Jay.

Mechanic's legs gave way and she crumpled onto the boardwalk. She bit her hand to stifle the sounds from her mouth as her chest heaved. Jo was dead.

Inside the house she heard Jeb shouting, 'There's someone out there!' She saw his head and shoulders silhouetted on the ground as he looked out of the window. 'Who's there?' he called.

Mechanic pressed herself hard against the wooden slats underneath the sill. She couldn't breathe.

'Who's there?' Jeb called again.

His silhouette disappeared and she heard more agitated chatter.

Mechanic seized her chance and ran from the house into the blackness of the Mojave desert. Remembering Jeb Huxton's liking for guns, she had to get away fast. She ran thirty yards then threw herself into a shallow indent in the ground facing the house. Jeb was on the porch looking around the property.

'I got a gun and I'll blow you away!' he shouted into the night, waving a twelve gauge in the air.

Mechanic lay flat and allowed the darkness to conceal her. Jeb stomped around the perimeter brandishing his gun and yelling. After a few minutes he ran out of steam, happy that the bad guys were now running for the hills. He went inside.

She pushed her face into the dirt and began to cry. Covering her head with her hands she screamed into the gravel and sand. Waves of convulsions racked her body. Jo was gone. The woman who had protected her for most of her adult life was no more. She slammed her fists into the red soil and kicked her legs like a toddler having a tantrum.

Jeb appeared on the porch again.

'I'll fucking come out there and waste your asses.' Mechanic lay rigid against the scorched earth and buried her face into it.

Jeb went back into the house. Mechanic watched him go and resumed her silent screams. Eventually the consequences of her actions began to slow her down, her knees, elbows and hands were bleeding and her face was red raw. She spat sand and gravel from her mouth.

Her face stung as the tears washed over the broken skin.

Jo was gone.

The very sound of it inside her head made her want to tear the world apart. Car headlights swept into the Huxtons' driveway, Mechanic leapt from her prone position and ran into the night.

* * *

Harper came round and felt as if he was in a dryer. He bounced around in the pitch black, it was roasting hot.

He thrust out his arms and legs to stabilise himself and realised he was in the trunk of a car. They were travelling fast and it was a bumpy ride. Suddenly it stopped, and while he could still feel the sensation of movement, it was smoother with the hypnotic hum of rubber on tarmac.

Harper's head pounded and he brushed his fingers against the large swelling on his temple. *Shit, that hurt.* He forced his knees against the trunk lid but it didn't budge, he tried to lever the catch with his fingers, but nothing doing. The atmosphere was stifling. Harper struggled to breathe. His head was swimming. His clothes clung to him, his body drenched in sweat.

He drifted in and out of consciousness as the hum of the tyres resonated beneath him. Suddenly he felt the heavy clank of metal hitting the front wheels, the car lurched up and down, then shuddered to a stop. Harper heard the doors open and slam shut and the chatter of voices. The trunk popped open and rough hands hauled him over the lip and dumped him on the floor. He felt sick.

Someone grabbed him by his collar and yanked him to his feet.

'This way.' Harper was marched across the concrete floor of what looked like a huge warehouse. Rows of empty racking reached up to the roof forming the skeleton of the building, their stark metal outlines silhouetted black against the orange glow of sodium lights. A route map of black skid marks left by forklift tyres criss-crossed the floor. The air tasted of dust and fuel oil. They headed for a roller-shutter door which opened as they approached and the ratcheting clatter of folding metal echoed around the vast space.

Harper tripped, struggling to maintain his footing – he was disorientated and nauseous. The strong hands flung him inside a room and the shutter door clanked shut. He was once again in darkness and sat cross-legged trying to collect himself. His head throbbed. His stomach spasmed and he retched on the floor.

As his eyes became accustomed to the light he could make out whitewashed block walls and a low ceiling with cladding hanging down through the broken tiles. There were no windows. The room was cool and he began to feel better. Harper pressed his ear to the door and listened for any noises or voices on the other side. Nothing, all was quiet. He bent down sliding his fingers under the concertina metal and heaved, it was locked solid. Harper felt his way around looking for anything he could use as a weapon. The room was completely empty.

He sat in the corner with his back against the brickwork and rested his head against his raised knees.

There was nothing he could do but wait.

The taste of bile burned the back of his throat.

Chapter 56

Mechanic drove around all night dazed from the horror at the Huxtons'. She careered from one emotion to another – one moment filled with the crushing grief of knowing she would never see her sister again and the next consumed with a raging fury, determined to avenge her death.

She arrived back at her new apartment as the early morning sun scattered low shadows across the building. Mechanic slammed the front door and rushed to the bedroom, tearing at the slit cut into the mattress. She felt around and retrieved two guns, ramming them into the rucksack along with a box of shells. *Those fuckers are gonna pay.*

Swinging the bag across her shoulder she opened the front door and stopped.

Mechanic rested her head against the doorframe and began to sob. Her legs crumpled and she slowly slid down to the floor, crying uncontrollably. She kicked the door closed. Tears streaked down her face and onto the laminate floor. Jo was gone, she felt hollow and cold inside.

Mechanic wiped her eyes on her sleeve and tried to catch her breath. The thought of killing Lucas, Harper and Bassano was all consuming. Blowing their faces apart one by one was what they deserved. But that was not the plan.

'Those bastards,' Mechanic said out loud. 'They took her and now she's dead.' She slammed her fist into the floor. They would die for what they did, but now was not the time. Mechanic had to focus on staying clear of Bonelli's men and delivering the penance.

She got to her feet, went to the kitchen and flicked on the kettle.

Focus on the penance. Jo's gone, I can't change that.

Mechanic had to maintain control, however painful that might be.

The phone rang.

She picked it up but said nothing. After several minutes she replaced the receiver and allowed herself half a smile. It was her colleague who worked in military intelligence, the one with a liking for being beaten up during sex. Mechanic had contacted him as soon as she'd placed the penance ad in the paper. She needed a favour in return for the usual brutal service and it looked like he had delivered.

The call was the news she'd been waiting for. The preparations for the penance were complete. Mechanic blocked out her grief and feelings of revenge, she needed to focus. She needed to get out of there.

An hour later she shuffled out of her apartment and along the sidewalk. The hijab helped to mask her face and the long robes covered her feet. The bracelets on her wrists jangled when she walked. Mechanic kept herself hunched over with an uneven gait. Small, round reflective sunglasses and deep brown skin completed the disguise. She was confident in her altered appearance and made her way to the shops nearby – sometimes the best place to hide was out in the open.

As she walked she noticed more than the usual number of cars cruising around with heavy-set men looking out of the windows. They were scanning the sidewalks but didn't seem to be looking for any action. A blue Ford with dropped suspension turned the corner and Mechanic recognised it as a car she had seen earlier – these guys weren't looking for hookers, they were looking for her.

Ten minutes later the same car passed again with a big guy in a yellow baseball cap hanging out of the window. They pulled over to the side of the road ten yards ahead. Mechanic immediately stopped and sat on a nearby bench. From her position she could observe what was going on. She sat back and hunched her shoulders, feeling the 9mm press into her spine.

The front doors swung open and two men jumped out. Mechanic moved her hand and gripped the gun. They shouted something to each other over the roof of the car and walked off. Mechanic relaxed as the men disappeared into a Walgreens. This was not about her, it was about buying breakfast and a bathroom stop.

She was about to continue walking when the back window buzzed down and an elbow rested on the ledge. A man's face poked out scanning up and down the sidewalk. Mechanic saw the bruised features and the molten scar running down his neck and his arm. It was Ramirez.

Mechanic watched over the top of her sunglasses. It was definitely him.

It made sense – if Bonelli's guys were out looking for her, who better to know what she looked like. Besides, Ramirez was probably still trying to keep his family alive.

Mechanic felt a pit of rage building inside her. She pictured Ramirez grinning as he crushed her finger with the pliers. She was filled with an overwhelming desire to kill him there and then. She dug her fingernails into the back of her hand trying to distract herself with pain. The urge grew and she gritted her teeth as the skin broke.

This is not in the plan, the thoughts bounced around in her head. *Get what you need and head back to the apartment. Focus on the penance.*

Ramirez stuck his head out of the window again and looked directly at Mechanic. Not a flicker of recognition.

Don't be stupid, this is not part of the plan.

Mechanic gathered up a pleat in her robe and emptied a handful of change into it. She stood up and walked slowly towards the car muttering in English and Arabic. The coins clinked as she held the material out in front of her. People avoided her and looked away not wanting to make eye contact with a beggar. Mechanic reached the car and peered through the open window, Ramirez was sat in the back, his black-and-blue face still a mess. She jangled the coins, mumbling something incoherent. He leaned forward to wave her away.

The driver and the man in the yellow hat came out of Walgreens with several bags full of goodies. Mechanic ambled past them as she continued towards the parade of shops. They jumped in and she heard the roar of the engine. The car pulled away, then screeched to a halt. The yellow hat bolted from the car and flung open the back door. Ramirez tumbled onto the sidewalk, his throat sliced open.

Onlookers screamed as they saw the almost beheaded man crash to the ground, spilling blood across the paving slabs. The man in the yellow hat flapped around trying to pick Ramirez up and bundle him into the back seat, but he was too heavy, so instead he slammed the door shut and flung himself through the passenger door as the car skidded away.

Mechanic hobbled off leaving a crowd of screaming people clustered around the dead man on the floor. She needed to hurry if she was also going to make one final check on her prey.

Chapter 57

Harper was woken by the sound of a gearbox cranking up as the roller-shutter door slowly lifted. He had no concept of time but figured it was morning. Shafts of sunlight burst from under the metal door as it opened to reveal three people. One of them was Bonelli.

Harper scrambled to his feet feeling much more stable than the day before. Bonelli stepped inside and immediately wrinkled up his nose. The stench of stale vomit hung in the air.

'You and I are going to try again,' he said.

'You didn't like my answers yesterday,' Harper replied rubbing the purple raised bruise on the side of his head. 'Not sure they're gonna be any different today.'

'You've had time to think. Let's hope that has made you more reasonable.'

Bonelli was flanked by two men in signature white shirts.

'Get him up.'

They stepped forward and grasped Harper under his arms, frog marching him into the open space of the warehouse floor. The bigger man cuffed Harper's hands behind his back and drove him to his knees. Bonelli produced the three photographs and spread them on the floor.

'You lied to me yesterday, Harper, and I want to know why.'

'I didn't. I don't know Silverton.'

'Not that part. You lied about not knowing the people in the other two pictures.'

'I don't—'

Bonelli interrupted. 'It would have been far easier to kill you, but frustratingly that would have left me none the wiser. You are only alive so I can ask you the question again. Who are the men in the photographs?'

Harper looked into Bonelli's eyes and realised lying was useless.

'Go to hell,' he said through clenched teeth.

Bonelli waved his arm and from the other side of the building Harper heard the grunt of a big diesel engine starting up. A massive forklift trundled its way along the floor belching black smoke from a stack above the driver's cab. The men in white shirts yanked Harper to his feet. He could hear the roar of the truck behind him as it got closer and the feel of cold steel against his wrists. The sound of whirring filled his ears as his arms were lifted up behind his back. Harper stood on tiptoes straining to keep his weight off his shoulders. His wrists were hooked over one of the forks.

'Are you sure you want to play the hero?'

'Fuck you!' Harper shouted.

Bonelli pointed to the sky and the engine roared as the forks raised lifting Harper off his feet. His shoulder joints cracked as they took his full weight. He screamed as pain tore through his body.

Harper swung back and forth as he was lifted into the air.

'You need to reconsider quickly before this does permanent damage.' Bonelli shouted.

'Fu ... ck you.' Harper croaked the words and spat on the floor.

The forklift started to move. The big wheels bounced on the uneven floor causing Harper to dance around high in the air. He kicked his legs and screamed as his shoulder joints cracked again.

'Who are they?' Bonelli shouted over the thunder of the diesel engine. 'We can do this all day.' The truck trundled around the warehouse with Harper swinging helplessly from the forks.

Harper's screams echoed off the walls of the building.

'Who are they?' Bonelli shouted again.

Harper couldn't hear him, he was fighting to stop his arms being ripped from their sockets. Pain consumed every inch of his body as bones and tendons grated together.

'You will tell me eventually. Who are they?'

The truck swung in a tight turn and Harper jerked around like a maniac puppet.

Suddenly his screams stopped.

Bonelli motioned to the driver who lowered him to the floor in a heap. He was unconscious.

* * *

Moran hated the morning briefings. Under normal circumstances she relished them as an opportunity to flaunt the headway she had made since the previous session, but now she reported on nothing and hoped it sounded like progress. This morning was no exception.

'And what about Silverton?' asked Mills dressed in another blue shirt with a button-down collar and cufflinks.

'I followed two leads.' Moran cleared her throat. 'Silverton stayed at the Hacienda while in Vegas. The hotel suite had been ransacked by the time we got there. We dusted for prints but nothing as yet. Silverton has disappeared without trace and no one has seen or heard from him. The hotel is none too happy about the unpaid bills. His bodyguard has recently had some previous with us, which came to nothing. Her apartment hasn't been occupied for the past few days, so we are assuming she has done a runner as well. I'm waiting on a warrant to enter her apartment.' She leafed through a wad of notes in a vague attempt to make herself look thorough.

Mills tapped his pen on the desk in impatient thought.

'Not much to go on.'

Moran nodded her agreement.

'Okay who's got the Turks?'

Each officer gave an account of their investigations and talked through any new lines of enquiry. Moran couldn't concentrate. Her mind was racing with what needed to be done to trap Mechanic. Lucas had placed the advert for today's Bulletin, a copy of which sat unread in her briefcase. These damn briefings were getting in the way.

Officers droned on about the people they had interviewed and Mills asked inane questions. Moran was more bothered about Mills and his sudden change in fashion sense. Then an awful thought barged its way into her head – had he smartened himself up to impress her? The prospect of Mills wanting to make himself more appealing in order to catch her eye turned her stomach. *What the hell is he playing at?* Moran preferred it when his clothes matched his work – a colourful shambles. She was suddenly jolted out of her daydream.

'Moran, isn't that Silverton's bodyguard?' Mills asked.

'Er sorry, sir, I missed that.'

'Say it again, Mick, and pay attention this time, Moran.'

'Yes okay,' said Mick, a forty-year-old guy wearing a suit which was probably new when he joined the force twenty years ago. 'The word on the street is that the downtown crew who operate out of Fremont street were hit a couple of days ago. Their head honcho Enzo Bonelli was killed along with one of his men. The jungle drums say they were both murdered by Jessica Hudson.'

Moran processed the information as fast as she could. 'Yes that's her. That's Silverton's bodyguard.'

'We need to find her and fast. If she was responsible for killing Bonelli, she's a dead woman unless we get to her first. Put out an all-points bulletin, I want her found and I want her here.' Mills emphasised his words by banging his hand on the table.

'Shit,' Moran said under her breath. Not only was Mechanic on a drug baron's walking-dead list, now she'd have the whole of the Vegas Police Department out looking for her. And it was Moran's job to keep her at large, at least for the next three days.

What a screw up.

Chapter 58

Moran inhaled deeply as she walked through the door of the ice-cream parlour. The sickly sweet aroma gave her a slight buzz of euphoria and given her current predicament she needed all her lungs could hold.

Lucas sat in their usual seat. He clutched the Bulletin and had the look of a worried man.

'Don't tell me it hasn't printed?' Moran asked.

'It's printed alright.' Lucas opened to the personals and showed her the column.

MECHANIC
OLD MAN SELECTED

'Phew,' Moran said. 'I thought that had gone tits up as well. Everything else has.'

'We got a bigger problem,' Lucas said.

'I know, you don't have to tell me—'

'Harper has gone AWOL,' Lucas cut in.

'What?'

'He went missing last night and his bed's not been slept in. We don't know where he is.'

'Shit, that's all we need, where could he be?'

'Don't know. Me and Bassano checked the bars close to the hotel and no one has seen him.'

'Do you think he's got cold feet and done a runner?'

'No, that's not his style. He put himself forward for this, remember. No, something has happened.'

'He's an ex-alcoholic who is slipping back into old habits, do you think he's gone on a bender?'

'He could have but, again, he wants this. He wants to take Mechanic down as much as anyone. I'm not sure he would jeopardise that.'

'Do you think Mechanic has jumped the gun and killed him?'

'That's not how she works, she would have waited for confirmation that I'd made my choice.'

'What do we do if he doesn't turn up? That fucks everything up.'

'He'll show, I'm sure of it. We have two days until the deadline and Mechanic needs to get in touch somehow.'

'Or not. She might choose to kill Harper with a bullet to the head while he's walking down the street. No fuss, no drama, bang!'

'I keep telling you, Mechanic loves the drama, she lives for the game. To her this is a piece of theatre to be played out in all its glory. No, she'll be in touch and then we can take her out.'

Lucas and Moran sat in silence as two coffees arrived.

'Harper has to turn up or we're not going to have a game at all.' Moran felt it was slipping away. Her dreams of stardom and ramming her success up Mills' ass were evaporating before her eyes.

Moran continued with the bad news.

'A few days ago Mechanic killed the head of the drug gang who run downtown Vegas.'

Lucas nearly spat his drink on the table.

'What!' He managed to swallow it down.

'So now we have the situation where Bonelli's crew will be scouring Vegas looking for her while LVPD have her on their most-wanted list. They are desperate to get to her before she gets fed to the fish.'

'I'd worry more about Harper if I were you. They won't find her,' said Lucas.

'Did you not listen to me? She's being hunted by drug-fuelled hoods on the street and cops in cars. That's serious shit. She might be lifted before we get our chance.'

'They won't find her, trust me. She could be in here right now and we wouldn't know it.'

Mechanic eyed Lucas from across the restaurant in the reflection of the tall glass display cabinet. She wanted one last look before he paid his penance. This was a blissful moment, one she would savour for a long time. One last look before his world came crashing down around him in two days' time.

Who's the woman sitting with him?

* * *

Harper regained consciousness sprawled on the floor. His arms were stretched above his head and he could see his blood-engorged hands cuffed to a metal ring set in the wall. He was about to move but thought better of it as footsteps approached. He slumped his head forward and closed his eyes.

He could hear voices and strained to make out what they were saying.

'What do you mean he's fucking dead?' Bonelli shouted in the face of the man trembling in front of him.

'That's what I'm saying, Mr Bonelli, Ramirez is dead.'

'Who did it? How did it happen?'

'Don't know yet. The two guys who were with him took a leak and when they came back his throat was torn out.'

'And no one saw a damn thing?'

'No sir.'

'People don't get their throats slit in broad daylight and no one sees anything. I want those two in here now. I'm working with fucking amateurs!' Bonelli was tramping around waving his arms in the air. 'And get this sack of shit out of here too. I'm sick to death of nothing but problems.'

'Sure thing, boss.'

'He's too much like hard work. Take him back to the desert and finish it. We'll find the other two without him.'

Footsteps came closer. Harper felt the cuffs click open and his arms flopped to his side. He was lifted bodily off the ground and thrown into the trunk of a car. The pain in his shoulders was excruciating but he had to remain silent. The lid slammed shut. Harper heard the doors closing and the engine revved hard.

He clawed at the flooring with his bloody hands until he found the join in the carpet. Twisting he lifted enough of the flap to get his hands inside. He felt around as the car jerked its way across the yard heading for the road. Then he found it. All he had to do now was judge when they were far enough away from the warehouse.

The enclosed space resonated with the gut trembling base notes of gangster rap music blasting out of oversized speakers. After what felt like a lifetime Harper could feel the change in road conditions. The smooth buzz of rubber on tarmac was replaced by the bone-shaking judder of rubber on desert rock.

He braced himself against the back of the trunk and kicked his feet into the corner. He heard a crack as his boot shattered the Bakelite casing of the tail-light. He thrashed out his legs, slamming his boot through the back of the fitting, and the whole housing fell out. A shaft of light filled the confines of the trunk. He sucked in the cooler air.

The squeal of the back brakes was deafening as the vehicle skidded to a halt. Harper heard a door open over the cacophony of music followed by cursing and seconds later the trunk lid flew open. The driver peered inside silhouetted against the bright sunlight.

Harper threw the tyre iron with all his might and hit the man in the forehead. The guy reeled backwards clutching his face as the tool bounced off his skull. Harper heaved himself out of the trunk and watched him stagger around, blood pouring through his fingers. He picked up the wrench and lashed out, hitting him in the neck. The man fell backwards as Harper repeatedly brought the tyre iron down on his head.

Harper patted him down and pulled a gun from his waistband. The man in the passenger seat switched off the music, opened his door and called out.

'Hey Nico, where are you man? What's going on?' He waited but there was no reply. He stepped out of the vehicle. Harper scrambled on his hands and knees and sat with his back tight against the rear fender.

'Nico,' the man called again, his view obscured by the raised lid of the trunk. He stepped sideways and saw his partner face down in the sand. He drew his gun and swung around in a three sixty, stepping slowly along the length of the car, his weapon levelled at head height.

The bullet entered below his jawbone and blew a ragged hole in the top of his head. The impact lifted him into the air and dumped him onto the hot ground. Harper jumped from his seated position and scanned the scene. All was clear.

He took the second man's gun, then climbed into the driver's seat and sped away showering gravel and sand onto the bodies.

Chapter 59

Mechanic's day was a mix of making her final preparations and evading Bonelli's men. She was still enjoying the rush of having sliced up Ramirez. Her bags were packed and laid on the bed, a copy of the Bulletin sat on the kitchen worktop open at the ads. There in bold capitals was what she had been waiting for. She knew Lucas would cave in and offer one of his friends as his penance. It was so like him to choose Harper, probably on the basis he had lived longer than Bassano – very predictable.

The important thing was that he had made a choice and the turmoil that must have caused gave Mechanic a warm glow inside.

She picked up the phone and punched in numbers. It rang at the other end.

'Oh hi, I wonder could you pass on a message to Captain Mark Jameson please.'

'Go ahead.'

'The message is, call Carla.'

'Okay caller I will pass that on.' The line went dead.

Captain Mark Jameson worked in military intelligence and was Mr Fixit to everyone who knew him. Jameson could lay his hands on anything and deliver it direct to your door, he could also compile intelligence reports on the movements of your favourite pet if you asked him. The man was a legend.

Mechanic had saved his life when a covert op went badly wrong, and when an ex-Navy Seal says he owes you, he means for life. His other redeeming feature was that he had absolutely no scruples whatsoever and never asked questions. Jameson had his regular mercenary clients but had a special place in the pecking order for Mechanic.

Jameson provided services that were eye-wateringly expensive and very good. His business model dictated he always insisted on being paid up front but where Mechanic was concerned he always took a part payment transferred directly into his account and the rest to be paid in kind.

The phone rang and she picked it up.

'Hi, it's me,' said Jameson. He was now talking on a secure line, the 'call Carla' routine worked every time.

'Hey, I wanted to check last minute details. Did you get the transfer?'

'Yup, that landed yesterday. The package is in the specified place and the schedule is clearly set out.'

'Transport?' Mechanic asked.

'All sorted, you need to be in the right place at the right time.'

'That sounds perfect.'

Jameson paused. 'Will I see you anytime soon?'

'I'll be in touch. I appreciate this one has been a big ask, so I reckon I should reciprocate.'

'Oh how?'

'When I see you next it would be wise to get yourself a cover story and a few days' emergency leave. You're not going to be in a fit state to go back to work straightaway.'

She could hear him breathing heavily on the end of the line, Jameson's erection was obviously robbing him of his power of speech. Mechanic waited.

'That would be good,' he finally croaked.

'I'll be in touch.' She put the phone down.

Jameson had pulled out all the stops for this one but the extra payment in kind was not all for his benefit. She couldn't recall the last man she'd fucked. Her life consisted of two things – providing for her sister and trying to act normal, which, for a crazed serial killer, left precious little space for any 'me time'.

Now Jo was dead, there was no need to worry about either.

Mechanic picked up the phone and dictated the advert to the business operator at the Bulletin. That left the rest of today and tomorrow to finalise preparations ready for the following day. Penance day.

There was a rap at the door. Mechanic pushed a gun into the back of her belt and peered through the peephole in the door. It was a uniformed cop.

Mechanic cursed and ran across the living room to close the bedroom door.

'Wait a minute,' she called out in a thick Middle Eastern accent, putting on the hijab. She opened the door.

'Good day, ma'am,' said the young officer, holding out his badge. 'We are conducting house-to-house enquiries with people who've recently moved into the area on a short-term rent. It's nothing to worry about, just a routine check.'

Mechanic went cold. The police must have traced her from the Bonelli murders and found her flat deserted. Investigating newly rented properties was a smart option. Either that or this was one of Bonelli's boys using the uniform as cover. She looked up at him from her stooped position. This was no Bonelli boy, this one looked like a cop.

'How can I help?' she asked, mangling the words with her accent.

'How long have you lived here?' He took out his notebook.

'Not long.'

'And who is your real-estate agent, ma'am?'

Mechanic waved her hand in a gesture which meant 'wait' and went inside to collect several sheets of paper from a drawer.

This was not what she needed right now. The false identity and papers were fine but her changed appearance had been done in a hurry and would not stand up to close inspection. She hovered inside and gave the officer the documents.

'My English is not so good.'

He looked at the papers and then at her. Something bothered him.

'Do you mind if I see some ID, ma'am?' He knew he was overstepping his remit, Mechanic knew it too.

Mechanic's mind raced. *Give him the ID and get rid of him.*

She disappeared again and came back with an Omani driving licence. Her picture was embossed on the front.

Please go away, Mechanic thought. *Just go.*

He looked at the licence and at the rental agreement.

'My name is Nassra Shamon,' Mechanic said trying to move things along. 'I come from Muscat, on a visa.'

The young officer returned the licence and the documents.

'Sorry to trouble you, ma'am. Thank you for your time.' He smiled and touched the peak of his cap.

Mechanic mumbled something in return, bowed slightly and closed the door.

'Shit,' she said putting her hands on her knees, exhaling deeply. Mechanic looked through the peephole and watched the officer walk back to his patrol car.

* * *

After an hour of phone calls and last minute packing Mechanic checked her watch. It was time to go. She sipped the last of her coffee, rinsed the cup and put it in the cupboard, running through the plan step by step.

There was a knock at the door.

She peered through the peephole to see the cop standing there again. Mechanic ducked down hoping he hadn't seen the lens change colour when she looked through it. He knocked again. She held her breath.

Fuck, what was he doing back?

'Mrs Shamon, I have a few more questions if you would open the door please.' He was persistent. Mechanic remained quiet.

'Mrs Shamon, I saw you look through the peephole, so I know you're in there. I have a few more questions.'

Mechanic pulled the hijab over her head, unclipped the safety chain and opened the door.

'Yes,' she said weakly.

'Thank you, Mrs Shamon. Can I take a look at your visa for entry into the US?'

Mechanic's head spun into overdrive again. *So this is an immigration issue, not a 'you killed two people' issue.*

Mechanic needed to get rid of this cop fast. Time was ticking away, she needed to leave.

She scurried back inside and returned with an official-looking document. 'Here.' She handed it to him.

Mechanic repeated the same words over and over in her head. *Please don't, please don't, please don't …*

He looked up and then uttered the words she'd prayed he wouldn't.

'I'm afraid you'll have to accompany me downtown, Mrs Shamon, I need to get these checked out. I'm sure everything is fine but if you wouldn't mind.'

'But why do I need to come with you?'

'It is simply routine, Mrs Shamon. I need to check out your documentation.'

Was this an immigration check or was she underestimating the young officer? Had he rumbled her?

Mechanic stepped away from the door. 'I need my things,' she said beckoning him into the apartment. 'Come in, you wait.'

The officer stepped into the small hallway. Mechanic closed the door and ushered him into the living room.

'Please sit, I need my medicine from the bathroom. I have asthma.'

He removed his hat and perched on the edge of the sofa.

Mechanic went into the bathroom and clanked around with cupboards and bottles.

The officer scrutinised every detail of the apartment, his intuition running riot, screaming at him that something wasn't right. There was not a cup or plate to be seen. No washing up in the sink and every worktop wiped clean. Not a single article of clothing or possession was on show. The bedroom door was ajar and he could see a holdall and rucksack on the bed. This was a woman who had paid a month's rent in advance and it looked like she was about to make an early exit.

Mechanic was still in the bathroom, he stepped across the living room to the bedroom and slipped inside.

'Looks like someone's been packing in a hurry,' he said under his breath.

He reached out his hand and ran the zip down the bag. The butt of a 9mm poked out.

The officer went for his gun.

Mechanic blew a neat hole in the back of his head.

The suppressed spit threw him forward onto the bed. An arc of blood spattered the quilt and the wall.

'Couldn't leave it alone, could you?' she said to the corpse lying face down in front of her.

Now it really was time to leave. The penance was waiting.

Chapter 60

Harper spun off the dirt track and was relieved to be on the solid road again. He needed to get rid of the car fast for two reasons, firstly, Bonelli's men might recognise it and, secondly, the back tail-light was missing and he was in danger of being pulled over by the police. Neither was a good option.

He reached the outskirts of Vegas and swung into the first shopping mall he came to. Harper selected the fullest car park and pulled over, resting his forehead on the steering wheel and breathing deeply. His whole body ached and when he moved his arms it felt as if red hot nails were being hammered through his shoulders.

Harper was hungry, thirsty and looked like shit. He had no money and two handguns, not a great combination. The driver's door swung open and he stepped out looking towards the Strip. The MGM was about a mile and a half away, he had no choice but to make it on foot. He flicked up the trunk and fished out a cap and a brown leather coat and set off.

An hour and a half later Harper arrived at the Lucky 6. He'd kept to the side streets and alleyways as much as possible. Men in cars cruised around but he managed to keep himself out of sight. He couldn't risk returning to his room – Bonelli knew his name, so there was a good chance he knew where he was staying. He also couldn't turn up at Lucas or Bassano's door with a cheery 'Hello I'm back,' because that might be followed by a hail of bullets.

Harper hid himself away against the back of a transformer which was tucked in the corner of the motel grounds from where he could see Lucas's room. He would have to wait.

He heard Bassano before he saw him, he was coming around the upper-level walkway heading for Lucas. Harper broke cover and waved his arms as far as his damaged shoulders would allow. Bassano looked down and shouted, 'Where the hell have you been?' *Nice one* thought Harper putting his fingers to his lips with a 'Shhh' gesture. Bassano met him at the bottom of the steps.

'Shit, what happened to you?'

'I'll explain later. Both of you pack your gear, we need to move out fast. The guys who did this to me want to do the same to you.' Harper ran back to the transformer and out of sight.

Fifteen minutes later Lucas backed up the car and Harper flung himself onto the back seat.

'What the fuck happened?' Lucas looked back over the seat at his friend. Bassano tossed him a bag containing bottled water and a sandwich. Harper tore open the packaging and bit into the bread and meat.

'The short answer is there's a guy named Silverton and our pictures showed up in his place. There's another man by the name of Bottelli or Bonelli or something, who looks like a drug lord and he's mighty pissed at us. I have no idea why, but the bastard nearly killed me, twice.'

'Where the hell have you been?' asked Lucas.

'They took me off the street at gunpoint, drove me to the desert and almost blew my head off. That's when he showed me the photographs of all three of us. I wouldn't talk, so he hung me from a fucking forklift.'

'Jesus.'

'His goons took me back to the desert to finish the job but I got away.'

'Where are they now?' asked Bassano.

'The two who drove me are lying in the gravel being picked clean by buzzards and the rest of his crew will be looking for you two.'

'You shot two of his guys?'

'No. I shot one of his guys and beat the other to death with a tyre iron.'

'Shit! We thought you'd gone on a bender,' said Bassano.

'Are you sure this wasn't Mechanic using someone else to take you out?'

'Not a chance. I have no idea why Bonelli is interested in us but it's not about Mechanic.'

'Where are we going?' asked Harper, still lying between the front and back seats.

'Moran is meeting us at the top of the Strip near the Sahara.'

'What about the leak down at the station, is she playing that right?'

Lucas had forgotten all about the storyline of the investigation having a leak. With the stresses and strains of the last few days, it had completely slipped his mind.

'Yes, that's working well,' he said trying to recover. 'She's placed the story that you'll be meeting with a senior LVPD officer the day after tomorrow and is confident Mechanic will take the bait.'

Lucas bit his lip. He hoped Moran had remembered the storyline as well.

Chapter 61

Lucas leaned against the wall watching the empty news-stand across the street. It was 5.45am and he hadn't slept a wink. Moran had met them in a car park the previous evening and put them up in a rundown motel at the top of the Strip. In an attempt to keep Bonelli's men off the scent they hadn't checked out of the Lucky 6. Each one took enough clothes for two days and Harper had what he stood up in.

That evening, he had spent an hour soaking in the bath allowing the warm water to ease his aching muscles while he ate a mountain of food. Despite Bassano giving him a lecture on healthy eating, he washed it down with a bucket of Jack Daniels and Coke.

Moran was not a happy woman. She hated shopping for herself, so the prospect of shopping for Harper did not go down well. He needed new clothes and toiletries. Lucas and Bassano were confined to the hotel, they couldn't risk being spotted by Bonelli's henchmen, so the purchasing duties fell to Moran. She bought the items, returned to the motel and threw it on the bed.

'Does this mean we're married?' Harper called from the bathroom. Moran never missed not having children on account of the fact that she worked with them every day. It was the first time she had cracked a smile in a week.

Lucas leaned against a wall enjoying the early morning breeze and watched a spotty kid hop off his bike by the side of the road. He unloaded a stack of newspapers from the back, slit the string with a penknife and dropped the papers into the Perspex box. Lucas was on them in an instant. He spread the pages on the wall and skimmed through the columns.

PENANCE DAY TOMORROW – APRIL 28
CHRISTCHURCH MALL MULTISTORY
8TH FLOOR, BAY 864.
5am SHARP

His stomach turned over as he read the ad. This was it.

'Moran has been in touch, it's game on,' Lucas lied marching into the motel room. Bassano emerged from the bathroom with a toothbrush sticking from his mouth.

'What's the plan?'

'Christchurch mall, tomorrow morning at 5am. We are going to take that bitch down.'

'Get Harper, we don't have much time and there's a lot to do,' Bassano said spraying flecks of white paste onto the carpet. Lucas lifted the phone and called the station.

Moran was already in work and picked up straight away. She listened to Lucas read the advert.

'That's good. We have a situation here which means I won't be with you till later. You know what to do.' She hung up.

The station was in complete freefall.

An officer had been found shot through the head at a low-rent property on the east side of the city. He was one of the team doing the house-to-house calls on recently rented properties taken out on short-term leases. The alarm was raised when he failed to call in. Another cop went to investigate and found his patrol car parked outside his last known location but there was no sign of him. The investigating cop could hear the sound of a police radio coming from inside the apartment, so he kicked the door in and found him dead. The rest of the place was empty.

Moran tried to stay focused. The morning briefing had been brought forward to 7am, which made Mills a very unpopular guy. The team gathered in the evidence room and went through the orders for the day. Lucas had been right. Despite every officer out looking for Mechanic there was not a single sighting. She'd vanished. When it came to Moran's turn she reported a ton of activity but very little progress. The briefing was over in forty minutes and Moran rushed from the office to meet with Lucas.

She found the three of them at the mall checking out parking lot 864, on the eighth floor of Christchurch Mall multi-storey. Despite her distractions at work, Moran delivered a totally convincing performance describing how she had fed the storyline at the station about Harper talking to the police. The meeting was set for tomorrow at 5am. Mechanic was bound to show up to protect her sister.

Realisation was dawning on Harper that he had put his head well and truly into the lion's mouth. Volunteering to be the bait to draw Mechanic into the open at some time in the future was completely different to the stark reality of actually being the bait tomorrow. The others rallied around him in support, each one relieved it wasn't them.

Lucas was suffering crushing feelings of guilt. He'd offered up his friend to be killed and lied about it. He felt like shit. Moran was the only one not feeling bad about anything, all she could think about was that this was her big chance. Her career would be guaranteed when she took Mechanic down.

By 10pm all was set. No more strategies to formulate, no more contingency plans to rehearse, no more checking of comms equipment and guns. They were ready to go, all that stood between them and catching Mechanic was seven sleepless hours.

There was one more thing left to do.

Back in his motel room Lucas reached for the phone and dialled home. There was no answer.

Damn, he thought. Now he would have to navigate around Heather the Rottweiler. He dialled anyway.

'Hello.' Heather answered.

'Hi Heather, is Darlene there please.'

'Jesus, Edmund, do you not understand about time zones? It's one in the morning. She is here but she doesn't want to speak to you.'

Lucas clenched his fist to stop himself exploding.

'Please, Heather, I'm begging you. It's important, put her on.'

'It's not me you need to beg to, it's Darlene. She's the one who spends her evenings crying. She's the one watching her marriage fall apart and all that's down to you.'

'That's why I need to speak to her. I'm coming home soon and I want to put things right.'

'She told me.'

'Can I speak to her please?'

'She doesn't want to.'

'Put her on the fucking phone!' Lucas could hold back no longer.

The line went dead.

He slammed the receiver into the cradle and redialled. It was engaged. He tried again. It was permanently engaged. Once more, the phone ended up on the floor.

Chapter 62

Mechanic was at the Huxtons' house walking towards Jo's bedroom. The pictures in the hallway told of a different life, before Mary-Jay was in a wheelchair. Images of a life full of church outings, eating ice-cream sundaes on the lawn, riding a bicycle … The framed photographs floated by as Mechanic reached Jo's door and eased it open.

The room was ice cold despite the sun pouring through the window. A figure lay on the bed covered with a white linen sheet, Mechanic stood beside it and reached out her hand. The material felt slimy to the touch and she couldn't grip the fabric. Try as she might the sheet slipped through her fingers.

The shape beneath the covers stirred.

Slowly the head lifted off the pillow and the body started to sit up. Mechanic grappled with the sheet but it glided through her hands. The cover slipped down the face. She was welded to the spot. Her legs wouldn't work. Try as she might she couldn't move.

The cover fell away to reveal the body beneath, it was Lucas.

He threw his head back and laughed. Mechanic's legs refused to move, she couldn't get away. His head jerked backwards and forwards, the inside of his cavernous mouth was black and his breath reeked of rancid meat. He raised his hand and pointed to the corner of the room. Jo was sitting in her chair and behind her stood Harper. He reached around with one hand and grabbed her forehead pulling it back against his chest. In his other hand was a long serrated knife. Lucas filled the room with manic laughter. The foul smell coming from his gaping mouth was overpowering.

Mechanic felt her legs come to life and slowly she slid one foot in front of the other edging towards her sister, Jo's eyes were pleading with Mechanic to help. She was mouthing words but Mechanic couldn't hear what she was saying. Laughter echoed off the walls.

Mechanic's feet inched along the floor, moving her ever closer. Then she found her voice and screamed at Harper, 'No!'

Jo's eyes were bursting from her head, she mouthed the words *'Please, please help me.'*

Harper raised the knife and the serrations ripped through Jo's throat. Her mouth still moved as a gaping slash opened up across her neck. Her head rolled back. Her mouth still moving – *'Please help me. Please …'*

Mechanic jumped and gasped for air. She sat bolt upright gripping the bedcover, her arms and chest glistened with beads of sweat. She focused on the surroundings and her head flopped down.

She took a moment to steady herself, threw back the covers and sat on the edge of the bed. It was early and the alarm hadn't gone off yet. She reached for the remote and flicked on the TV. The morning news was full of an employment bill not being passed in Congress and forest fires raging in California. The tickertape headlines ran across the bottom of the screen telling of a celebrity who had been found dead from a suspected drug overdose at the age of thirty-one. Mechanic walked to the bathroom.

The programme didn't include the most important news item of the day.

Today was penance day.

* * *

Mechanic pulled up next to the black SUV and looked out at the multi-storey opposite. There was a clear view of her target. She got out of her car and groped around under the back wheel-arch of the SUV. She removed the keys, pushed the button, and the indicator lights flashed. Next she went to the back and let down the tailgate, which cleared the metal crash rail against the outer wall. She slid open the side door and climbed inside closing it behind her.

* * *

Harper was late. The traffic was awful and he swerved and honked his way to Christchurch mall. It was 4.45am and this was not going well for a 5am rendezvous. Where the hell were all these people going, shouldn't they still be tucked up in bed? Lucas, Moran and Bassano were already in position. Moran and Bassano were in separate cars parked on the eighth floor and Lucas was on the ground floor by the lifts.

* * *

The back seats of the SUV were missing, replaced instead by a raised wooden bed about six feet long and four feet wide. Mechanic reached underneath and pulled out a long black case. She placed it in front of her, snapped open the clasps and lifted the lid to reveal a military sniper rifle.

The gun was long and matt black, with a cut-out metal stock and precision telescopic sight. A silencer was screwed into the muzzle. Mechanic removed it from the soft foam interior and rotated the bipod feet into place. She took a box containing 0.3 Winchester centre-fire cartridges, picked one out and slid it into the chamber with a soft metallic click. The rifle smelled of fresh gun oil.

* * *

Harper could see the multi-storey and began to relax, he would make it with time to spare after all. Moran popped the clip from her gun, confirmed it was loaded for the umpteenth time and snapped it back in place before placing it on the passenger seat. Bassano flicked the gun safety on and off and watched the entry and exit ramps. Lucas was trying not to think of the terrible consequences which might unfold in the next fifteen minutes. He felt like throwing up.

* * *

Mechanic lay on her stomach with her legs apart, her toes digging into the wooden surface. She pushed the butt of the rifle into her shoulder and rested against the cheek piece. Her non-trigger hand supported the stock as she looked through the telescopic sight. Through the back of the vehicle she had a clear line to the car park opposite. She checked the rangefinder, it read 210 yards.

Harper didn't wait for the lights to turn green. He sped over the pedestrian crossing, to howls of protest from the people halfway across. Moran checked her watch, it was 4.56am.

Where the hell was Harper?

* * *

Mechanic scanned the car park, the crosshairs dancing along the empty parking bays. She trusted the sight was accurately calibrated to the distance, and with very little wind drift it should be a clean shot. She slowed her breathing and could feel her heart rate drop as she relaxed into the rifle. Mechanic released the safety catch.

* * *

Harper roared up the ramp to the eighth floor and circled around the one-way system. He spotted the parking bay and skidded into it. He unfastened his seatbelt and looked around. The floor was empty apart from Moran parked in one corner and Bassano in the other.

Mechanic saw the front of the car pull into the space. There was movement inside the vehicle then the driver's door opened. Sunlight glinted off the window. She zoned everything out and focused on the target.

Harper gripped his gun in his belt and stepped from the car. The ceiling was low, which amplified every sound. He looked around him. Nothing.

Mechanic saw the head emerge, then the shoulders. Her breathing was slow and shallow. The crosshairs bounced slightly in time with her heartbeat. Up and down, up and down, always fire at the bottom of the down stroke.

Harper drew his gun. This didn't feel right. He twisted around and checked all the angles. Something was wrong.

The driver's door obscured Mechanic's view but that didn't matter. She placed her finger on the trigger. Her heart pulsed sending the crosshairs dancing once more.

Harper didn't like this. Every sinew in his body was screaming to get the hell out of there. This felt wrong.

Mechanic's body was completely relaxed. Always shoot on the respiratory pause at the end of the exhale. Always shoot on the down stroke.

1 … 2 … 3 … squeeze.

Point three of a second later the shell sent a shower of blood and brain tissue into the air. The rifle angrily spat out the empty casing against the side of the SUV. Mechanic continued through the trigger pull and slowly released it back to the rest position. She stayed in place, focusing on the magnified image, counting down the seconds. Nothing moved.

Mechanic sat up, packed the gun into the case and fed it back under the wooden bed. She picked up the shell casing, closed the tailgate, locked up the vehicle and placed the keys under the back wheel-arch.

She looked at her watch. It was 8.03am.

* * *

Lucas wiped the perspiration from his face and felt light-headed. Why was nothing happening? Then it dawned on him, Mechanic must have killed Moran, Bassano and Harper.

Lucas panicked. The only thing he could think of was Harper lying in a pool of blood on the eighth floor. Mechanic must have got all three of them.

It was over. The penance had been paid.

His earpiece crackled.

'She's a no show. Repeat, Mechanic is a no show.' It was Harper.

Lucas looked at his watch. It was 5.04am.

Chapter 63

Friday 27 May 1983
Tallahassee, Florida

The warm spring rain drummed hard against the umbrellas as the sun scorched steam off the grass. Only in Florida could that ever be considered normal weather.

Lucas stared blankly ahead completely immune to the fifty or so faces staring back at him. He had no more tears to cry, no more emotion to give. His hands shoved deep into his pockets, letting those around him do the job of keeping the rain off. His crushing sadness permeated everyone that was there.

The priest read from a book and the words floated past Lucas without being heard. The ground was awash with white flowers, all with handwritten cards stuck between the folds of cellophane. In stark contrast the mourners all wore black.

A pale wooden casket stood above the grave. Raindrops danced off the coffin onto the grass.

The priest was coming to the end: '… and so we commit this body to the ground. Earth to earth, ashes to ashes, dust to dust.'

There was a soft whirring sound and the coffin descended out of sight.

'So let us go in peace to live out the word of God,' the priest continued from his script, crossing himself.

Lucas stepped forward, scooped a handful of wet soil and dropped it into the grave. The dirt rattled against the wood. Pain shuddered through his body and he struggled to keep his balance. He stood motionless while the rain cascaded down his face, dripping from his eyelashes. He didn't blink, staring into the middle distance. An arm reached around his shoulders and guided him back under the umbrella.

Others filed past the grave, wearing their masks of grief and allowing soil to spill through their fingers onto the coffin lid. Lucas was escorted back to the black limousine. The crowd milled around chatting as the car silently pulled away.

Lucas twisted in his seat and looked out of the rear window. He could just make out the white marble headstone with black writing.

There was no way to come back from this.

HERE LIES DARLENE ANNABEL LUCAS
DIED AGED 53 YEARS
BELOVED WIFE OF EDMUND
TAKEN BEFORE HER TIME
HER SOUL RESTS IN PEACE

Harper was never the intended target.

Mechanic had put Lucas through the emotional turmoil of choosing between his friends as a sick game, one she enjoyed over and over while she was planning how to kill Darlene. This was a penance with a sting in the tail. This was a punishment worthy of the death of her sister.

Darlene was an easy prey. When she worked out of the Tallahassee office she always had the same routine. She would drive to work and park in the multi-storey at 8am, in her designated slot on the eighth floor. It was like clockwork, every morning was the same. Every morning that is until Mechanic put a bullet through her head.

Jameson had been thorough in his surveillance report and the multi-storey was the natural choice. The SUV and sniper's rifle were procured with the usual no questions asked and returned three hours later to the military compound from which they originated. It was a relatively straightforward assignment for a man with no scruples.

Mechanic had picked up the airline tickets from a baggage locker at McCarran International Airport and had taken the six-hour flight to Tallahassee. There was a perfect symmetry in killing Darlene Lucas at precisely the time Harper was at the multi-storey eighteen hundred miles and three time zones away. It had taken meticulous planning but it was a lovely touch. Mechanic hoped the subtlety was not wasted on Lucas, after she had gone to so much trouble.

Lucas and the others were completely stumped when the morning had turned into a non-event. Moran couldn't believe her moment of fame had failed to materialise. The single biggest moment of her whole career had evaporated into nothing.

For two days they waited for further contact from Mechanic, but none came. It was all a big fat zero until the cops tracked down Lucas. They found him at the motel and gave him the news. When the realisation finally struck home, he cried for days.

* * *

Mechanic used to think that eight months was a long time to go without killing someone of consequence, and the only thing of consequence was slaughtering Lucas and Harper. In the end that turned out not to be true. She found as much pleasure in knowing they were still alive, while Darlene Annabel Lucas lay prematurely in Rose lawn cemetery.

After all, killing them was not to be rushed. This was a dish to be savoured. When the time was right she would give herself a treat and kill all three.

As for Lucas, his every waking moment used to be consumed with finding Mechanic and killing the psychotic bitch, though in public he used the phrase 'bring her to justice'. This was still the case, but from now on justice didn't get a mention.

Chapter 64

11 Months Later
April 1984
Queens, New York City

Bassano relished the distractions of the second Friday in the month. Some wore dresses, some wore suits, some primped and preened for hours while others came straight from work. But they all wore the same expression when they met him. And today was distracting as hell.

The dance floor heaved with a writhing mass of bodies, the music thumping out a beat which punched you in the stomach from thirty feet. People gyrated and rubbed themselves against perfect strangers, hoping it would lead to something more.

The Venetian masks added to the sense of abandoned pleasure. They gave the green light to enjoying doing things the wearers would be horrified to do minus the anonymity. When you're wearing a mask, anything goes. The strobe lighting made the whole scene look like a single organism pulsating to the beat. It was hot and it was loud.

Bassano wore his mask and was leaning into a woman with long dark hair. Her back was against a pillar and his arm was outstretched marking out his territory, his hand resting inches from her head. She bent forward to hear him over the noise. They broke away and threw their heads back laughing. Bassano would like to say she was exactly his type, but in truth any woman this close was his type.

He leaned in again and put his face next to hers. He lingered, whispering in her ear. The woman laughed again and slapped him on his chest, playfully reprimanding him for something suggestive. She slipped her hand in his.

Bassano smiled his best Italian American smile. She tilted her head to the floor in a false parade of coyness and sipped her drink holding his gaze.

Bassano didn't have a drink. In his one hand he held the warm, strong fingers of the woman in front of him, and his other was a metal hook. He still didn't trust himself to grip a glass with his prosthetic and he wasn't about to let go of her in preference for a glass.

His mask was black and hers glistened pearlescent white. The invitation had said 'Girls in white, guys in black. Masks obligatory'. For Bassano, singles clubs were a welcome diversion from real life, and the masks made the parties a total blast.

He scored every time. Not only was he tall and ruggedly handsome, but he definitely had the curiosity factor. The faint lace cobweb of scars on his face, and his missing arm, seemed to hold a deep fascination for certain women. They were crazy to find out about it, and the more they had to drink the crazier they got.

When he laid on the Italian charm, coupled with the story of how a vicious serial killer nearly murdered him, he was home and dry. It worked every time.

He wasn't interested in taking any of them home to meet his folks. He'd done that once and it was a disaster. No, this was distraction time, that's all.

Huge speakers banged out some techno rubbish, which only people wearing masks would ever consider dancing to. The DJ shouted over the distorted sounds from the PA and the crowd in front screamed something equally unintelligible in return. Bassano placed a kiss on her cheek. She smiled and squeezed his hand. This was going good.

He reached down and cupped her hand holding the drink, brought it up to his lips and drank it dry. She slapped his shoulder and sent him away for another. There is something about being over six foot tall with a hook for a hand which makes getting close to the bar a relatively easy process. Bassano ordered two more drinks, paid for them and walked back with both glasses pinched between his thumb and first two fingers.

He reached the pillar, she was gone.

He scanned the room trying to find the dark-haired woman in the white dress wearing a mask, a description which didn't really narrow down the field. Then he saw her standing against the wall by the restrooms. She was wearing her coat with a look that said 'catch up, boy'.

Bassano pushed through the tight knot of people and offered up the drinks. She took one and downed it, crunching the ice between her teeth. She fed her arm around his waist and said something in his ear. Bassano smiled, gave his drink the same treatment and allowed her to lead him through the crowd towards the emergency exit next to the stage.

She hit the bar with the heel of her hand and the door flew open, the fresh air hitting them like a blast freezer. They spilled out into a narrow alley at the side of the club. A row of trash cans and dumpsters lined up against the opposite wall. She slammed the door behind them. The music carried through the walls as if they were still on the dance floor, it echoed and reverberated off the high brickwork.

She pushed Bassano against the wall and kissed him. Her tongue was hot in his mouth. Her hands caressed his face pulling him in.

Bassano's arm curled around her, feeling the contours of her body. She pulled back and ran her fingernails down his chest. She kissed him hard. Her fingers slid down to his belt. He began to breathe heavily. He tore off his mask and spun her round, pinning her against the wall, grinding his hips into hers.

She sank to her knees and unzipped his pants. He was hot and hard in her hand. She gripped him tight and freed him from his clothing. Bassano steadied himself against the wall and closed his eyes.

There was a blinding flash of pain.

He recoiled to see blood running down his legs. The dark-haired woman knelt with her back against the wall holding a knife in one hand and his cock and balls in the other. Bassano staggered around, holding the gap in his crotch where his genitals used to be, his mouth wide open in a silent scream.

She slid the blade underneath the band on her mask and cut it free. Bassano stared at her face as blood pumped from his body.

She looked familiar.

She was smiling at him.

He recognised the smile.

The face was different, but the smile was the same.

The last time he saw it, a woman broke his face and severed his arm.

His legs gave way and he toppled backwards. The scream finally left his throat, only to be drowned out by the noise of the club.

Her high heels clicked on the concrete as she walked away, confident that this time she had done a proper job. The bloody contents of her bag were a fitting trophy.

One down, two to go.

The End

Acknowledgements

I want to thank all those who have made this second book possible – My family Karen, Gemma, Holly and Maureen for their blunt, painful feedback and endless patience. To my band of loyal proofreaders Yvonne, Lesley, Christine, Penny, Christine, Nicki, Jackie, Anne, Frazer and Simon who didn't hold back either and finally my talented editor, Helen Fazal, who once again did an amazing job and made me a better writer in the process.